Elizabeth Beacon has a passion for history and storytelling and, with the English West Country on her doorstep, never lacks a glorious setting for her books. Elizabeth tried horticulture, higher education as a mature student, briefly taught English and worked in an office before finally turning her daydreams about dashing piratical heroes and their stubborn and independent heroines into her dream job: writing Regency romances for Mills & Boon.

Also by Elizabeth Beacon

The Duchess Hunt
Candlelit Christmas Kisses
The Scarred Earl
The Black Sheep's Return

A Year of Scandal miniseries

The Viscount's Frozen Heart
The Marquis's Awakening
Lord Laughraine's Summer Promise
Redemption of the Rake
The Winterley Scandal
The Governess Heiress

Discover more at millsandboon.co.uk.

A WEDDING FOR THE SCANDALOUS HEIRESS

Elizabeth Beacon

MILLS & BOON

Chapter One

You're three and twenty, Isabella Alstone, and far too old to hide in the dark. You should stay in the ballroom and pretend to be happy, not creep out here as if you're planning to steal the silver.

Isabella was tired of being the perfect lady, though, so she stripped off her gloves and waved them in front of her overheated face, ignoring the voice of her conscience. It was hot even outside on this sultry late summer night and she wasn't going back until she was cooler, calmer and more resigned… No, not more resigned, more collected. Yet promises so logical and right when voiced to a friend seemed strange and wrong now and how could she be calm about that?

'Now, why is a lady of quality lurking in the shadows with the likes of me? Better go back to being belle of the ball instead of getting caught out here in bad company.'

The voice from the shadows startled Isabella from her reverie. The sound of his velvet-and-darkness voice told her he was right, but she was in the mood to be reckless.

'Why?' she demanded, peering into the gloom to try to see through the shadows.

His gruffly masculine voice had a pleasing hint of danger along the edge of it she shouldn't want to know more about, but she had left safe, respectable Isabella inside and it was wonderful to be a different person altogether for a few stolen moments. She could be the sort of female who'd dive into wild encounters in the dark, as if she was put on this earth to be foolish and bold with the first rake she stumbled on in the shadows. Her fantasy of being a brash and sophisticated lady who took what she wanted from life and laughed at the future, as if it wasn't heading towards her at the speed of a runaway horse, was too alluring to turn her back on just yet.

'Because I'm here,' the mysterious voice explained, as if that was all she needed to know to send her running. She stayed exactly where she was, refusing to scuttle inside like a scared rabbit, and heard him sigh, as if he couldn't believe how stupid she was not to listen and do as she was bid.

'You're no debutante, so the Bond Street Beaux must have told you how beautiful you are by now and that will make everything worse if we're caught in the moonlight together.'

He stepped forward so the light from the few hundred wax candles could illuminate his face and form and show her how right he was. With a face too much his to match any ideal of classical perfection, he wasn't the most handsome man Isabella had seen. He wasn't the tallest or broadest or most obviously powerful male she had ever met either. Of course, he *was* leanly fit and quietly muscular as well as deeply, darkly intense. *And* uniquely formed to make her shiver in her dancing slippers with an unexpected and delicious anticipation of something she'd hardly dared think about until now and usually shuddered away from when she saw that feral light in other men's eyes. Only seconds ago she'd been hot and weary and now she felt so alive there could be air and stardust under her feet instead of solid York stone. If this was how being irresponsible felt, it certainly topped being her usual sensible and reasoned self.

'I haven't the faintest idea who you are, so if you're trying to scare me, it's not working. Although you're right about one thing,' she said as lightly as she could when the world seemed to have stopped and they were the only two people left moving. 'I have been out for a long time now and know false flattery when I hear it.'

'I don't flatter, Mrs...' he shot a steely gaze at her ring finger '...apologies, Miss, and there's no need to pretend to be middle-aged,' he said with a wry smile that did hot and disturbing things to her insides. 'We'll both be old soon enough.'

'We will?' she echoed in a breathy whisper that must have given him doubts about that maturity, but she did *feel* like a giddy girl when he took her gently by the arm and urged her further into darkness and away from the pool of golden candlelight spilling out of a ballroom that now seemed almost as remote from her as the Arctic.

'Will someone come dashing out to find you any moment now, ready to usher you away?' he asked with a smile, but she felt a tension in his sleekly powerful body that made her frown briefly.

'No,' she told him like a silly debutante desperate to be ruined by a rogue. 'My family trusts me to behave,' she added with a late tilt at sophistication and a flutter in her heartbeat that suggested they shouldn't tonight.

'They don't consider the basic needs of the human heart often enough, then, or, in my case, even baser masculine ones you're better not to know about until you really are a Mrs Belle,' he replied with a cynical thread in his voice that made her frown for another sensible, bone-jarring moment before the darkness and scent from some exotic hothouse flower nearby wafted it clean away.

'So you're not to be trusted?' she heard herself ask like the fledgling idiot she'd never allowed herself to be in polite society.

Nobody was ever going to lure *her* in with showy good looks, false promises of love and passion, and heady nights like this one. She remembered her eldest sister, Miranda, falling for evil, charming Nevin Braxton at seventeen and all the horror her elopement and ruin had brought down on her family's lives too well for that. Isabella had shuddered away from rakes as if their kisses would poison her ever since. This man hadn't flattered and flirted and fawned on her, though. He seemed to see beyond her golden looks, exquisitely fashioned gown and neat figure and was speaking to the real Isabella.

And out here she could forget what was waiting for her inside the hot room only feet away. On this terrace with the scent of exotic flowers heavy in the air, only now mattered. Just enough light shone from the ballroom for her to see his eyes were ice blue and hot at the same time. Her breath stuttered when he pulled her further from the lights of the party and the glow of a waxing moon gave them a world of their own.

'You should not trust me, Belle. I'm dangerous,' he said almost seriously. 'I'm a wolf in wolf's clothing,' he added as if he believed it.

'It's not full,' she told him and sensed his bewilderment. 'The moon,' she explained with a nod towards it where it seemed almost touchable, on the horizon, 'so you can't claim the moon made you do it.'

'Do what?'

'Kiss me,' she heard herself say rashly. A sane part of her was so shocked it was as if it flopped down on to the stone bench nearby and sat there with its mouth open.

'Oh? And why would you let me do that, Belle? Perhaps you're as wild as I am,' he murmured, suddenly closer than she remembered.

She should run, dash back into the familiar noise and heat and glitter of a *ton*nish ballroom, and find the nearest respectable female to chaperon her. Instead she stayed as if her feet were rooted into the still-warm stones under their feet. She could touch and taste him if she stayed, hear the urgent saw of breath he'd been holding too long. Moonlight fell on high cheekbones and dark, dark hair springing almost to disarray despite all his efforts to tame it. The hint of a frown at his dark eyebrows told her a goodly part of him thought he ought to fight this basic, gut-deep attraction as well. But there was enough light for the sensual curve of his mouth to betray the fact urgency and passion were getting the upper hand even without her exploring touch and silent encouragement to get on and kiss her and to hell with the real world.

'I think you're right,' she whispered as she padded her fingertips against his tense jaw, feeling how it clenched and suspecting it was taking everything in him not to fall on her like the wolf he claimed to be.

But reason gave way to madness and suddenly she was in his arms. This was the kiss that would bring Isabella Penelope Alstone fully to life. The one she'd been so secretly waiting for since the day she began to be a woman. She hadn't even let herself know she wanted it until now. His mouth fitted lushly against her eager lips and he felt so familiar against her. He murmured something as if he agreed with her unspoken thoughts and she opened her mouth to say *Yes, please*, but he dipped his tongue inside first, as if he had to know more, had to know everything now she was here at last. She was melting from the outside in, or should that be the inside out? Heat beat through her in time with his hurried breaths and the dart of his gently exploring tongue, as if he knew she'd never felt passion like this before and it was a shock that echoed through them both.

Yes, *there* was the shake of novelty and wonder in his fingers as he danced them across her cheekbone and down to outline her chin as if he was learning her with every sense he had. Never before had she been tempted to burrow into a man's arms, to try to become a part of him by melding her heat with his, her mouth with his. For a minute reality threatened to pull her back and her mind told her body to flinch away, but the alluring stranger snatched all her attention back by sliding his wickedly exploring tongue over her lower lip, deepening the kiss.

She shifted even closer and copied his exploration. His cheek and jaw felt so firm under her touch and her fingers were intrigued by the contrast between her own softer features and his hawkish ones. She could feel the suggestion of his beard despite a careful shave and she spared a moment to scent the clean, sharp smell of soap and something tangy used to take the sting of the blade away when a gentleman was making himself civilised and smooth for the company of ladies.

Real life threatened to jump in again, but she told it to go away and muttered something encouraging instead. Nothing in reality could beat a meeting outside time and all the rules of polite society. Her heart beat so fast and her breath demanded air while pleasure and hope and a big, wide *yes* to life and this stranger and all he could be opened up inside her. She was shivering like a thoroughbred and rode a tide of heat more intense and deep and demanding than anything she'd ever felt before. There were no words to describe how right it felt when he pulled her closer to show her what she was doing to him. She felt the tension of deep desire in his rigidly muscular form. This was the carnal, primal need that carried men and women to places they'd never intended to go to when they started an evening not even knowing one another.

Instead of flinching back and telling him, no, they couldn't go any further down that road when they didn't even know one another's real names, she pushed her curious hands under his unbuttoned evening coat and gave a pleased little grunt at the feel of a hot, needy and intriguingly muscular male under her exploring touch. Her fingers soothed the tight muscles at the base of his spine, whispered inquisitively downwards, desperate to know the difference between his spare male flanks and her own sleekly feminine curves. He gasped as if she'd stung him, then sucked in breath as if he might need more if she was going to carry on, so she did. She could feel his muscles shift and soothe, then tense again as she explored the sparseness of his buttocks and the honed, pared-down line where they met long, strong legs. Her own legs wobbled and almost let her down as their stance thrust his unmistakably eager manhood emphatically against her.

This was what uncontrollable desire felt like. This was how a woman felt when she was desperate for the man she loved to take her somewhere magical. That old taboo, that stark little four-lettered word sounded like a death knell in a corner of her mind, but she was moon-mad and curious enough to ignore it for a little longer. It put a hiccup in her sigh, though, a caveat in her exploration even as she buried a gasp of awe and need against his shoulder, then stood on tiptoe so that every bit of her felt it knew every bit of him.

But they didn't, they couldn't; not with so many sharp eyes and curious minds dangerously close by. She felt him stand a little straighter, pulling back his leanly powerful shoulders so he stood more sceptically apart from her as she burrowed against the warmth and strength and certainty of him and tried to hold on to this moment for a little while longer. If she let go, she'd have to see what she'd done and what she ought to have been doing instead. Ever since she'd given in to impulse for once and stepped outside the stuffy ballroom behind them, the way her life was planned out from now on was weightless in the balance against this rebellious encounter under the stars. Let him go and that weight would tumble back and she would end up more wrong than she had ever been in her life.

As she stood in the stronghold of his arms, trying to hold the real world at bay for as long as she could, voices started to disturb the fog of her mind.

'Isabella can't be out here,' she heard Magnus Haile's voice say in the vast, close distance between his world and the one she and the stranger and the moon inhabited.

Now just a few yards away his voice sounded pacifying with forced casualness. She stiffened and felt her fellow moon-led simpleton do the same. Magnus must be with his father for him to sound like that. The Earl of Carrowe was a despot with his family, but so sleekly charming in the polite world the stark difference between public and private man still took Isabella's breath away.

'Where is she, then? Get your engagement puffed off so I don't end up in the sponging house or have duns to breakfast. You have shilly-shallied for far too long, so you find her before her upstart brother-in-law withdraws his consent or I'll spill your secrets.'

'She's of age and so am I. We need no consent,' the Honourable Magnus Haile asserted uncomfortably, as if he was trying to remind himself that he and Isabella were two free and unencumbered adults.

Even as she stood in another man's arms and felt him go rigid before he let her go as if she'd suddenly grown horns and a tail, Isabella frowned at the flatness in Magnus's usually pleasant tenor voice. He had spent last Season courting her so half-heartedly it took her until the end of it to notice. Then he had asked his fateful question and it shocked her even now to recall she had agreed. They were *friends*, she reassured herself. They would run in harness well together and she had never met anyone who made her heart race or her inner wanton melt with greed and heady desire. Until tonight. When it was too late.

Isabella stepped cautiously away from her stranger; stiff as he was now reason had rushed back in. A sluggish breeze stirred the sticky heat and fluttered her pale gown as space opened up between them.

The Earl of Carrowe pushed his protesting second son aside and stepped away from the pool of candlelight. Still as a statue now, Isabella froze and held her breath. This familiar stranger standing so stiffly next to her felt remote and withdrawn as an iron statue. She desperately hoped the night was deep enough for the Earl not to see them standing here like guilty lovers. Who would have thought a man she never laid eyes on until tonight could show her Isabella the Undone? All in the space between the ballroom and here and now.

'You don't need consent, you need a pitchfork up your…' the Earl said in the coarse manner he saved for his family. Or at least those who depended on him for a leaky roof over their heads. Here at Haile Carr he had to hide his true self or risk the fury of his wealthy daughter-in-law and her even wealthier father.

'You'll keep a still tongue in your head about my future wife if you want me to go through with this marriage.' Magnus sounded as austere as a monk and halted his father's trail of obscenities in their tracks.

Isabella stifled a hum of sympathy as she felt the weight of real life settling back on her shoulders. It felt even more of a burden now than when

she had first decided to share Magnus's responsibilities. They weren't in love, but she never
wanted to be in love anyway. Love was a trap
and an illusion, nothing like the fairy-tale emo-
tion three-decker romances portrayed. Isabella
had agreed to Magnus's proposal for one reason—to get him and his sisters out from under
the Earl's thumb—to give her best male friend
outside her family a chance to be free of the
monster she had heard bully and even beat his
children. She had had no idea until a visit to
the Haile ladies showed her the insults and foul
language of the real man under the Earl of Carrowe's urbane outer shell. The Countess had hidden Isabella's presence and even took her out
down the backstairs so the Earl wouldn't know
she had been there. From that moment on she
was filled with a passionate desire to help the
Earl's daughters and Magnus had given her a
chance to do it, so she took it and him and told
herself all would be well because she didn't want
to be in love with her husband anyway.

Except it felt as if they had missed something
vital out. Isabella had been restless and hot and

uncomfortable in her own skin in the ballroom and bolted outside to get away from what she'd done with her eyes wide open. And look where that had got her; she'd taken light in the arms of a stranger and now had to live with the memory of it on her conscience while she pretended to be Magnus's glowingly happy bride-to-be.

'Renege on our deal and I'll tell the world what you did last year and who you did it with,' the Earl threatened Magnus as if he couldn't bear to be bested by another son after his heir married a rich woman and got control of his own purse strings. The atmosphere in the ballroom had felt oppressive with Viscount Haile and his wife holding court while family tensions simmered just below the surface. Or maybe she was making excuses for her own bad behaviour.

But what did Magnus do last summer? A couple of times since she arrived here Isabella had sensed something was deeply wrong with Magnus. It felt as if she knew only half of what was going on. Their engagement was supposed to be a surprise that would make this annual party even happier, but it didn't feel very joyous to Isabella. Her money and family power were pitted against the Earl's extravagant self-indulgence and his cruel grip on his family. He'd traded control of his unwed daughters for part of her fortune; Magnus would save his sisters and Isabella could start the family she longed for. But then she arrived here and the reality of marrying the man who'd been her friend since she made her debut finally hit home. To make those babies they would be intimate together and it felt like a giant factor she left out of her calculations about marrying for sense and companionship. Much as she liked Magnus she wasn't sure she wanted to couple with him. She was a country girl at heart and three and twenty; she knew enough about the mechanics of marriage to shiver at the very idea of the one she'd committed herself to while she stood so close to a man who had nearly taught her a lot more than she needed to know about how a man and a woman were together when they wanted each other so urgently they couldn't even wait for a bed.

'You need money too much to risk Isabella jilting me,' Magnus was arguing now and she felt the man at her side wince.

Not for her sake, she sensed, or for the Earl's. So he must be on Magnus's side. She could feel fury arcing across the few bare inches of late summer air between them. The shame of her own betrayal was bad enough—the wrong she'd done Magnus with this stranger. So what about him? He was furious with her, but fairness whispered he hadn't deserved to kiss another man's affianced bride as if she was free as air, then find out how wrong he was before their lips were cool from kissing. Even more guilt twisted in her belly and finally saw off the wanton Isabella who still longed for more from a lover and never mind who he was and who he wasn't.

'No, damn you, I need all that gelt to keep the duns at bay,' the Earl was saying now. 'You find the wench so we can announce the engagement before all the local clodhoppers go home.'

'I'll see if Isabella is mending a flounce or visiting the ladies' withdrawing room, because she's clearly not out here. You shouldn't judge her by your low standards. Not everyone has your genius for sin.'

'Speaking of sinners, where's your mother?'

'Maybe she's with her prospective daughter-in-law, avoiding you.'

The string of obscenities that greeted that provocation faded as father and son turned to go back inside. Isabella wasted a few moments wondering how quickly the Earl could put on the mask of genial host after his unpleasant tirade. No doubt it would be plausible as ever by the time he was back in the crowded ballroom that she now dreaded so deeply she would almost prefer to stay out here with a furious male of a very different kind than re-enter it and face the future.

'I presume you know your fiancé's mother, Miss Alstone?' he asked coldly.

She shivered despite the sticky heat that hit her again now the magic of the moonlit night had flown. 'How do you know my…?' she began, then her voice trailed off when he turned to face her.

'Who else but you would skulk on the terrace at Haile Carr, trying to avoid her fiancé in the arms of a stranger? Who else did I come here to see and maybe even steel myself to meet?'

'I don't know, but why *are* you here?'

He grasped her arms as if she was the last person he really wanted to touch and walked her towards the pool of golden light on the still-warm stones. Her gaze ran over his hawkish features and heat and excitement flashed through her once again, but there was such fury in his uncannily light blue eyes it suffocated.

'Can you see it now?' he demanded roughly, shaking her a little when she stayed silent. 'The mark of Cain you have put on me tonight,' he bit out and the rage and guilt beneath his bitter words felt formidable.

For another cowardly moment she let her gaze linger on features that seemed uniquely his. Eyes clear and pale and steely blue, yet so alive and passionate even the fury in them seemed better than the cold aloofness he was striving for. Eyebrows and wild curls so dark above his icy gaze that looked so hard now. His features were so strongly marked and masculine she couldn't sort them from a softer, more blurred version that nagged at her memory.

'The Countess, you're Lady Carrowe's...' Yet again she let her voice tail off as if she was an incoherent and bedazzled debutante. Even the thought of being so silly and unguarded made her stiffen her spine and meet his eyes as if it didn't cost such an effort. She felt sweat bead her brow. 'Youngest son,' she ended, because she knew who he was and still refused to name-call over one thing that certainly wasn't his fault.

'Say it, Miss Alstone,' he ordered with weary impatience. 'I'm my mother's publicly denounced shame since the day I had the bad taste to be born alive. I'm the cuckoo in the Earl of Carrowe's nest; Lady Carrowe's disgrace; destroyer of innocent ladies' reputations and all the names they call me if I'm stupid enough to enter a room full of your kind. And what about you, Miss Alstone? You're Magnus Haile's affianced wife and far more of a disgrace than my mother ever was in private. She married a monster and you're about to wed his very opposite; you have no excuse for luring in a lover before you even marry my big brother.'

'That's between us and none of your business,' she said coolly.

'Tell him about this and I'll tell the whole world what you did tonight. Dare whisper a word to hurt him and I'll make sure the world finds out what we've done.'

'You can't ruin me,' she defied him and knew it was cheap to invite him to throw mud at the Earl of Carnwood's youngest sister-in-law if he dared.

'Wulf FitzDevelin may not get past generations of rank and privilege and be-damned-to-the-rest-of-you, but Dev can do it with a few flicks of his pen and a lampoon from a scurrilous friend who owes him a favour.'

'You're him; a famous writer? That Dev?' she said, incredulous he was the scourge of liars and hypocrites and fools she'd found so irresistibly funny when he wasn't directing his fury at her.

His more usual style of showing the folly and misfortune of his fellow man took his writing beyond satire. She admired his compassion and delight in ordinary and extraordinary people of great cities and small places alike. In his mind she probably qualified as liar, hypocrite and fool. That idea added a layer of sadness to her guilt she didn't want to think about right now.

'Luckily for me there's no law to stop a bastard being a writer or vice versa. And I thought I was so cynical nothing could shock me, but you proved me wrong tonight, Miss Alstone; I hope you're proud.'

'Not really,' she made herself say as if she was thinking about something more important than a trifling sin she could take to church with her on Sunday and come away with a feeling of absolution.

'Mention this aberration to my brother and I'll not only deny every word and ruin you, I'll take your family and friends down with you.'

'Don't threaten me,' she flared back at him, even as fear for those she loved and wanted to protect flared fiercely in her heart and hurt more bitterly because he was the one trying to put it there. 'Nobody will rule me or mine with fear or beatings or nasty little lies ever again,' an Isabella even she hadn't known was so furious about her childhood spat like a cornered tigress. 'Stay away from me and mine and your brother as well,' she went on in a forceful whisper for fear of being overheard. 'I'll do what I can for your half-sisters, Mr Wulf, as long as you're not glowering at me from the sidelines as if I'm the She-Wolf of France and Lucrezia Borgia rolled up together.'

'Your namesake the Queen Isabella, so-called She-Wolf of France?' he taunted her.

'A poor choice of words doesn't change facts.'

'I doubt you worry very much about them at the best of times, miss. Luckily for you I haven't the stomach to stay here and watch you promise to wed my brother as if you're worthy of even a single hair on his head.'

'You love him, don't you? All those stories about you being heartless and impervious to love and affection are more of Lord Carrowe's lies,' she said, so shaken by the fact the notorious Wulf FitzDevelin had turned out to be nothing like the man he'd been painted she forgot she was the one doing battle with him right now.

'I feel very cold and resistant to you, and if you don't hurry back inside, your undeserved reputation as a cool and lovely lady of fortune will be blasted for good. I'd be the first to dance on her grave, but Magnus wouldn't like it.'

'I certainly won't risk notoriety for the sake of someone who thinks he can threaten all I hold dear because I was stupid.'

'Stupid? A little more than that, Miss Alstone,' he said with such revulsion in his voice she decided to let him have the last word, since he liked them so much.

She gave him one last challenging look to dare him to do his worst, then turned her back. He was a mirage—a wonder that turned out nothing of the kind. Magnus and his sisters and her own loving family were real; they mattered. She used her memory of the ballroom's layout and decorations to sneak back inside unnoticed. She would get her breath back and confess to nodding off in a quiet corner from exhaustion and nerves. Yes, she could put Isabella Alstone back together and even look glowingly happy when her engagement to a good man was announced. Just a few more moments away from the stares and speculation of the cream of local society and she'd be able to playact with the best of them.

Chapter Two

Six months later Isabella wished she couldn't remember that night of rebellion as if it was only moments ago. She watched her very pregnant middle sister walk towards her like a ship in full sail and did her best to swap prickly memories for here and now.

'Are you hiding up here because you think it's the last place anyone will look, Izzie?'

'If I was, it clearly hasn't worked and, no, I'm not hiding,' she lied concisely when Kate reached her. The need to find peace felt urgent after all these weeks and months of turmoil, so here she was on the top floor of the newest part of Viscount Shuttleworth's grand and sprawling mansion, watching the spring landscape below and trying not to think.

'That's your story,' Kate said sceptically. 'I never believed them when you were the baby of the family and a sweet smile and tall tale got what you wanted nine times out of ten, and I don't believe you now.'

'Well, I'm not a baby anymore, so stop thwarting me for the good of my soul and trust me to know my own mind.'

'You're my little sister, Izzie, and trying to pretend all's well with your world when it obviously isn't won't work. I can tell how sad and confused you are about whatever has happened between you and Magnus these last few months while I've been stuck in the country like a cow out at pasture. Don't shut me out, love; I'm on your side whether you want me there or not.'

'You wouldn't leave me alone even if I wanted you to, so it's as well I don't,' Isabella joked, then sobered when she saw genuine hurt in her sister's eyes. 'I know how lucky I am to have a lionhearted older sister like you, Kate. When we were little and Miranda eloped, then Jack died, you protected me like a lioness. You must have been so sad and lost yourself, but you somehow forced our aunt and cousin to stop beating and bullying me until I was as silent and cowed as Magnus's poor little sister Theodora. I'm sorry it cost you so much to keep me safe, but you have a family of your own to spoil and protect now, my Lady Shuttleworth, and I can take care of myself. I'm sad about the end of my betrothal to Magnus, but I expect I'll get over it soon enough.'

'I don't think you will,' Kate argued as if wistfulness and guilt were written all over Isabella's face and she really hoped they weren't. 'And you were quite right to put an end to it if you didn't love him.'

'Although you're the worst-tempered and most infuriating sister I have, Katie darling, you're loyal to a fault,' Isabella tried to joke; because she had a sore heart and conscience she didn't want Kate to know about. And she did love Magnus, just not in the way a wife should love her husband.

'You only have two sisters.'

'Exactly.'

'Hmmm, I know when I'm being led away from a subject, so trying to make me angry won't work. I'm not as gentle as Miranda is most of the time, but I can control my temper when you're not around to goad it. And you should humour me, since I'm in a *very* interesting condition,' Kate said with a rueful rub of her swollen belly.

'You'd hate it if I did.'

'True, but I might secretly be flattered you wanted to cosset me so badly you held that clever tongue of yours for once in your life.'

'You don't need flattering. You and Edmund have a lovely little daughter and a new baby on the way. No doubt all three of you will spoil him or her to the edge of reason the moment they are born and what does anyone else's opinion matter when you're the centre of their world?'

'I love them so much I pinch myself to make sure this is really happening at times, but you're my little sister, Izzie. I couldn't *not* care about you while there's breath in my body, and, come to think of it, even if I was dead, I doubt I'd be able to stop loving you.'

'Oh, Kate, I love you so much,' Isabella said, feeling shaky at the very thought of losing her beloved sister. They were all trying not to dwell on the ordeal of childbirth as Kate got closer and closer to her time, but the thought of ever having to live without her beloved sister cut through Isabella's fragile attempts to be cheerful like a grim bolt of lightning on a sunny day.

'Then tell me the truth,' Kate demanded relentlessly as if she knew she had an unfair advantage and was determined to use it.

Isabella avoided her eyes and tried not to think about the ridiculous mess her life was in. The truth? She didn't even know what it was herself, so how could she tell anyone else? 'Magnus and I found we did not suit,' she said carefully. 'So I had to break the engagement, since he couldn't.'

'And we both know a lady can change her mind if she really must, but a gentleman's word has to be his bond. It's quite absurd when you think about it, but you're too passionate to be Mr Haile's convenient wife for the next forty years because neither of you had the courage to say *no* before it was too late.'

'As I'm now considered a jilt, I doubt I'll have a chance to marry another man I respect, so we'll probably never know. I haven't met anyone else

I would want to marry in five years on the marriage mart,' Isabella said with her fingers crossed under her skirts.

She'd met a man she simply wanted that night at Haile Carr, but Wulf FitzDevelin wouldn't marry her if she was the last single woman left on earth, so he didn't count. 'Half the eligible bachelors avoid me now and the rest find my fortune irresistible,' she told her sister breezily. 'I expect they think I'm desperate after whistling Magnus down the wind as if handsome and intelligent gentlemen are ten a penny.'

'You're ridiculously lovely and an heiress in your own right, Izzie. If you were desperate, you'd have clung to him like a limpet.'

'I didn't say it was logical, but at least as an old maid I'll be spared such nonsense in future.'

'You're three and twenty, love, and won't be on the shelf long,' Kate argued with a wry smile. 'There are a few other gentlemen with good eyesight and a modicum of sense in their handsome heads, so you don't need to wear the willow.'

Isabella felt tears threaten at her sister's steadfast love and loyalty, just as they had when she'd seen Kate and her husband, Edmund, stood waiting for her on the gravel carriage sweep this morning, too impatient to wait to greet their guest at the top of the wide stone steps as befitted their station as Lord and Lady Shuttleworth. Kate, Edmund and their daughter had hugged and inspected Isabella for damage, as if they were afraid she'd been broken since they saw her last. Louise Kenton, née Alstone, was the youngest sister of Miranda's husband, Kit, Seventh Earl of Carnwood. Kit and Louise and their sister Maria were distant cousins of her and Miranda and Kate and he was probably the most reluctant lord in the House when he succeeded to the family titles, but marrying Miranda seemed to have reconciled him to it and Louise simply added Kate and Isabella to her family when her brother married their big sister and she felt like another sibling now. Isabella wasn't quite sure she wanted Louise's sharp eyes on her, though she was glad Louise was here for Kate during this time. At least she knew a good deal about childbirth after bearing six children since marrying Hugh.

Isabella didn't know how Edmund convinced his wife she was too near her time to go to Derbyshire and join Kit and Miranda for the Easter festivities, but she was very glad he had. This way Kate must play hostess to as many of the family as he could assemble and what a good thing her sisters had married men who respected as well as loved them. Kit and Edmund found ingenious ways around their wives' sore spots and stubborn streaks when an invigorating argument wasn't advisable and that was the sort of marriage Isabella had tried to convince herself she could build with Magnus.

She felt like a fool about that delusion when she watched Edmund and Kate, and Hugh and Louise, together and realised she'd left something vital out. Magnus was a handsome and civilised gentleman with a clever mind, a dry sense of humour and a good heart, but he wasn't the love of her life. Although she didn't want one of those, it was probably better not to marry at all than accept less. She had spent six months at odds with herself and at the end of it found out Magnus was in love with another woman. He had offered for Isabella to silence his obnoxious father about the child he and his beloved Lady Delphine had made together and he loved *her* so much he'd been ready to sacrifice himself and Isabella for the sake of her precious reputation. So if she wasn't going to risk marrying for reason again and loving a man with all of her heart was a terrifying step she refused to take into the unknown, she would do better not to marry.

'I'm not pining for Magnus, Kate. He was the first grown-up gentleman I danced with at my come-out ball and I suppose I fooled myself into thinking we could make a good marriage out of our long friendship and mutual interests, but I was wrong. I miss him as a friend, but I won't collapse in a tearful heap whenever you say his name.'

'If you like him that much, maybe you should marry him anyway, since you always said you'd never wed for love,' Kate suggested half-seriously, as if it had been wedding nerves that made Isabella call off the wedding and the whole thing might still be salvaged. Since Kate took three years to discover she loved Edmund far too much to let him marry anyone else, Isabella forgave her sister for doubting her.

'No,' she said firmly enough to nip any well-meant schemes to throw her and Magnus back together in the bud. 'It would be a disaster.'

Never quite measuring up to a lover your spouse couldn't have would make a marriage hideous. Lucky for her it was only passion on her side and not love. Still, it was probably unfair to compare every other man she met to broodingly handsome Wulf FitzDevelin and his devilishly seductive kisses one impossible night when she took a few minutes off from being cool and careful Miss Alstone.

'You don't think you could come to love him in time, then?' Kate said with memories of her own slow-burning feelings dreamy in her dark blue eyes.

'No.'

'Then I'm glad you found out before it was too late. Edmund is my best friend, but he's also my abiding passion and it baffles me how you thought you could settle for less. A civilised and passionless marriage could never work for you, love.'

'You were hell-bent on making one yourself once upon a time,' Isabella pointed out to divert her sister from this uncomfortable topic of conversation.

'I'm not sure that's a proper way for an unmarried lady to express herself, sister dear. And, as Edmund was the man I was determined to make it with, I had perfect taste, even if my judgement was a little clouded,' Kate replied smugly. Isabella was certain Kate and Edmund still enjoyed the odd passionate, invigorating argument about it even now.

'Take a lesson from me, Izzie,' Kate persisted because she knew Izzie far better than she wanted her to, 'marriage lasts too long for any Alstone to risk it without being in love with our spouse.'

'Don't upset yourself because it didn't happen. I miss Magnus and his mother and sisters, but I'm glad we agreed to part before it was too late.'

Are you going to tell your sister what blinded you to the truth for so long, Isabella? the sneaky inner voice she wanted to ignore whispered.

I was confused, she told it firmly and it was a wonder she didn't have a permanent headache with all these contrary feelings clashing about inside.

'Gentlemen can be the most dreadful cowards about losing their freedom,' Kate said sagely as if she was an expert on the breed now she had a subtle and determined lord to try to order about for his own good.

'I don't think Magnus was waiting to say "I do" through gritted teeth because of prenuptial nerves, love,' Isabella tried to joke, then went back to staring out of the wide sash windows because it wasn't funny. 'Oh, look who's outside again, Kate. Louise did say Sophia was to stay in the schoolroom today, didn't she? The wretched girl obviously wasn't listening since she looks as if she's off to explore the lavender maze you designed by the wilderness and never mind her governess.'

'It's a lovely day and I don't blame Sophia for wanting to be outside instead of stuck in the schoolroom staring out of the windows at a blue sky and dreaming. I'm not going to lumber up to the schoolroom to betray her. You could find Louise and tell her what her youngest daughter is up to if you really want to, but she's probably doing her best not to know.'

'We were never allowed to use the weather as an excuse to avoid our books,' Isabella said half-heartedly.

'Charlotte never took her eyes off us long enough for us to escape, but I'm not sure even she could keep Sophia in on a day like this if she was still a governess instead of Ben Shaw's wife and mother of their vast tribe of children,' Kate said, peering over Isabella's shoulder at the half-grown girl.

'The Kentons would be a challenge even for her,' Isabella said absently. Sophia had reached the broad walk now and her scarlet cloak flew out behind her as she ran. She made a splash of vital colour against the sunlit grass and a richly periwinkle-blue sky and was nearly at her destination now. Isabella wished she was out there with her, running away from adult cares and all the gossip her cancelled wedding had brought down on her and her family. 'With parents like

Louise and Hugh none of them are ever going to be pattern cards of proper behaviour.'

'They'd have to be changelings,' her sister agreed.

'Sophia and her littlest brother certainly aren't and, speaking of young Kit, I wonder where he is. Perhaps Sophia locked him in a cupboard, because I can't see him minding his primers if he can get into mischief with his big sister instead.'

'Louise could be keeping a closer eye on him as she knows what a restless little devil he is, or he could still be on his way and that's why Sophia's running to get away before he spoils her adventure.'

'You're probably right,' Isabella said and wondered if it was too late to chase after Sophia or let little Kit lure her into mischief. 'It's a good thing their brothers are at school or I might have to go and restore order and it looks cold out there.'

'Much you'd care. Miranda is always scolding you for ruining your complexion in the sun or the wind and you don't take much notice when you're not in town and the tabbies can't make snide remarks about her negligence.'

'Miranda will listen to their spiteful gossip and feel guilty.'

'She's never quite learnt to ignore the nay-sayers, has she? As well Kit doesn't care or we might still be wearing hair shirts because she ran off with Nevin when he was secretly wed to our vile cousin Celia. Oh, look, Izzie. Who on earth is hurrying after Sophia? I'd certainly remember if I'd met *him*, happily married or not,' Kate exclaimed and pointed at the lithe and vigorous figure striding after Sophia Kenton with a wildly gesticulating master Christopher Kenton on his shoulders.

No, it can't be him, Isabella. Wulf FitzDevelin is on the other side of the Atlantic and he wouldn't follow you to Herefordshire on a private family visit if he wasn't. He wouldn't cross the street to pick you up if you'd been knocked down by a dust cart, she told herself firmly, because her heartbeat was loud in her ears as she watched the powerful male figure hurry after Sophia and wondered if she'd really fainted and this was a nightmare.

His drab greatcoat swirled out behind him in

his hurry and even from up here his crow-black locks looked wild, but there was such leashed power and energy in his loping walk, encumbered or not, that she couldn't escape the reality of him. He was here, now. She remembered the defiant set to his head and shoulders too well and couldn't fool herself her eyes were deceiving her.

How dare he? He wasn't on visiting terms with Kate and Edmund and it couldn't be because he couldn't stay away from her. He had put vast and empty miles of ocean between them after that night at Haile Carr and now he was back. A silly, moon-led part of her was dancing as if he'd come to claim her now his half-brother wasn't engaged to marry her any longer. She shook her head to deny the idiot any say and decided she must find out what he wanted before he made his contempt for her clear and Kate put two and two together.

Feeling the force of his impatient personality even from up here, she noted he was even more leanly fit and unforgettable by daylight. Large chunks of his overlong sable hair were being held captive by Master Kenton and she almost winced in sympathy, but he deserved it, didn't he? She shivered as if she was out there, in spring sunlight, close enough to see him frown as she fought to read the thoughts in that austere, almost handsome dark head of his.

'He's the Haile family ghost; Wulf FitzDevelin,' she muttered, but Kate heard and raised her eyebrows. 'I can't imagine what he's doing here, so don't ask me,' she added as coolly as she could with Kate gazing at her as if she thought differently.

'That's Lady Carrowe's Folly? Well, I never, ever did,' Kate said slowly. 'If his father was anything like him, I almost understand her fall from grace. If I wasn't married to the love of my life and Edmund wasn't such a potent lover, I might be tempted to lure a man like him into my bed and the devil take the consequences.'

'You only say that because you know it's never going to happen. Any woman who sends out lures in his direction will reap trouble and heartache. If he has a heart, he's hidden it so well nobody knows where it is.'

'Your Magnus is said to be as close to him

as if he was a full brother and you think *him* a good man.'

'Magnus *is* a good man and can't see his half-brother's dark side because he loves him.'

'Whatever side you catch him on I'd wager my best bonnet debutantes' hearts beat nineteen to the dozen when they set eyes on the two of them. Their elder sisters will do more than sigh over a rogue like that and I expect he has to fight them off, if he's careless enough to venture into Carrowe House at the right time for the Countess to be at home to callers.'

'If you weren't such a country wife nowadays, you'd recall not even the most dashing of the young matrons are brave enough to visit her ladyship openly and they'd be idiots to accept a dare like him even if they did,' Isabella said with a fierce frown at the man's back as he strode away.

'Or so besotted they couldn't help themselves,' Kate suggested with another overt glance at that powerfully lean masculine figure as his long legs ate up landscaped gardens and a much sneakier sidelong look at Isabella.

The inner voice she was trying to ignore whispered Kate was right: he did improve the scenery even on such a shining spring day. Familiar little demons were whispering in her ear and how dare he wake them up when she'd tried so hard to silence them? The long, sinful nights in his bed her inner fool yearned for wouldn't be as wonderful as his leanly honed body and moody looks promised. No, of course they wouldn't; not now he despised her. No point risking her all for an itch she wanted to scratch so badly it still kept her awake at nights.

She tried to divert herself by wondering if his mother had loved his father or simply wanted him. Lady Carrowe never refuted her husband's assertion Wulf was her by-blow, but had she thought what illicit passion could cost when she lay with her lover long enough to get with child? If he was anything like Wulf, she probably couldn't see past the blind haze of wanting and so it was a good thing Wulf FitzDevelin disliked and distrusted Isabella Alstone so much, wasn't it?

'He's probably here to lecture me about his

brother,' she told her sister crossly and at least he was oblivious to her fast-beating heart and weak knees as she followed his every move with hungry eyes.

'Hmmm, well, he looks to have made a firm friend of young Kit. Sophia won't be so pleased her little brother caught up with his help, or should I call it endurance?'

'Young Kit is a force of nature,' Isabella agreed absently.

'You could call it that,' Kate replied as they watched man and boy close in on Sophia, 'but your FitzDevelin is one as well and grown-up with it.'

'He's not my FitzDevelin. I wouldn't give him a ha'penny worth of goodwill if he stooped to beg it from me and he never will.'

'Why ever not?' Kate asked so innocently Isabella bit back a groan.

'We hardly know each other and don't like what we do know,' she said flatly.

'Because he's the Countess of Carrowe's by-blow and they whisper dark scandals about him and all the lovers he's had who ought to know better?'

'He had no say in the sins his mother and father committed before he was born,' Isabella said absently as she tried not to think about all those bored society matrons rumour credited him with seducing. Kate was probably right and they lined up to be seduced and that was one more reason not to join in.

'They say the Earl made sure his wife's byblow got an education and would have set him up in a profession if your Wulf hadn't run away. Kind of him to raise his wife's bastard, but he didn't get much thanks, did he?'

'Kind? Do you really think so?' Isabella asked absently.

She was busy watching Wulf move so fluidly he might actually be a wolf padding after his prey if he had another pair of lithe legs and a fine pelt to go with those ice-blue eyes. For a hungry moment she wished she was at his side, close enough to admire the ease of sleek muscle over elegant bones and wonder at his total focus as he ruthlessly tracked his quarry. Except he wasn't a predator and she wasn't fascinated, so it was as well she wasn't close enough to fall under his spell.

'You don't?' Kate said, sounding intrigued.

'The Earl isn't a kind man, Kate. He would have sued his wife's lover for criminal conversation and divorced her if he was.'

'She does seem very inoffensive and quiet now,' Kate said and Isabella could see her acute mind working on Lady Carrowe's unfortunate situation.

If the lady had even one more supporter among the *haut ton*, she might be less oppressed and her daughters more welcome in polite society. Isabella stared down at the empty garden where Wulf and the youngest Kentons had disappeared from view. She half-expected to see a mark in the air, a magic rune perhaps to tell unwary females danger lay ahead.

'You have given a good deal of thought to Mr FitzDevelin's shocking birth and stormy upbringing during your engagement to his brother, Izzie,' Kate said airily.

'No more than I would about anyone in such a situation,' she replied and fought not to cross her fingers against another huge lie, because not a single night had gone by since she met him when he didn't haunt her sleeping and waking.

'Of course not, but whatever you think of him he's here and can't have come all this way to see anyone but you. In your shoes I'd hear him out before Edmund and Hugh chase him away.'

'I doubt he'll go or stay unless he wants to,' Isabella muttered, but Kate was right. She didn't want her overprotective male relatives running him off before she found out what he wanted. 'Can you keep them busy long enough for me to be rid of him before they find out?'

'I'm in no fit state to stop anyone doing whatever they want, but if Hugh and Edmund think we're having a feminine coze about babies and lying-in, they won't interrupt unless the house is on fire or someone falls off the roof. We can go to my boudoir and tell my maid to be sure we're not disturbed, then you can use the garden stairs to go and find Mr FitzDevelin and I can escape the fuss Edmund will surround me with until I'm safely delivered.'

'He loves you, Kate.'

'I know and I love him, but I can't take a step

without having to account for it to someone who has better things to do if they'd only get on with them.'

'Not as far as he's concerned they haven't and you'd be mortally offended if he went off to discuss crops with his tenants or horses with his cronies and left you to birth his child alone.'

'I would and quite right, too.'

'Stop being contrary and go and have a rest, then. Edmund will need to be revived with smelling salts if you don't stop behaving as if you're about to throw a trifling entertainment instead of giving birth to his second child.'

'If you promise to stop being wise about the rest of us and look at your own motives and feelings, I might.'

'There truly is a first time for everything, then,' Isabella said crossly.

'Anyone would think I was the contrary one of the three of us,' her sister said as if she really thought she wasn't. 'And stop looking like that, because Miranda and I know you're wilful as a donkey even if you fool so many with that angelic face.'

'I almost wish I'd stayed in London to be gossiped about by strangers now.'

'Really? When there must be so many more sharp eyes to watch your assignations with Mr FitzDevelin when you're in town?'

'Nonsense, I've never met him in town and this isn't an assignation.'

'You would have to know he was coming for it to be one of those, wouldn't you?' Kate said as if she was quite convinced Isabella had been waiting for him to catch up with her ever since she broke her engagement to his brother and how much more wrong-headed could one woman get?

Chapter Three

Wulf cursed himself for not being able to resist the shine of tears in a little boy's eyes when he begged for help to catch up with his big sister. He'd been excluded from so much as a boy that the little rascal couldn't have chosen a better bid for sympathy. Yet what would such a young girl think when confronted by a strange man with her brother aloft, especially one this unkempt and in need of a shave? His windswept, travel-stained appearance would probably terrify her and exhaustion was making it easier for him to frown than smile.

'How did the infernal brat persuade you to hunt me down?' this girl demanded when she saw her brother riding triumphantly on a stranger's shoulders. 'I do wish people would ignore him when he pretends to be an ill-treated waif. Every time someone believes him it only encourages him to keep doing it,' she went on and he should have known this sturdy little rogue couldn't have a shrinking violet as a sister.

'Thank you for the advice. I'll bear it in mind if I'm not invited again,' he managed to reply with a straight face. He had ridden here too hard to get this over with. Lack of sleep and a decent meal must be making him light-headed, because there wasn't anything here to laugh about.

'We don't live here, so that won't do any good,' she told him with a resigned sigh that almost set him off again.

'I promise to learn from my mistakes, then,' Wulf said, swinging his giggling passenger down so the boy could run into a clever lavender labyrinth and gallop its paths as if he'd had enough energy to run from Herefordshire to the distant Welsh Mountains all along.

'He's a horrid brat and should be beaten at least once a day for the good of all our souls, but who the devil are you?' the girl demanded as if she'd only just taken in his windswept, bearlike appearance and realised he wasn't the sort of visitor a grand house like Cravenhill Park usually attracted by daylight.

'I'm Wulf FitzDevelin; who the devil are *you*?' he replied, wondering if the young men of the *ton* had any idea what a whirlwind was going to hit them when she was old enough to be presented at Court.

'I'm Miss Sophia Kenton, because my older sister Julia got to be Miss Kenton when our aunt married Mr Sandbatch, and Wulf's not a proper name for a gentleman.'

'I'm not a proper gentleman, but it's short for Wulfric if that helps.'

'He's my horse,' young Master Kenton shouted breathlessly from the labyrinth and this time Wulf did laugh out loud. The sound sent a pair of crows cawing into the treetops and broke the almost uncanny peace of this place.

'I'd have thrown him off a lot sooner if I were you,' Sophia said with a frown at her little brother.

'I really don't think you would,' Wulf said, seeing reluctant affection in the girl's eyes and contrasting it with the open dislike in the eyes of his two eldest half-siblings when he'd been a scrubby brat himself.

'Probably not, but I'd be tempted,' the girl said with a wry smile.

'It *is* you, Mr FitzDevelin; I thought my eyes were deceiving me. What a very *unexpected* surprise,' Isabella Alstone's cool voice said from behind them.

Wulf felt his heart thunder; instinct should have warned him she was there. The sound made him feel as if parts of him he didn't want to think about right now could burst into flames. 'Good day, Miss Alstone,' he said flatly.

Somehow he managed to meet her dark blue eyes calmly and she obviously couldn't imagine why he was polluting the clean air of her brother-in-law's fine estate and ought to go back where he belonged. In the gutter presumably, he concluded and hoped a cynical half-smile would divert her from the ravenous hunger roaring through him like the hottest and most ill-timed lightning.

'Is my brother-in-law expecting you?' she asked

as if she had no idea how she made red-blooded males feel by being so perfectly, femininely arrogant. All he wanted right now was to kiss her and it took too much effort to recall why he'd come. She'd jilted Magnus—Gus, as he'd always been to Wulf—and he'd done so much damage between them already even the idea was madness and he should be ashamed of himself.

'I doubt Lord Shuttleworth has the least idea I'm here, but *you* should have known I'd come, Miss Alstone,' he said stiffly.

'Why would I? There's no reason for you to intrude on a private family gathering and I could hardly believe my eyes when I saw you walking up the Broad Walk with young Kit on your shoulders,' Isabella said stiffly.

Now she was faced with the real man her silly heart was racing as if she'd run all the way from the house to simper at him. She half-wished he was still on the other side of the Atlantic, building the new life he'd claimed to want when he left England. If he'd stayed away, she wouldn't have to face the fact he still stirred her as no other man ever had. She wouldn't have to feel the

Isabella he woke up that night straining against the leash.

'You didn't send your brother-in-law to throw me out, though, did you?' he challenged in the husky undertone she found so ridiculously enchanting that moon-mad night.

'I don't want to embarrass my family, Mr Fitz-Develin,' she said primly.

'I presume you are part of Miss Alstone's family, Miss Sophia? Am I making you uncomfortable?'

'Yes, I am and, no, you're not. I'm far too interested in how Aunt Izzie knows you and what you've done to make her glare daggers at you. I don't think Kit has ever been embarrassed about anything in his life, so I shouldn't bother to ask him.'

'Oh, please run along, Sophia, and take young Kit with you,' Isabella interrupted before this meeting turned into an even bigger farce.

'I can't; it would be improper to leave you alone with a strange gentleman, Aunt Izzie. It's our duty to chaperon you,' Sophia said so virtuously Isabella frowned to say she was overdoing it and should do as she was bid for once.

'Maybe so, but show your little brother the way to the middle of the lavender labyrinth and at least try to mind your own business while you're doing it,' she said, in lieu of Sophia turning into a proper young lady by a minor miracle.

Sophia crossed her arms and stared back as if Isabella was the one being difficult. 'For that I should stay here and insist on listening to every word.'

'Go away, Sophia. Please?' Isabella gave up trying to reason her out of eavesdropping. 'Please?' she cajoled as she was desperate to get this over and Wulf back on the road before Edmund or Hugh knew he was here.

'Oh, very well, but you owe me half-a-dozen favours.'

'And she'll make me pay,' Isabella muttered gloomily once Sophia demanded little Kit's attention until he found something more interesting to do.

'You don't treat her as an irritating little girl, though, do you?' he asked as if he was surprised.

'If she had any idea how difficult being grown-up is, Sophia wouldn't be in such a hurry to be one.'

'You find being a society beauty burdensome, then, Miss Alstone?'

'I do when people throw it at me like an accusation, Mr FitzDevelin.'

'I apologise,' he said impatiently.

'I doubt it, but you must have come here to speak to me, since you don't know my family and I doubt if you're a business connection of my brother-in-law. A strange man on the strange horse I assume is resting in my brother-in-law's stables as we speak won't go unnoticed long, however much you tipped the groom to look the other way. My brother-in-law will want a good reason why you came here uninvited now his family are arriving for Eastertide and my sister is in an interesting condition.'

'Before I'm grabbed by the scruff of my neck and thrown out I admit I came to plead with you.'

'*You?* Plead with *me*?' Isabella exclaimed, although he'd come a long way to play a trick if he was lying. 'I doubt you even know how.'

'Then I must learn, mustn't I?' he said impatiently. 'Magnus is a broken man,' he accused with such fury in his ice-blue eyes he must think it was her fault. 'He's shockingly thin and can't shake off the influenza I'm told he contracted at Christmas. He needs you. I can't imagine why when you kiss strange men at the drop of a hat and threw him over when you got tired of being engaged to marry him.'

'Please don't bother stretching your poor, underused imagination any further, then, because I'm not the woman your half-brother needs.'

'You really are stony-hearted, aren't you?'

'Apparently,' she said calmly.

Letting him know his accusation hurt as if a knife had been plunged into her chest would be even more stupid than finding the air at Cravenhill Park fresher and the sunlight brighter because he was here, even while he was flinging insults at her. If she had any sense, she'd turn her back on him and walk away; prove how indifferent she was to him *and* his misconceptions. A foolish part of her was far too pleased he was here to do that, despite the fury in his gaze as he let it slide over her.

'What will get me past the ice between you and nobodies like me so I can reason with you?' he asked and began to pace, as if that was the only way he could stop himself shaking her.

'Nothing you can say,' she told him steadily and refused to let him know he'd hurt her. His picture of events was so wide of the mark she'd laugh if she wasn't feeling so sick.

'And I dare say you'd turn his life upside down and treat him like a fool if you did agree to wed him after all, but even that would be better than watching him waste away for the lack of you in his life.'

'I shall not and certainly not to please you. Please me by going away and avoiding me like the plague from now on, Mr FitzDevelin. Your brother and I had our own very good reasons not to go ahead with our wedding, but not one of them is any of your business.'

'Yes, it is. I got back to England a week ago to find Magnus half the man he was when I left and he's worth a hundred of either of us. I won't let you set him at naught because his devotion has become tiresome.'

'Find a fresh horse and go home, because you've had a wasted journey. Your insults won't change a thing and next time you set out on a wild goose chase you should talk to your brother about it before you begin.'

'He won't talk to me,' the wrong-headed idiot mumbled as if he didn't want to admit he'd failed.

'Neither will I,' she said quietly.

Was it right to enjoy the blaze of anger and frustration lighting his eyes to purest ice blue before he turned to pace up and down the path again to stop himself taking her back to London by force for his brother like a juicy bone someone stole?

'He obviously loves you to distraction,' Wulf FitzDevelin threw out as he paced close enough to vent his fury without Sophia hearing. 'Heaven knows why when you treat him like a whining dog you can kick aside when you're weary of it.'

'I don't kick dogs. Your arguments are so persuasive I'm surprised you're not employed as a diplomat, Mr Wulf,' she retaliated sweetly. She was stoking an already scorching fire and it felt wickedly enjoyable as well as oddly powerful to bait him when he couldn't lay a finger on her without having to explain it to a pair of children and her furious male relatives, but she really should stop it. 'You'll scare the children and as they're Kentons it takes a lot of doing.'

He frowned even more fiercely and looked over at Sophia, who was staring at him while little Kit ran round the maze making war whoops as if he witnessed fiery adult battles of will every day of the week. He might well, given who his parents were and the fact they were notorious for enjoying a good argument. This wasn't a good argument, though, was it? Still, Wulf looked a little sheepish when he turned back to her.

'I'm sorry,' he said abruptly, as if every word cost a fortune.

'Are you? Now I've seen your true colours I'm not surprised Magnus doesn't confide in you.'

'We were close as real brothers until he got engaged to you. He's been closed as an oyster ever since and now just drinks and looks miserable as sin whenever someone mentions your name.

You broke off the engagement days before you were due to marry; you've broken his heart.'

'Don't be so melodramatic; it was two months until our wedding and the invitations hadn't even been sent out.'

'Be grateful we're being watched by innocents, Miss Alstone. I'm so tempted to find out if there's red blood in your veins I doubt much else would hold me back.'

A hard and feverish sort of wanting blazed in his ice-blue eyes as if his steely will was all that stopped him kissing her witless, so she'd have to be grateful Sophia and little Kit were nearby, wouldn't she? 'I'd bite you if you tried it, Mr FitzDevelin, then we'd see what yours is like and never mind mine.'

'How very *uncivil* of you,' he snapped back sarcastically as if he hoped his words would freeze in mid-air and physically hurt her.

Isabella was hard-pressed not to wince. 'Lucky we are being watched, then, since I don't care to lower myself to your level,' she replied and she needed to feed that fury; keep him standing across the green dell glaring at her like an enemy.

She was almost terrified by the wild emotions burning the frosty air yet fascinated by the idea of exploring them and never mind conventions, relatives by marriage or her thorny Alstone pride.

'You're afraid you might kiss the bastard back, again.'

'No, I could never want a man who despises me,' she lied.

'Why not, you did last time, Isabella,' he reminded her with such deadly softness she felt his words scorch as if he'd written them in Greek fire on her flinching skin.

He was quite right; that night she kissed him as if her last breath depended on it and why was she such a confounded idiot as to want him and not his half-brother? She felt the merciless heat of longing for a dark and dangerous man she'd never been able to feel for gentlemanly, handsome and much kinder Magnus Haile. Raw wanting ran through her like wildfire, but this time she'd keep it to herself.

'Go away,' she demanded in a voice rasped and on the edge of admitting something dreadful.

'And tell Magnus he's right, you're cold as an iceberg under all that golden beauty?'

A shard of pain her good friend could say such a thing about her threatened her serenity. She managed a haughty stare and told herself he'd made it up.

'I can't persuade you to drag my half-brother out of the pit of despair he's tumbled into since you jilted him? He doesn't deserve to be treated like a piece of rubbish by a woman he loves for some reason that's beyond me.'

'No, you can't and find out what he really wants next time you set out to get it for him by fair means or foul,' she replied so sweetly she heard him grind his teeth and was savagely glad.

Chapter Four

Wulf struggled with a powerful urge to shake Isabella until she was as disarrayed as he was after galloping all the way here as if the devil was on his heels. But he couldn't do that with the young Kentons looking on. Even if their softly hostile words didn't carry on the clear air, such acute children must already know something was amiss and that would send them running for their father. Tension was stiffening every muscle and sinew he had and he wanted Isabella with a burning hunger he'd never felt the like of before. It roared to life the instant he set eyes on her hesitating on the edge of the terrace at Haile Carr while he was trying to convince himself to go inside the hot and brightly lit ballroom because Magnus needed his support and never mind the Earl and his eldest half-brother's order to stay away. If only he'd fought his doubts a little harder, he might have been introduced to this golden-haired and lovely heiress as Magnus's intended bride instead of kissing her as if his heart and soul depended on it.

An image of his brother six months on, pale, bony and unshaven as he brooded over a brandy glass at the breakfast table, reminded him why he was here. But as Isabella Alstone was as cool as the frosty air around them as she stared back at him, there seemed no point repeating the speech he'd put together word by painful word as he rode here. His inner devil took over his tongue at first sight of her and hurt was still screaming for air inside him. For months this sense of betrayal had wanted to tumble out in a toxic stream of bitter words, but they weren't for Magnus, were they?

'Quiet men have unquiet souls and dark needs and it could be too late to draw back and say a polite "no, thank you" to the next one you hook as firmly as you caught my brother,' he warned. The thought of her playing with another idiot in the dark made him feel as if madness was lying in wait.

'You have no idea what your brother and I mean to each other. *You* should be wary of thinking you know him better than he does himself, Mr FitzDevelin. I would like you to leave before you cause the sort of scene I would rather not put my family through at Eastertide with my sister so near her time.'

'No doubt your brothers-in-law will enjoy crushing my pretensions if they find me, but I rode here for my brother's sake and would rather be a thousand miles away for mine. Will you mend this public rift and take up your betrothal to Magnus again?'

'No,' she said stiffly.

Was it the hint of hurt too deep for an ice princess that made his breath catch and a whisper of forbidden longing catch at his heart? No, she was his brother's dream and Wulf FitzDevelin's worst nightmare. 'You don't care a fig for my brother,' he said flatly and turned away in disgust. Yes, that was it; her regal indifference to Magnus's sufferings disgusted him. He should disregard the little part of him that was dancing a jig because she was free to enjoy all kinds of forbidden mischief with Magnus's bastard brother at last.

'Maybe I care too much,' he thought he heard her whisper and his inner devil tripped up in mid-skip and fell flat on its ugly face.

Wulf spun on his heel to glare a challenge at her and she met it, nodded at their youthful audience to remind him to be quiet. 'Why break your engagement, then?' he rumbled gruffly.

'Because it was the right thing to do,' she murmured, watching the Kenton children explore the labyrinth as if they'd been the centre of her interest all this time and the hard tension in the air between them didn't fascinate her as well.

'And you always do the right thing, do you?'

'No, but I own my mistakes when I realise I've made them, Mr FitzDevelin.'

'Was it because I kissed you at the Summer Ball?' he finally gritted out the question that had alternatively appalled and elated him since he read a notice the marriage between the Honourable Magnus Haile and Miss Isabella Alstone would not take place. The newssheet had appeared just as he returned from running away from his stark betrayal of his brother's trust.

'You do have a high opinion of yourself, Mr FitzDevelin.'

'Was it?' he persisted.

'No, I might have managed to forget that outrage…'

'You didn't respond with outrage at the time; I wish you had.'

'So do I and stop interrupting—it's rude as well as a waste of time. Where was I? Oh, yes, I *might* have forgotten that outrage, but I chose to keep it in my memory as a reminder never to wander out of a hot ballroom and expect to find a gentleman in the dark. Your conduct that night had no influence on my decision not to marry your half-brother. Be glad of it, Mr FitzDevelin, and stop glaring at me as if I made you do it when we both know you fell on me like the lust-driven yahoo you are.'

He ought to be as furious as she was trying to make him, but when she put on that high-nosed lady manner, it lit a fire inside him she ought to be a lot more wary of. It had burnt out of control that night at Haile Carr; heat had scorched the sense out of both of them, as if being close as they could get was all that mattered in this life. Gus would have every right to despise him if he found out what they nearly did the first night they laid eyes on one another, but this wasn't about them and stealing illicit kisses in the moonlight. He had come here to plead with her to take his half-brother back and marry him, not to remind them both how disgracefully they behaved when they forgot who they were. *So how is that going, Wulfric?* Badly. The uncomfortable truth was he didn't want her to wed anyone else. Fury at the very idea of her in another man's arms thundered up against his love for his brother and trumped it. He made himself recall the sickening fall back to earth that night after he'd kissed this beautiful, vital woman as if his life depended on it, then found out who she was. A Miss Alstone of Wychwood would never truly want a misfit like him. Even if he had half a kingdom to offer her, she'd turn up her nose and say a chilly 'No, thank you'.

'Did Gus ever kiss you like that?' he heard

himself ask and only just smothered a groan of disbelief.

'He never asked for more than a lady cares to give before marriage.'

'Less than nothing, then,' he stated flatly and she blushed and lowered her eyes. He tried to stamp on a low sense of satisfaction he'd ruffled her ice-maiden calm when Gus could not.

'I gave your brother his freedom, and if you want to know more, you must ask him,' she ended with so much ice in her voice he shivered.

'Do you think I haven't?'

'Ah, but you don't ask, do you? You demand.'

Wulf blushed and was surprised he still could. 'I'm sorry I was rude,' he said a little more loudly so the children might hear him, if they hadn't run off to find enough strong men to throw him out. He flicked a glance in their direction and saw they were still there, keeping half an eye on him as if he might do something very interesting if they turned their backs and they didn't want to miss it.

'You only ever wanted me because of how I look,' she accused so softly he could barely hear her. 'And don't twit me on being vain, because it's more of a trial than a blessing. Men have wanted me since before I left the schoolroom because of my fortune and a set of even features, but I was always more than that to Magnus— would I could say the same for you.'

'Marry him, then,' he said harshly, secretly hurt she thought him wanting and why wouldn't she when Magnus was worth a dozen of him?

She sighed and shook her head. 'Do try listening for once,' she said as if she was running out of patience. 'Magnus confided in me, and if you can't trust my word we should not wed, ask him to do the same for you.'

'You could marry me,' he heard himself say as if his voice was coming from a great distance.

'Because you kissed me once and feel guilty? No, thank you. I wouldn't marry now unless I was so deep in love I couldn't help myself, which means I shall never marry because I don't want to be in love.'

'Perhaps you won't have a choice, but you wouldn't wed a bastard even if you loved me from head to foot, would you? Miss Alstone of

Wychwood and the by-blow of an erring countess? Unthinkable.'

'I would dislike you if you had a ducal coronet,
vast numbers of houses and thousands of acres
to your name. Being housed and fed by a vindictive man during your early years has bent you
out of shape, Mr FitzDevelin. Maybe Lord Carrowe isn't the tolerant, sophisticated gentleman
the polite world think him, but you're not either.'

'I hope you don't mean he raised me in his
own image.'

'No, but I think you became hard and angry
in order to survive his harsh regime and you
shouldn't let him shape your view of the world.'

'You have no idea how it feels to be blamed for
anything amiss in your family's life.'

'My sister Kate and I were left in our great-
aunt and cousin's hands as small children. I
doubt there's much your stepfather could teach
them about humiliating those too small or poor
to thumb their noses and walk away. You ran
as soon as you were old enough, didn't you? I
can't tell you how we would have envied you
the strength and cunning to survive in the wider

world when we were to blame for anything that went wrong at Wychwood before our brother-in-law inherited it.'

Wulf felt his heart lurch at the thought of tiny, defiant Isabella surviving such a harsh regime. She ought to have been doted on and valued from the moment she was born, as the outgoing and confident children on the other side of this coolly peaceful garden obviously were. He itched to drag the hags who inflicted such cruelty on two little girls to the nearest Bridewell and show them how it felt to be whipped and humiliated until tears and pleas sank into despair and your only refuge was unconsciousness. He'd sworn as a boy never to lay violent hands on a woman or child, so he'd have to trust the Earl of Carnwood to make sure those harpies never had control of a child's life again and reminded himself the Alstone sisters were nothing to do with him, then or now.

'You do understand, then,' he admitted gruffly.

'I do, but we were rescued by my eldest sister's godmama after she spent a year or two nagging my grandfather to send us to school so persistently he gave in to get some peace. Then Miranda married Kit and we had a fine governess and all the love we were starved of when Miranda left and my brother died. So Kate and I only had a few years of being wronged before our older sister and brother-in-law showered us with enough love and attention to make up for that time.'

'Those women left their mark on you,' he argued quietly and at least now he knew why she held herself a little aloof in case she met gleeful spite in a stranger's eye or saw a bully under their skin.

'Not as big as the one your stepfather left on you,' she countered.

'He doesn't rule my life; I won't let him.'

'Then if you get over this conviction you know what's best for your brother and anyone else you care about, we might get on better.'

'We might, except Magnus is still miserable and you're still here. Relations between us won't improve until you change that situation.'

'Here we go again, so it's probably as well my brother-in-law is about to interrupt us.'

'Damn it, I'm not done.'

'Well, I am and here he comes anyway. Go back to London and talk to your half-brother before you blunder into any more private homes without an invitation. If you tell Magnus half the wrong-headed nonsense you spouted at me, I'm sure he'll confide before you dash about the countryside doing more damage.'

Two purposeful males were striding ever closer and she was pushing him aside as if he was a problem she'd confronted and solved. Except Wulf felt more like an arsenal of gunpowder ready to blow with the smallest spark. He wouldn't be going away satisfied he could now forget Miss Alstone's vital beauty, acute mind and waspish tongue as if he'd never met her one hot and spellbound August night.

'Papa, Papa, we're over here,' little Kit shouted as if he and his sister must be more important than any mysterious stranger.

'Mr Fitz-something helped him catch up with me,' Sophia informed her father with an exasperated look at her brother, as if she already knew he wouldn't get the rebuke she half-wanted him to have for spoiling her adventure.

'And your mother has a great deal to say about you setting him a bad example twice in one day, so I'd keep quiet about his sins if I were you,' her father told her gently as he sat young Kit on his shoulders. 'Did you invite FitzDevelin here, Shuttleworth?' Sir Hugh Kenton asked very coolly indeed and Wulf no longer wondered how the man kept six children almost in order. He had an urge to go and stand in a corner until he'd learnt how to behave himself and he was supposed to be grown-up.

'No,' Lord Shuttleworth said baldly.

Wulf felt as if his fur was being rubbed the wrong way, but he couldn't accuse either of them of the sort of lazy prejudice his stepfather lived by. They clearly disliked him for his own sake and never mind the bed he shouldn't have been born in.

'Mr FitzDevelin is on his way into Wales and has called in to pass on a message from his mother, Edmund,' Miss Alstone said as she rashly stepped in to protect him from making a very sudden exit with the force of a gentleman's boot to speed him on his way.

'How unexpected of her ladyship to send you as her envoy, FitzDevelin,' the Viscount Shuttleworth said blandly.

'And how invisible her letter is, too,' Wulf thought he heard Sir Hugh mutter as if he'd been looking forward to throwing the unwanted guest out for his whatever he and Lord Shuttleworth were to one another. Brother-in-law; cousin-by-marriage? Whatever complex relation his lordship was to Sir Hugh Kenton, the Alstone clan moved as one formidable whole when threatened. How Wulf wished his own family were so uncomplicated.

'I suppose your horse has had a short rest, Mr FitzDevelin, so you can be on your way to Brecon again,' Isabella said as if a mythical journey would save him from her relatives' protective wrath.

Tempted to argue he had nowhere else to go just for the hell of it, Wulf obliged with a silent bow because he didn't feel like lying outright to these two aristocrats.

'A shame we can't put you up for the night, Fitz-Develin, but I must be inhospitable,' Lord Shuttleworth said as if he was only mildly amused by playing host to such an unwelcome visitor for however short a time it took to get rid of him.

Wulf read the warning underneath his bland comment and decided to go quietly. No point arguing when he'd wasted a long ride hoping he could put the world right for his half-brother. For once in his life he'd tried to be unselfish, noble even, and Miss Alstone was so obstinate he wondered why he'd bothered. He'd fought all the way here to blot out the snide, self-mocking voice that whispered he was a fool in time to the pounding of hooves as he ate at the miles between him and Isabella Alstone. It argued he was desperate to see her again and never mind his brother. And now he was here why had he ever thought anything he had to say could make a difference when Magnus couldn't change her mind?

'You'd best hurry. I'm told it could rain so hard tonight the roads will be impassable,' Sir Hugh warned and even his son stopped telling his father about his day so far as if he'd caught something implacable in his quiet voice.

'Then I'd best get on my way before I'm marooned,' Wulf agreed blandly, although they all knew he'd be heading back to London and it didn't look like rain.

'Thank you for delivering the Countess's message and do give her my best wishes when you see her next, Mr FitzDevelin,' Miss Alstone chimed in to speed him on his way.

What else could he do but bow as gracefully as he could, then smile a quick farewell at Miss Sophia Kenton and the little rogue sitting on his father's shoulders? Miss Alstone was already discussing the weather with Kenton while Lord Shuttleworth waited impatiently to see Wulf off the property.

'My wife is very near her time, FitzDevelin,' his lordship told him as they strolled away. 'Come here again and I'll have you roped on your horse and left to wander wherever he takes you. And stay away from my sister-in-law.'

'I came on my brother's behalf, my lord,' Wulf made himself argue. He wanted to thump someone to make himself feel better as well, but it would do neither of them any good to alarm the very pregnant Viscountess.

'I trust my sister-in-law to know her own mind and so should you. She and Mr Haile will only have parted after a lot of heartache and I hate to see her troubled.'

'You are in her confidence, then?' Wulf heard himself say urgently, as if he was her rebuffed suitor and not Magnus.

'No, but she hates to break a promise and you can tell your brother so when you get back to London. He obviously doesn't know her as well as he thinks if he thought sending you to plead his case would get her to change her mind.'

'He doesn't know I've come.'

'Then you'll be the butt of his displeasure as well, won't you?'

'Probably,' Wulf said with the sort of defensive young man's shrug he thought he'd grown out of.

'I suppose you cared enough to come here on a pointless quest bullheaded,' his lordship said as if he was trying to find excuses for the sort of boyish mischief Wulf never had the chance to commit.

'My brother is eating his heart out. He's taken to the bottle and refuses to shave for days on end and not even our younger sisters can get a smile out of him. If you had a half-brother you loved, wouldn't *you* do anything to see him happy when he's hurting so badly?'

'Yes, which is why you're walking to my stables to collect your horse and not being carried there by my grooms to be put on it and driven off fast as the nag will go.'

'I'd best be grateful for small mercies, then,' Wulf said with a rueful grin and decided he'd like this man under other circumstances.

'Don't try too hard until you're away without arousing my wife's suspicion you're here on a mission of your own,' Lord Shuttleworth said as if he knew Wulf's reasons for coming here were only half-unselfish and that was impossible, wasn't it?

'Consider me warned off, my lord.'

'A shame, but I won't have my wife or her sister upset if there's anything I can do to prevent it and that's a fault I've long shared with Sir Hugh and the current Earl of Carnwood.'

'I'm not your equal, my lord, but there's no need to point it out with every second word. Trust my stepfather to be sure my irregular birth is engraved on my heart, much as Mary Tudor claimed Calais was on hers.'

'It's not a matter of quality or inequality, but common sense. Tangling with you or your brother now will drag my sister-in-law's good name through more mud and I can't have that.'

'Nobody will know I was here if you don't tell them and I didn't give your stableman a name.'

'Which was why he sought me out and, as a reward, I'll be granting him a cottage of his own this Eastertide so he can wed his sweetheart. So some good came of your impromptu visit.'

'I shall preen myself even as I ride away with my tail metaphorically between my legs, my lord,' Wulf said and was surprised by a bark of genuine laughter from his reluctant host.

'Smug or not, that will be a challenge.'

'I'm used to it,' Wulf said ruefully and wasn't that the truth?

'I suppose you must be and as a rule I care more about a man's head and heart than the way he came into the world, but I know my sister-in-law has been hurt and I care more about her than your sensitivities, so I'm prepared to be inhospitable in your case.'

'I came here on my half-brother's business,' Wulf said as his temper began to tug at its tethers. Magnus was ill and Isabella Alstone was clearly in perfect health and coolly composed, so why was she the one who needed protecting?

'And you think me rude to harp on it, but I don't think you're sure how you feel about my wife's little sister, are you, FitzDevelin?' he added unexpectedly.

Wulf almost cursed aloud again and gave even more away to this frighteningly acute and deceptively mild-mannered man. 'What can I say? You threatened me with indignity if I breathe even a bad word about her and now you want to know how I feel. I feel my brother is sad and ill after the abrupt ending of their betrothal, but things may not be as simple as I thought when I rode here to plead his case.'

'Against your own interests as well,' the man said cynically, as if he knew Wulf's inner devils lusted for Isabella and never mind fraternal love. 'I'm in love with an Alstone sister myself, FitzDevelin. Did you really think I wouldn't recognise the dazed look in a man's eye when he gazes at one of them as if he hasn't a hope in hell of ever laying hands on her but can't help himself longing all the same? I longed unrewarded for three very long years and know everything there is to know about longing and not having, but still doing it.'

Wulf frowned moodily at the neat stable yard they were nearing so rapidly, aware he'd better guard his tongue even more carefully. 'I'm not in love. I have no personal interest beyond my brother's welfare and sanity,' he bit out, feeling as if the lie might snap back and bite him.

'Then you're wilfully blind or a fool. I'm not your enemy, but I will be if you harm my wife's little sister.'

'If my half-brother marries your sister-in-law, I'll go abroad and none of your kind will miss me.'

'Hmmm, Lord Carrowe makes no effort to

provide for your younger sisters, so they'd miss you and Magnus Haile seems to like you,' Lord Shuttleworth argued.

This clever man clearly had all sorts of wrong-headed ideas about the passion Wulf had for Lady Shuttleworth's younger sister. Passion was all it was. He'd get over it.

'Magnus and my mother will find the girls a good husband each and I expect they'll be abetted by your sister-in-law even if she doesn't marry him.'

'They're your family, FitzDevelin, not Miss Alstone's.'

'Have you tried telling her that?'

'No, I've no fancy to get my nose snapped off and you're right, she won't let a broken engagement stop her matchmaking,' Lord Shuttleworth admitted.

'My sisters' welfare comes first and they'll do better when I'm gone,' Wulf said.

'You're set on leaving England again, then?'

'Yes,' Wulf said gruffly.

'Then I must wonder why you came back.'

'So must I.'

'Although the Earl can't stave off his creditors much longer,' this lord warned as if Wulf ought to weigh that in the balance when planning his future.

As if the problem of how his mother and sisters would survive hadn't haunted him all the way across the Atlantic and back. It was the idea of his mother and sisters being destitute that dragged him back to England, wasn't it? He'd been desperate not to see his brother marry Isabella. This fiery need for her, from the instant he had laid eyes on her, sent him across the Atlantic in the teeth of winter storms, but it was wrong to have been elated for even a minute when he came back to find the wedding had been cancelled. He rode here dogged by guilt and pity for Magnus's low state of mind mixed with irritation he hadn't come here to plead for himself.

'Lord Carrowe has the legal right to dictate his wife and unwed daughters' lives. He doesn't thank me for interfering,' he said carefully.

'You might need help if he's in the Fleet for debt,' Lord Shuttleworth replied, taking a visiting card out of his pocket and scribbling on it with a fine silver pencil before he handed it over. 'Ben Shaw is a lord's love child but has a powerful enough reach to make your stepfather wary of tangling with him.'

'Thank you, although I've no idea why you'd help me.'

'My wife and her sister were neglected and abused by those supposed to care for them as children and I'd hate to see your sisters left vulnerable, even if they are grown-up and too old to be bullied and coerced.'

Wulf frowned his disagreement because his youngest half-sisters were so terrified of their father they might walk off a cliff if he told them to. The twins were eighteen and Aline seven years older and more stubborn and defiant than her little sisters, but Shuttleworth was quite right and he had to put their needs before his own. Any scheme to leave the country with his mother and three unwed sister would need a lot of fine tuning, and if Ben Shaw, whom he'd already met causally, could help, he'd lower his pride and ask for it if the time came.

'I will put them first,' he promised curtly as

they walked into the stable yard and he thought that he and the Viscount might have been friends in different circumstances.

Chapter Five

'Another fool's comin' gallopin' up the drive 'ell for leather, your lordship,' a different groom from the one who had first greeted Wulf told his master gloomily as they waited for Wulf's horse to be saddled. 'Seems like a day for them, don't it, m'lord?'

'Indeed,' Lord Shuttleworth responded with a frown that made Wulf glad he was playing first intruder today and not second. 'I'll see who it is and what he wants while you bring that nag out for this gentleman, Alworth.' His lordship invited Wulf to precede him out with an impatient gesture.

'Hell and the devil, that's Gus,' Wulf was shocked into exclaiming when he saw a hard-ridden horse tearing towards them with his weary rider looking as if he was barely hanging on to the reins. 'What is he doing riding here as if his life depends on it when he's supposed to be convalescing?'

'The same thing as you, I expect,' Shuttleworth replied shortly.

Had Miss Alstone's family secretly opposed what seemed a perfectly good match to the rest of the world? Wulf felt contrary emotions churn inside him as he waited for Gus to gallop across Lord Shuttleworth's park and tell them why he was in such a hurry.

'Wulf, thank God I was right although you're a damned fool,' Magnus gasped out when he was close enough to be heard.

He hadn't bothered with the shave he had needed even when he set out and looked more the wild man than Wulf and quite unlike his usual dapper and gentlemanly self. He wondered fleetingly if Miss Alstone would like Gus better thin as a rake, romantically unkempt, wild-eyed and even looking a little bit dangerous. Wulf's heart plunged, then hammered to a marching beat at the thought of having to watch them blissfully reunited.

'I'm leaving,' he said coolly. 'No doubt you'll have a warmer welcome.'

He turned to reclaim his horse and ride away. He could leave Magnus to it now he'd pushed him into doing what he should have weeks ago: beg Isabella Alstone to take him back. Wulf turned away to hide his feelings and Gus scrambled off his horse with such haste Wulf turned to stare at him open-mouthed. Gus seemed more interested in Wulf than finding the woman he had ridden here so hard to see.

'Damn it, Wulf, don't you turn your back on me as well,' his brother gasped out as if he was the social outcast of the two of them. He swayed so alarmingly Lord Shuttleworth started forward to stop him falling to the ground as if he was having a seizure. Deeply shocked by his brother's wild state, Wulf got there first and felt the lesser shock of Gus's newly bony body under his supporting grip. No woman was worth this much agony, he silently chided his brother, certainly not one who could coolly dismiss his sufferings as if they had nothing to do with her.

'Brace up, Gus,' he ordered as if impatient instead of sad and furious at the effort it cost him to get out the words struggling on his tongue.

'He's been murdered, Wulf—dead as mutton,' his brother managed before he went limp and Wulf was left to wonder for a terrible moment if his brother was mad.

'Who's dead, Gus?' he asked urgently as he fought to stay upright under their joint weight. 'And why would you think he's been murdered?'

'Saw him with my own eyes, Wulf. My father. Stiff as a doornail and covered in his own gore, but at least he won't trouble us any more.'

For a terrible moment relief sang in Wulf's heart, but he smothered it and shivered when he remembered their startled audience. 'My brother is not in his right mind,' he informed the Viscount, not sure a temporary derangement of spirits could cover the fact Gus had given a magistrate good reason to suspect him of patricide.

'The gentleman is exhausted,' Lord Shuttleworth said brusquely. 'Alworth, get both these nags stabled, then find a hurdle to carry him into the house to be cared for. We need to get him out of the cold and stop this faint turning to an ague.'

'Aye, m'lord,' the groom said with one last glance at this latest strange gentleman who seemed only half-alive after his long ride.

Wulf was battling shock and terror at his brother's hastily gasped-out words. Magnus must have been struggling with such terror ever since he set out in Wulf's tracks. No doubt he'd had to deal with the magistrates and get the corpse out of the house before he set the Runners on the killer's scent. And then he'd set out to fetch Wulf back when he was far too weak from his illness to withstand another shock. He'd always thought Gus the sensible one, a steady hand who would keep the rest of his family functioning despite their father's worst efforts.

If the Earl of Carrowe had been murdered, Wulf must get to Carrowe House as fast as he could and whisk his mother and sisters out of there. Torn between his concern for Gus's welfare and the urgency of getting back to London as fast as he could, he watched Miss Alstone arrive breathless in the stable yard with a familiar thump in his heart even now, when he should have nobler things on his mind than longing for a fine lady in a state of mild disarray. She looked as if she'd been running since she saw Gus dash over the horizon like the hero out of a ballad. She came to a hasty stop to stare down at his unconscious brother as if she couldn't quite believe her eyes. Not sure if she was delighted or horrified, Wulf used the excuse of brotherly concern not to watch love warm her shocked blue gaze as she examined Gus's pale face for signs of life and at last his brother blinked and opened his eyes.

'Why have you come dashing all this way in such a headlong fashion?' she said as if Gus was in a fit state to reply. She seemed to realise he was drifting in and out of consciousness when she shot Wulf an impatient glare instead. 'What's the matter with him? What have you done?' she said and the accusation made his gorge rise.

How could she think he'd harm his brother when Gus had dared the Earl's wrath to protect him as a boy and he loved him for it? How could she think him so little? 'Nothing,' he said coldly.

'You should look closer to home for a cause, since I'm told he hasn't been the same since you jilted him.'

'Be quiet. I won't listen to you two trading insults at a time like this.'

Shuttleworth's rebuke jolted Wulf and the man was right, he mustn't lose his temper, however much her accusation hurt. He had to keep a cool head and get his brother home as fast as a coach and horses could carry them, since Gus was obviously in no state to ride. Scandal was about to descend on the Haile family yet again and there was nothing he could do to keep it quiet if Gus's grim tale was true, but Shuttleworth and his family shouldn't be involved.

'You're right, my lord, and I'll be very grateful if you could let us borrow a carriage as far as the next coaching inn.'

'Wait until our local physician arrives, man. The moment he says your brother is fit to travel I promise to set you on your way as fast as can be.'

'As nobody knows who we are here, you can call us Smith or Butcher or Baker if it makes life easier,' Wulf offered distractedly and gazed down at his brother's haggard face. If the Earl had really been murdered, the Viscount wouldn't want the notoriety of having one of the Haile family as his guest and Wulf almost wished Gus would faint properly so he could forget the blind terror on his face when he gasped out his reason for coming.

'Or Candlestick-Maker?' Miss Alstone offered sarcastically. Her scorn pulled him back into every day, which was where he needed to be if he was going to get his family out of this latest calamity unscathed, so he ought to thank her.

'A bit long-winded, don't you think?' he argued against the uproar as three grooms and a foot-man arrived at the same time as Sir Hugh and his two available offspring.

'Forgive me?' she asked rather sheepishly, as if she thought her accusations were appalling as well, but he should absolve her, since she'd asked nicely.

'I'll try,' he said, making it clear he was pre-occupied. Magnus helped by jolting out of his trance at the noise and staring about him in a panic. Lord Shuttleworth was right; if this was

Gus's reaction to people who ran to help him, then a party of Bow Street Runners and a constable or two galloping in his wake could send him into a decline. Wulf shuddered for his brother's life and his sanity and decided who he chose to marry didn't seem very important now. 'Quietly, Gus,' he cautioned as the rescue party eyed his brother warily as if horror might be contagious. 'My brother exhausted himself tracking me down as our mother has been taken ill,' he explained as if that was the top and bottom of their woes.

And it wasn't an outright lie; the Countess's usual method of coping with problems was to be too delicate to face them. A murder in the house would require at least a nervous collapse and how her husband would have raged at her for it. At least the Dowager Countess of Carrowe could have hysterics whenever she chose from now on and Wulf doubted he or Magnus had the heart to deny her such a small solace for her hard life under the Earl's thumb. The word *Dowager* echoed dully in Wulf's head as he supervised the lifting of his brother on to the hurdle and soothed Magnus when he protested at being carried about like an invalid.

The Earl is no more, long live the Earl, Wulf mused numbly as he watched his brother's pallid face while the little procession slowly made its way to the house. Gresley would inherit little more than his father's title and Wulf already knew there was no point expecting very much from the new Earl. Gresley had never taken much interest in his younger brother and sisters and Wulf couldn't see that changing. Gresley would inherit Haile Carr officially and his wife had long ago decided she preferred it to London and the snobbish reminders the high sticklers knew how to make that she wasn't a born lady even if she was a countess now.

Indifferent to the new Earl at the best of times, Wulf turned his attention to the half-brother he did love. If Magnus had discovered the Earl's dead body, it might explain his half-crazed state when he got here. After he ran away from Carrowe House as a lad himself, he'd seen things that would shock a trooper, but Gus was far more sensitive and sheltered than Wulf had been and the Earl *was* his father. Add the stress and heartache of his parting from Miss Alstone and his

illness earlier this year and it seemed little wonder Gus had buckled under the burden of it all.

'Carry him to the green bedchamber in the
old wing,' Lord Shuttleworth ordered as they
got Gus up the steps and inside the mansion. 'I
don't want my wife to get wind of this yet,' he
added. 'Even without your brother's current state
of health this is an awkward situation for my
wife and sister-in-law,' the Viscount murmured.

'His news has put everything else out of my
head,' he admitted as Miss Alstone's exasperated
snort of impatience seemed almost to argue that
propriety and the gossips be damned. However,
he couldn't quite believe in her anxiety for a man
she'd brushed aside like a buzzing fly when she
broke their betrothal and talked of so coldly not
half an hour ago. He wished she'd go away and
stop distracting him.

'Brandy,' Lord Shuttleworth ordered briskly
when the little procession reached a clean if
rather old-fashioned bedchamber. 'The rest of
you can go.' His lordship added a few words of
thanks for the grooms who had carried Magnus
upstairs and now stepped back obediently.

'You two as well,' Sir Hugh Kenton told his

offspring with a severe enough look to make them do as they were bid. 'And no listening at doors,' he added as they turned away.

'He might, but I wouldn't,' Miss Sophia said with an accusing look at her little brother and a saintly expression Wulf didn't believe for a moment.

'If either of you even try it, I'll tell your mother what you were up to this afternoon,' their father threatened. From their slumped shoulders they really would go this time and Wulf was glad they hadn't heard Magnus's startling opening statement and didn't realise what a fine, grisly story they were missing.

'My brother will be best out of these clothes; it looks as if he slept in them before he set out to track me down,' Wulf said, hoping to get Isabella out of the room as well.

'Yes, that's a good idea and here's the brandy you ordered, Shuttleworth. One exhausted man against three of us—I think we can cope, don't you?' Sir Hugh said with a cool look at the female too stubborn to have left the room.

'You're trying to get rid of me, aren't you?'

Isabella challenged him and Wulf realised he'd underestimated her yet again.

'Yes, is it working?' Shuttleworth asked blandly.

'Considering I'm a single lady, I don't see how it can't. You two think you're sharp as needles, though, don't you?'

'We are,' Sir Hugh said modestly.

Wulf pretended he was too busy pressing a brandy glass to his brother's lips to hear the by-play and shrugged aside a ridiculous urge to beg her to stay.

'It's very annoying of you and I expect a full account of whatever goes on in this room later, so if you don't want me to put Kate on your tail, you'd best give it to me as soon as you can,' she threatened, then left the room with her nose in the air, snapping the door closed behind her to make her feelings plain.

'She won't tell Kate,' Shuttleworth reassured himself out loud.

'Especially if we fob her off with some plausible tale,' Sir Hugh agreed.

Wulf thought they looked uneasy about the chances of her complying with anything she didn't want to comply with. 'Never mind Miss Alstone; where's the sawbones?' he demanded and hoped a lady wouldn't lower herself to listen at doors.

Isabella wouldn't dream of doing anything as unladylike as putting her ear to the keyhole when she was far too likely to get caught. She racked her brains for a better way to find out what was being said in a closed room. If they thought hiding Magnus in the older part of the house would stop Kate finding out he was here, they didn't know her sister as well as they thought and Isabella *had* to know why Magnus had galloped after his half-brother so hard he'd endangered his health even further. Her pulse thundered at the very thought someone might have told Magnus what she and his brother did at Haile Carr that night. No, that wasn't possible—nobody knew about that but her and Wulf and he loved Magnus. He'd never hurt him even if he despised her. Not even, her uneasy conscience whispered, if he had truly set sail for America to avoid her and his own sense of treachery to his half-brother.

She had to know what all this was about. If

someone had seen and whispered about her and Wulf's disgraceful encounter in the shadows at Haile Carr, she must decide now if she could deny her sins in public or dare to admit it and be pointed out as Wicked Miss Alstone for the rest of her days.

Inspiration suddenly hit as to how she could get answers to her questions. The poor state of the floors and ceilings in the older parts of the house had been a theme running through Kate's letters these last few months. Hopefully the carpenters had been put off thumping and hammering for a few weeks while the family assembled. Maybe their unfinished works could let her listen to what was being said by a pack of men who thought they knew best.

Creeping up the elaborately carved staircase that indicated this had once been a more important part of the house was a lot easier than she expected. The drop cloths and drugget put down to protect finely carved and polished oak against work boots and the dust and dirt nobody could keep at bay on a worksite muffled the slight noises of creaking treads and settling timbers as she moved as if walking on eggshells. She must be even more wary once she was above the room they'd taken Magnus to. If news got about of his hasty visit, the gossips would poke and pry for a reason, so she should know what had brought him here and she had to admit to herself she was more than curious to know what had happened between Magnus and his half-brother.

She grabbed the hem of her gown so she could tie it round her waist and keep her skirts out of the dust. At least ladies' waists were lower and skirts wider now; the idea of trying to do this in a narrow column of cambric or muslin made her shudder for the contortions it would cost her. Mentally apologising to her maid for the state she was about to get her petticoats in, she glanced out of the nearest window to orient herself to the room below. She crept past three dusty and half-repaired attic rooms before halting at the doorway of the one where she could see the fountain court from the same angle she'd glimpsed from Magnus's room. Yes, that was about right. Three sets of acute masculine ears would be directly underneath her, maybe even four if Magnus was less faint than he had been at first. Her maid would have more to scold about than dusty petticoats and Isabella sighed for her stockings as she removed her soft-soled shoes and stepped on to oak boards she was delighted to see in place over only half the floor. She held her breath as she measured every step like an acrobat. Maybe she should become a government spy, she decided when she got to the edge of the floorboards without more than a creak so slight it sounded like an old house settling. The gap was too wide to jump without giving herself away. If she wanted to hear more than the murmur she could pick out now, she would have to creep across bare joists and hope the laths were poorer or more worm-holed so she could hear through them. She quailed at the idea of stepping on a splinter or a nail and overbalancing and falling into the room below, or even being left suspended halfway with her legs sticking through. Listening hard to be certain they hadn't heard her as she crept closer to the gap, she bent over it in the hope of catching what the men were saying. Ah, here was a piece of luck. The plaster was exposed below and she could see a crack and a few slivers of daylight through it. She edged along a beam that looked sound enough to get her closer. Her stockings were ruined already and she'd scraped her knees, but at least she could hear words now instead of just manly rumbles and grumbles.

'Do you think your little demons have really gone this time, Kenton?' she heard Edmund ask.

'Aye, they soon get bored and it's still a lovely day and their mother isn't looking for them yet.'

'Good, then we'd best get on before anyone else tries to find out your secrets, Haile,' Edmund said almost as if he was joking.

Isabella nodded emphatically at thin air. *Yes, do get on with it. This position is uncomfortable in so many different ways.*

'The Earl—he's stone-dead and he was murdered,' she heard Magnus say and suddenly it didn't matter she was perched up here like a chicken. Murder, no, surely that was impossible. Murder happened in newssheets and sensational ballads, not to people she knew.

Chapter Six

No, it's a fever raging through him; Magnus is delirious. Even the Earl of Carrowe doesn't deserve to die like that.

Isabella shook her head in disbelief and all her blood seemed to rush to her head as Magnus's words echoed in her ears like the crack of doom. Murder? Her ears were deceiving her or Magnus was raving. He was so torn and tortured by the awful situation he was caught up in that his mind had been turned. Yes, that was it; he must be suffering from brain fever. She was praying the doctor would come and save his sanity before it was too late when his next muttered sentence disillusioned her.

'I found my father done to death, Wulf. He was murdered, foully murdered,' Magnus was saying and Wulf muttered something soothing she didn't catch because she was too busy lingering on the gruff rumble of his voice like a besotted debutante while poor Magnus was in the grip of horror. 'Foully murdered,' he echoed his own words as if he couldn't stop now he'd got to Wulf and told him his terrible news.

'So you said,' his brother said coolly. 'Tell us where and how the Earl died, Gus, before the sawbones gets here and pours laudanum down your throat. We'll not get even this much sense out of you for hours after that.'

She heard Magnus chuckle and could even imagine him smiling weakly, so perhaps Wulf understood him after all. She was suddenly glad they were as close as they were. They, too, had shared a harsh childhood and deserved something more than bitter memories out of it. For some reason the old lord had only seemed to care about his two eldest children. After half a year of trying to avoid her future father-in-law, she'd concluded he blamed his younger children for the disaster his marriage turned into. Isabella shuddered at the thought of being imprisoned in such a marriage herself and wondered how Lady Carrowe stopped herself from murdering him long ago. No! She mustn't even think such things. Tempted to rock back and forth on her beam to comfort herself, she shook her head at the very idea Lady Carrowe had put a knife into her husband. If she was going to do that, she would have done it when Wulf was born and the man denounced him.

'He must have come back home that night after his usual debauch and we didn't even know it,' Magnus was saying. 'We found him in the morning and by that time he was long gone, Wulf. He was sitting in the Small Drawing Room with his eyes wide open and staring at us as if he'd met the devil. Remember how it was called the Red Room before Mama had it painted white to try to make it seem less gloomy? Heaven knows it's red again now,' Magnus reported with a dash of hysteria in his deep voice again, as if he was remembering the sight of his murdered father and might truly run mad if they weren't careful how they teased this terrible story out of him.

Shivering like a greyhound in a thunderstorm

now, Isabella felt her heart stutter at the terrible ring of truth in his words. Now *she* couldn't shake off the awful image of the Earl staring into the pit of hell while his lifeblood drained out of him.

'I have to suppose he was stabbed, then, since there was so much blood,' his brother was saying as if they were discussing the weather.

Isabella shook her head; how could Wulf be so calm about a soul being snuffed out so horribly? Even if it was the Earl's. Surely he had a spark of pity in him for a life ended so violently? He'd be a lesser man if he didn't and she didn't want him to be somehow. He might be the most contrary, abrasive and downright annoying man she'd ever met and she was almost sure she didn't like him, but she didn't want him to be smaller than she'd thought when he stepped out of the shadows on that dratted terrace at Haile Carr.

'Maybe he was, but we couldn't see a knife,' Magnus was saying more steadily now, so she must listen instead of thinking uncomfortable thoughts she could dwell on later. She would have tried to soothe and calm him, but Wulf obviously knew truths this brutal couldn't be wrapped in clean linen. She supposed she ought to respect him for knowing better.

'From what little I could see before Mama had hysterics and I had to carry her to her bedchamber, he could have been stabbed as well, Wulf,' Magnus said, 'but he had certainly been hit on the head. That plaster bust of Ovid he used to throw his hat on when he came home drunk was lying broken and bloody by his chair. The side of his head was beaten in and he was covered in his own gore.'

'You're certain it was him?'

'Even I'm not fool enough to ride here on a maybe, Wulf, and before you ask me, yes, I made sure he was dead and didn't leave Mama and the girls alone in that house with his corpse. The sight of him lying in his chair like butcher's meat will haunt me to my dying day, so heaven knows what it'll do to poor Theodora, who found him first and ran to get me. I have to get back to them instead of cosseting myself like a Bath breakdown, they need me.'

'Lie back down, you idiot, you're exhausted.

I'll look after them until you're rested and fit to help—you're too ill to be any use to them now, Gus. We're both going to need our full strength to deal with what comes next. I've wished him dead in the past but never thought I'd see this day.'

'Don't say that, Wulf,' Magnus said a little more strongly. 'Someone might hear and think you had a hand in his murder. And think how happy he'd be to drag you down with him, even if he had to die to do it.'

'You're right,' Wulf admitted and Isabella could imagine him frowning. 'Don't expect me to pretend I'm sorry he's gone, though,' he added gruffly.

'That's too much to ask, but we'll all be suspects now. You'd best keep a still tongue if you don't want it to be more than an unproven suspicion we wanted him to die sooner rather than later.'

'Everyone knows I hated him, Gus. Shuttleworth and Kenton aren't the sort of men to grasp the first straw of suspicion that drifts their way,'

Wulf argued and Isabella silently nodded her agreement.

'FitzDevelin's right, Haile—you're going to need all the friends you can get, so you'd best not offend us,' Edmund said, sounding as calm and steady as if these two unlikely visitors had called in to pass the time of day.

'We need to leave as soon as we can so you keep you and yours safe from this grim business,' Wulf added.

'I can't lie about like this when we're needed at home,' Isabella heard Magnus fretting and was glad he wasn't absorbed in his own miserable situation for the moment, even if it was for such a terrible reason.

'If we can borrow a carriage to get to London all the sooner, I'll be grateful to you, Lord Shuttleworth. I shall send it back as soon as we can hire a decent vehicle and hopefully your family will hardly notice the horses have gone before they're back again.'

'You don't know our families like we do if you think that, FitzDevelin, but you're welcome to borrow my travelling carriage and a fast team the moment your brother is declared fit to travel. In the meantime, we three should prepare ourselves for a hard ride.'

Edmund sounded doubtful about it even as he spoke. As well he might with Kate in such an advanced state of pregnancy, Isabella thought, wishing she was down there and allowed a say in their plans. She had been Magnus's fiancée for half a year and knew the Countess of Carrowe and her younger daughters as well as any outsider. So she, too, must return to town only hours after she had arrived in the country. Edmund had to stay here with Kate, but there was nothing much Isabella could do to help her sister once Kate was in labour. A single lady wouldn't be allowed into the room to hold her sister's hand while she laboured with doctors, midwives and an experienced mother of six on hand.

'Can't stay here, must go back,' she heard Magnus mutter distractedly.

'You're in no fit state to go anywhere,' Sir Hugh Kenton argued briskly. 'And there's no question of you leaving your wife when she's about to give birth either, Shuttleworth. I'm the best person to go back to town with FitzDevelin and your job will be to keep Haile here and his identity a secret until he's fit to travel. I have experience of such dark matters and at least I can help FitzDevelin and the Countess untangle their affairs, so stop playing the dutiful lord, Edmund, and remember Kate needs you here.'

Isabella recalled how scandal had dogged Hugh for years after he had been suspected of murdering his first wife. The Navy decided to dispense with his services so he became a merchant captain for Isabella's brother-in-law Kit. He was still in Kit's service when he met Louise in some wild and scandalous manner they refused to discuss even now. As a result of his past, there was very little Hugh didn't know about false witnesses and the sort of vicious rumours that could blacken an innocent man's name. Of course he was the right person to help the Hailes, but so was she. Lady Carrowe was living in a broken-down, barely habitable mansion her husband had been plundering for years to fund his extravagant lifestyle. Then there were her younger daughters; their slender hopes of a decent marriage could be snuffed out by this latest scandal if it wasn't handled very carefully. Isabella might as well make herself useful to the Haile girls and their mother and she was sure she could stay out of the way of Magnus and Wulf if she tried hard enough.

'It's true; I shouldn't leave my wife,' Edmund admitted at last, 'but you'll need help to get your family out of this mess without a great deal of scandal and danger, FitzDevelin. Don't turn Kenton's offer down because you're too stiff-necked to accept help.'

'I know a good deal about danger and my mother and sisters are used to scandal; they have me to thank for that,' Wulf replied with bitter irony.

It was true, though, wasn't it? He'd lived where he wasn't wanted until he was old enough to run away and at an age when he should have been dreaming of wild adventures rather than facing them daily as he fought to survive on the streets. He was a strong man and the Haile family needed one now more than ever; no wonder his brother had ridden here so frantically to fetch Wulf back. Feeling uncomfortably disloyal, she reminded herself Magnus had been through his own private hell and a long illness these last few months, so it was little wonder he was felled by this heavy blow on top of all the others.

'I suspect you're the least of their worries right now, FitzDevelin. Time to stop harping on the past and get on with the present now your step-father is dead and his killer is at large,' Hugh warned.

Isabella shivered, listening even harder for anything she could catch through feet of dusty air and a crumbling ceiling.

'And your mother and sisters need you,' Hugh continued.

'I promised to do everything I could to get you back to London by tomorrow morning, Wulf,' Magnus said restlessly, as it was his fault they weren't on the road already.

'I can ride all night if I have to,' Wulf said dismissively. Isabella could imagine him doing it as well, despite the punishing ride he must have had to get here already, driven to confront her with her sins and bully her to take Magnus back and marry him. At least no self-respecting highwayman would hold up such an angry man for fear of being mown down as if as unimportant as a fly on a horse's ear, primed pistols or no.

'Start now,' his brother urged breathlessly, 'I'll follow when I can, but you'll be far more use than I am right now, Wulf.'

Silence descended while the men tried not to agree out loud and Isabella plotted her own hasty departure from Crayenhill Park and the rural peace and quiet she'd come here to find. If she stayed, news of Magnus's presence would leak out and the local gossips would seize on it as a sign of reconciliation in the teeth of the biggest scandal to hit the Hailes for centuries. She needed to get to London before the polite world had a chance to write off the Haile ladies for good this time.

'Give me half an hour and we'll set out together, FitzDevelin,' Hugh said so firmly she knew Wulf might as well accept his company as eat his dust all the way back to town, since Hugh could afford the best horses and he couldn't.

'My thanks, then, Sir Hugh. I hope you'll return here once I've got my mother and sisters out of that dusty old mausoleum and away from the gossips.'

'No, don't make them hide away as if they're guilty of something, you great manly idiot,' Isabella actually muttered under her voice before shaking her head at her own stupidity. It was high time she crept away and got on with frustrating all their well-meant masculine plans. She wriggled precariously around on her beam to face the door again, then shuffled along until she got to dusty floorboards and could take to hands and knees while the men were busy arguing about who was going where and what they were doing when they got there. They didn't seem suspicious of the sounds of an old building restless on ancient foundations and she knew enough to insist on returning to London now, whatever arguments Edmund thought up to stop her.

Isabella glanced down at her dusty person and undid her knotted skirts. At least they would cover grimy petticoats and her once-white pantalettes, but neither would ever be the same again. Even if her underpinnings were boiled for hours to get them white again, the lace was damaged.

The last few minutes would have been much trickier if she had to twist about on a beam with nothing to keep her knees from the splinters. Dirty feet and torn stockings were bad enough, she decided as she shuffled her shoes back on at the far end of the interconnected rooms. Now all she wanted was to get back to her room unseen and wash off the dust of ages before making her rapid departure.

Had Hugh and Wulf gone yet or were they still waiting for the doctor? She stole along make-shift corridors added long after this part of the house was built, musing how folk managed to live hugger-mugger in such times. The very idea of one room opening off another struck her as absurdly intimate, but maybe everyday life *was* more intimate in a rich man's house back then. Wulf FitzDevelin's latest intrusion into her life seemed to have made her think about things she usually accepted as everyday parts of life she didn't even need to wonder about. Perhaps she needed his abrasive scorn of fine ladies to make her question how her life ran along so smoothly she rarely questioned the rights and wrongs of it.

Somehow she found her way through the warren of rooms back to the main house without having to go back the way she'd come and risk them knowing she had heard most of what they had said. Now all she need do was explain her hasty departure to Kate and Louise, persuade her maid to pack everything she'd only just finished unpacking and retrace the journey they'd only just completed.

During the three frustrating days it had taken Isabella to journey from Herefordshire to London at a respectable pace, so nobody could accuse her of unladylike haste, she had far too much time to think. So much for her resolution to change the way she lived when they had to crawl along because she didn't want to draw attention to her return to the capital by doing it at the same breakneck speed Hugh and Wulf would be galloping at. At last, though, she was staring out of mud-spattered carriage windows at the busy streets and closely packed houses and sighing with relief that they were back in London when she had been so pleased to quit it less than a week ago.

Magnus would have to stay at Cravenhill until he was well enough for the long journey home, so it should be obvious why she left her brother-in-law's house for the time being. Louise and Kate would have sent out the right letters to the right people by now, explaining how poor Mr Haile was laid up at Cravenhill after foolishly riding all the way there at breakneck speed to beg for Sir Hugh's help in his family's hour of need. The poor man had some sort of brain fever earlier this year so how could they turn him away at the risk of his health being permanently broken? Although his timing was unfortunate to say the least and poor Isabella had been forced to leave Cravenhill for London in order to stay with dear Charlotte Shaw, her former governess, until Mr Haile was well enough to leave. Nobody could blame the Countess of Carrowe for being too bowed down with her own troubles and sorrows to drive all the way to Herefordshire to attend to Mr Haile herself, but really it was *most* inconvenient.

There would still be murmurs about why Magnus Haile was in Herefordshire when he should have been at Carrowe House. He would probably be portrayed as the devoted, broken-hearted suitor seeking comfort at the darkest time in his life; she would be the hard-hearted female who hotfooted it to London rather than give in and marry him after all. Enduring a few whispers and the odd sneer was nothing next to the horrors haunting Magnus's mother and sisters at this very moment, though. They had to live with the sort of wild speculation and storytelling that could cost an innocent life if the wrong person was found guilty of the Earl's murder. Her own lot in life suddenly seemed very easy in comparison.

'Drive straight round to Hanover Square, Samson,' Isabella ordered briskly. 'Carnwood House will be closed up, so there's no point in stopping there.'

'Very well, Miss Alstone,' Kate's well-trained coachman replied impassively.

Glad her personal maid, Heloise, was new and not given to arguing about anything that didn't concern fashion or her mistress being perfectly turned out whenever she left her bedchamber, Isabella sat back on the comfortable cushions and hoped Charlotte was home.

'Izzie, what on earth…?' Charlotte shifted the baby in her arms to kiss her former pupil, then raised her eyebrows at the small mountain of luggage piling up in her spacious hallway under Heloise's stern supervision. 'You'd best come into my sitting room and tell me all about it,' she said softly. 'Have everything conveyed to the Blue Bedchamber if you please, Harris,' she said to the butler before leading Isabella into the cosy parlour she favoured, because it was next to her husband's office and he frequently dashed in to join her for half an hour or so.

'What are you doing back in London less than a week after you left?'

'Magnus came to Cravenhill in great haste, then had to stay to be nursed through a recurrence of that illness he had earlier in the year.'

'Is it catching?'

'No, not after all these weeks. Edmund is a kind Christian gentleman, but he would have sent Magnus somewhere else to be cared for if there was the slightest risk of infection for Kate and the children. Oh, don't look at me like that; the babe hasn't been born yet. Or at least it hadn't been when I left. By now it may have come into the world, since Kate was the size of a small cottage.'

Charlotte raised her eyebrows again and looked unconvinced by Isabella's misplaced humour, as well as her telling of half the story. The horrid tale of the Earl of Carrowe's murder must be flying about London faster than a family of hungry kites by now, so it was little wonder Charlotte refused to be diverted.

'Oh, very well, Magnus suffered what the doctor called a "nervous collapse". It's not my fault he's been under so much strain of late, so don't you start blaming me as well. And don't expect me to tell you what *did* cause it either.'

'As well as whom?' Charlotte demanded. Trust her to latch on to the one part of her sentence Isabella wished she hadn't let slip.

'The rest of the world,' she explained so airily it ought to divert attention from her flushed cheeks. 'Who should mind their own business for once.'

'I doubt even the gossips care about your part in the Haile family's woes now.'

'They would have done if I hadn't left Cravenhill the day Magnus arrived unfit to ride another yard, let alone go a mile to the village inn. I didn't dare wait for Kate's baby to be born before I left, but why must the gossips tattle and fabricate stories and put me and the Haile family to so much trouble, Charlotte?'

'Mainly because you were born with such spectacularly good looks it's impossible to avoid it, but that's the burden you bear, poor love.'

'Don't mock me, Charlotte. It feels heavier than usual right now.'

'Because gentlemen can't see the real Isabella for your looks and fortune?'

'Maybe,' Isabella said cautiously.

If Charlotte ever guessed there was one man in particular who thought the social gulf between them so wide it was unbridgeable, she'd dig until she found out who he was. Charlotte was the only grandchild of a duke and she had wed a nobleman's by-blow. No argument about Wulf's unsuitability or the scandal he was born into would cut ice with Mrs Ben Shaw.

'Love can creep into even the most carefully guarded heart when you least expect it,' Charlotte warned with all that personal experience waiting to back her argument up.

'Not into mine it won't and Miss Margaret seems to have exhausted herself with her protests about her teeth coming through,' she said as the baby in Charlotte's arms let out a wail.

'I'll try putting her in her cradle so we can have a cup of tea and eat one of Cook's best sugar buns in peace.'

Charlotte rose very carefully and eased the child gently into her cradle. A little stir of protest and she sang softly until the little girl settled back to sleep with an angelic sigh of content.

'At last,' Charlotte breathed as she lowered herself to a chair. She looked so weary Isabella murmured she was going to order that tea herself instead of ringing for it and left them to sleep off their disturbed night side by side.

* * *

Isabella sat in her own private sitting room attached to the large guest bedchamber in the corner of the Shaws' house that was furthest away from the nursery wing and wondered how Wulf FitzDevelin was faring under very different circumstances. The murder of a peer of the realm couldn't quietly fade from public memory after a day or two of shocked gossip and a few soothing murmurs from the authorities. She hoped Hugh had managed to set the right hounds on the right trails to find the killer, because until he was tracked down and punished, the Hailes would be eyed with suspicion wherever they went. Isabella puzzled over the challenge of visiting the ladies of the family. It would have to be done in secret, however much she wanted to march in through the front door and make it clear she didn't care about the newssheets or the gossips. If she was an independent lady without close family and many friends and well-wishers, she could do just that, but given that she had two sisters and a clutch of very good friends whose reputations and wellbeing were bound up with her own she had to be discreet and careful about her own reputation.

If Magnus's supposed love, the woman who was too timid to admit to him even when his father hadn't been murdered, really loved him, she would come to town and stay at his mother and sisters' side even if she couldn't bring herself to support him as openly as Isabella thought she should. Lady Delphine's family estate marched with that of Haile Carr and the lady knew the family very well. Isabella frowned and couldn't recall much about her own past meetings with Lady Delphine Drace. She knew Lady Drace was widowed last year and her pompous husband had been the sort of political baronet she always avoided as carefully as she could herself. The man would prose on for ever about his own views and beliefs, then condescend to all women as if they were incapable of rational thought and put on this earth to listen to the wisdom of pompous idiots like him. The Lady Delphine she remembered had anxious blue eyes set in a thin face and hands that seemed restless and almost outside of the lady's control. Who would think a woman like that could inspire such passion in

Magnus he hadn't cared very much if he lived or died once she'd turned her back on him after he'd fathered her supposedly posthumous child?

Isabella was tempted to write and order the woman to live up to her obligations for once in her life. The Hailes needed a friend and Lady Drace was the logical person to be there for them, but she clearly wasn't coming. News of the murder must have reached Norfolk and the Drace Dower House by now and she hadn't driven up to town to show her support or even written a sturdy message of support for her old friends. Lady Delphine was clearly a broken reed, so Miss Alstone would step into the shoes of supporter and friend. Yes, now she was here and it wasn't quite time for the Season yet, she would be able to find lots of good excuses to slip away on errands for her sisters or fittings for a new gown or an endless search for exactly the right bonnet to match her new pelisse. If she also happened to visit the creaking old Carrowe mansion while she was out, that would be by the by, as long as she didn't allow herself to be seen by the hordes of spectators still haunting the scene of the crime like expectant carrion crows.

Chapter Seven

After another pointless and frustrating morning with the lawyers and magistrates, Wulf strode back to Carrowe House to fend off the curious. This morning he'd needed all Sir Hugh Kenton's clear-sighted logic to help him cut through the jargon and ritual as they went over the whys and how and perhaps of his stepfather's murder yet again. Until now he'd thought he understood his native language well enough, but he hadn't encountered a room full of legal minds hell-bent on contradicting one another as incomprehensibly as possible. Sir Hugh could cut through their nonsense and get to the nub of the matter as Wulf couldn't quite bring himself to, with the lives and reputations of his closest family weighing so heavily on his mind. He frowned at the thought of all the contrary forces tugging him in different directions right now and was doubly glad he'd listened to Lord Shuttleworth and accepted help when it was offered by a man who understood his situation all too well.

Wulf wanted to know who broke into ruinous old Carrowe House that night to murder the Earl and he didn't want suspicion falling on his family. Trying to weigh their lives and wellbeing against the mystery of who hated the old man enough to kill him was enough to give King Solomon in all his wisdom a headache and Wulf didn't feel very wise at all right now. Cutting down the list of suspects would mean his family could become more and more prominent on it. His mother and sisters had been there that night, as had Magnus, even if he had been out for a goodly part of it. If they knew where he'd been, he might be left off the inventory of suspects. Wulf was only missing from it himself because he was more than halfway to Cravenhill Park when the Earl was killed. There were too many reliable witnesses to his journey and nobody had been able to show how Wulf Fitz-

Develin could kill his stepfather and be in Herefordshire so quickly unless he'd mastered the dark art of being in two places at once. If not for his guilt-driven obsession with begging Isabella to take his brother back and marry him, he would have been in London that night and would likely be in Newgate awaiting trial for his life at this very moment.

Whoever killed the old man when Wulf wasn't there to take the blame couldn't have been thinking very hard. Or perhaps they loved him enough to make sure no sane magistrate could accuse him of the murder. That simply wasn't possible and implied careful planning, which didn't seem very likely given the impulsive, excessive violence of the crime. The coroner stated that the Earl had been stabbed *and* bludgeoned to death. It was apparently impossible to work out which wound had actually killed him, but both needed enough force to almost excuse Lady Carrowe and her equally slight, petite daughters from the list of suspects. But extreme passion could lend superhuman strength, one of the magistrates had pointed out unhelpfully.

Wulf tried to block that caveat from his mind as he went in through the strong, ancient oak back door of shabby and tumbledown Carrowe House. He walked past the kitchens without even noticing the soot and decay or the empty and echoing sound of his own footsteps as he strode past deserted rooms that had once bustled with life and hectic activity. It seemed better to consider the everyday annoyance of his eldest half-brother, Gresley—now Fifth Earl of Carrowe—than let his thoughts linger on the uncomfortable notion someone he loved could be a murderer. Early this morning he'd received Gresley's reply to his express telling him the Earl had been murdered and it was time for his successor to take up his responsibility as head of the family. Apparently the new Earl of Carrowe was too busy to come to town and the new Lady Carrowe too overcome by nerves and grief for him to leave her even if he wasn't. Wulf must sort it all out and keep the curious at bay, meet the old Earl's creditors and do whatever necessary to keep their mother happy until Magnus was well enough to take over. Since Gresley hardly trusted Wulf to put on his own shoes without detailed instructions, that was almost as bad as declaring he didn't give a damn what had happened to his father or the family he was born into. The old Earl had always favoured his eldest son and now Gresley wasn't even willing to come and fetch his body home. That was what undertakers were for apparently; something else to add to Wulf's list of things to do. At least Gresley would have to foot their bill, Wulf thought, the new Earl's callousness proving him a lot more like his father than he'd want to admit.

Wulf was tempted to whisk his sisters and mother off to stay at his own house on the wildest heath he could find near London and leave Carrowe House to the rats and the duns and the curious. Gresley would have no choice but to come and sort the poor old place out then, but it would look bad if they all ran away before the new Earl came to take up his responsibilities. Wulf paused at the bottom of the stairs and felt a sly glimmer of satisfaction at the neglect so obvious all around him now the Earl wasn't here to brazen out the shabbiness of his London home as if this was how he liked it. Not much of an inheritance for his successor, was it? Gilding was flaking off any fine plasterwork still clinging to the damp marred walls and cracked ceilings. The odd paintings the old man hadn't sold were so tattered or darkened by smoke and age not even the most optimistic collector was prepared to waste a few shillings to find out if a masterpiece lay under the gloom. Wulf couldn't even remember what colour the curtains, cushions and carpets were in their youth because it was so long ago they should be in a museum, if they took the moth-eaten debris of past glories.

Why wasn't Gresley here sizing up the value of anything that had escaped his father's careless eye and consigning the rest to the bonfire, though? Gresley could pretend he doted on his plump little wife all he liked, but Wulf knew money was his true passion. The new Countess of Carrowe's grandfather had owned the richest plantation in Jamaica and a fleet of slave ships and now she held the purse strings at Haile Carr. If not for her fortune, Gresley would never have married her, so it didn't ring true to stay away because she was feeling squeamish about her father-in-law's murder, not when something might still be salvaged from the wreck of his father's once-splendid assets. Perhaps the new Earl of Carrowe had the old ruin earmarked for a grand square and a few rows of neat town houses to bring him in a healthy income. Some enterprising architect could have ridden up to Haile Carr and be laying out his grandiose ideas to Gresley at this very moment.

Wulf shook his head, managing to relax the grim set of his mouth and unclench his teeth. After being bullied, then ignored by his eldest half-brother as soon as he got too big to terrorise, Wulf always looked twice at Gresley's motives. Maybe Gresley would be different now he was a true lord instead of a courtesy one. The sense of right and wrong Wulf had clung to even while being beaten for something he didn't do in this very house as a boy forbade him to pass the blame for the Earl's death on to Gresley simply because he wanted him to have it. Gresley's natural cowardice explained his absence every bit as well as guilt might do, but if any of his kin must be guilty of murder, he'd prefer it to be Gresley. Better if it was a passing maniac or some habitual criminal with a grudge and a capital sentence hanging over him already, but if Wulf had to sacrifice a family member, Gresley would do nicely.

'Ah, I'm so glad I have caught you at last, Mr FitzDevelin,' Isabella Alstone's dulcet tones greeted him brusquely from the shadows as if he ought to have been expecting her and he was deplorably late.

He groaned and why wouldn't he? She was the last person he wanted tangled up in this dark business. He had half-hoped she'd stay at Cravenhill Park to mop Gus's brow, or join her other sister in Derbyshire and stay out of his way.

'Are you now?' he replied concisely.

'Yes. We need to talk about your mother and your sisters,' she told him with such determination he might have groaned again if it wouldn't give too much away.

'What have you done; locked them in a convenient attic?'

Even in the gloom of a hall where the windows

probably hadn't been washed for a decade he saw her lips tighten. She seemed to be making an almost physical effort to hang on to her temper and he felt ashamed of himself for taunting her so absurdly when everything about his family was serious right now.

'If you're going to be difficult, at least do it where they can't hear you,' she said as if addressing a fractious child.

He could see the aunt of a variety of hopeful nieces and nephews in her patient expression and badly wanted to kiss her so they could both forget to be practical for a few blissful moments. 'The estate office is as neglected as the rest of this dust heap, but at least we won't be disturbed in there,' he said, waving her into the cobweb-decorated room behind what had once been the state rooms. If she was scared of spiders, she should have stayed away from Carrowe House.

'How busy and full of life this place must have been once upon a time,' she said after a cool look around dusty deed boxes and chaotic piles of faded and mouse-chewed paper scattered here, there and everywhere after several decades of lordly impatience when the Earl decided not to pay a secretary.

'It's quite busy with it now,' he said as a give-away scuttle in the corner of the room said some of those mice were still here.

She didn't even flinch. 'My maid will have hysterics if I take this home with me,' she told him calmly as she plucked a spider off her richly blue pelisse sleeve and put it on a tottering heap of official-looking parchment rolls.

'You have strong nerves, Miss Alstone.'

'Maybe, but I also have an aversion to being dismissed as a flighty female sure to bolt at the first sign of something I might not like the look or feel of, Mr FitzDevelin,' she told him with a very straight look.

'So I can't terrify you with our furtive wildlife. Foolish and ungallant of me to try, I suppose, but I've always been very protective of my mother and little sisters.'

'Good, it's about time someone was.'

'If you want us to have a civilised conversation, don't throw accusations of neglect at Magnus. He's not here to defend himself.'

'I didn't mean him. You know we badly wanted to get them away from here,' she said and he could see the truth in her deepest of blue eyes as she refused to be swerved from her chosen subject.

'You and your family?'

'No, me and Magnus. That's why we...'

Her tongue had clearly taken her further than she'd meant to go. He knew a truth she hadn't meant to let slip out when he heard it and, from her quick grimace and the frown knitting her brows, so did she.

'That's why you agreed to marry Magnus?' he said incredulously. 'You thought rescuing them was so important you were ready to wed my brother to do it?'

'No, of course not. Magnus is a handsome and kindly gentleman with a keen sense of humour and he'd been a good friend since I made my come out. I had more reasons than I can count to say yes when he asked me to marry him.'

'And they all dropped away barely a month before the wedding? They don't sound like the sort of reasons I could ever risk marrying for.'

'Two months and you're not the marrying kind,' she told him sternly.

'Neither are you if you needed all those reasons to say yes to my brother.'

'No, I really don't think I am,' she said rather sadly and stared at a dusty cobweb for a long moment before she seemed to recall who she was talking to. She shook her head impatiently and looked as if she wanted to be done with him and this shabby old wreck of a house now their conversation wasn't going to plan.

'But you wanted to be?' he guessed.

'I did; it was a mistake.'

He'd been right the first time he set eyes on her, then; she really did have a generous and yearning heart under all that cool poise and perfection. She *was* gallant and impulsive and protective and would make some lucky child a wonderful mother one day. How wrong-headed of Magnus to think friendship and common interests were enough to build a good marriage on with a woman like her. He'd had their mother's example of what happened when a passionate, loving woman married the wrong man in front of him all these years, yet Magnus still asked Isabella Alstone to marry him without loving her? Now Wulf was angry with his brother instead of himself or this unattainable woman he'd longed for all the way across a vast ocean and back again. What the devil was Gus thinking of to tangle such an exceptional female up in a mess like this one, then turn himself into a shadow of his former self when she saw sense and refused to marry him? No, he suddenly knew it wasn't her behind all the changes in his brother. There wasn't that sort of intensity between them, so there must be something deeper and darker behind Magnus's unhappiness than his broken engagement. At last he could see a malaise deeper than his brother's physical ills behind Gus's actions when he looked back over the last year or so and he wondered why he hadn't seen it at the time. Of course, he'd spent six months of struggling with a malaise of his own, so could a woman be at the root of Magnus's melancholy and irrational actions as well?

'A mistake you don't intend to repeat?' he asked now, feeling guilty at the sudden thought that although he couldn't have her in his bed, he didn't want her in anyone else's.

'Indeed not.'

When he rode to Cravenhill Park as if his life depended on persuading her to marry his brother, he'd almost hated her for the jealousy roaring through him at the thought of the union going ahead. He'd looked up to and loved Magnus all this life, but last year he left England so he wouldn't be able to do everything in his power to seduce Gus's bride-to-be away from him. Then Gus let her slip through his fingers as if she wasn't the most magnificent female either of them had ever laid eyes on anyway, and if the idiot *didn't* love her to distraction, he must be in love with someone else. Wulf couldn't think of any other reason why a sane and vigorous man wouldn't fall in love with her and Gus had certainly been one of those until whoever got her claws into him fixed them so deep she managed to blind Gus to Isabella's extraordinary beauty.

'How were you planning on helping my sisters?' he prompted to get them away from the nerve-jangling topic of her being anywhere near a marriage bed with another man.

'We made it a condition of the marriage settlements that they would live with us once we were married—' she began.

'The Earl must have been delighted,' he interrupted, because they were on that thorny subject of marriage again, and if he wasn't careful, he'd lose control and kiss her again to keep her quiet.

'He was so overjoyed at the idea of getting his hands on part of my dowry he would have put them on a boat to China if I had asked him to.'

'I'm amazed your brother-in-law was prepared to let him have access to even a penny of your fortune.'

'He didn't want to, but money didn't feel important when your sisters were so firmly under the thumb of a brute and a bully. Anyway, I'm three and twenty and Kit can't order me to do as I'm bid any more.'

'Can anyone?'

'Once upon a time they could, but never again.'

Another reason why she had agreed to wed Magnus, Wulf realised with a bite of something like pity in his heart for the bewildered little girl she must have been once upon a time. She trusted his brother not to dominate her or terrify their children, because Magnus was too terrified as a child himself to inflict it on anyone else. What would it take to get her to trust any man with all of herself when she had such gaps and grief still stark in her memory? More than him, he admitted, frowning down at the moth-eaten scrap of carpet under their feet as if he hated it.

'We have been in here alone long enough even if nobody else knows we're here. I can call on you in Hanover Square to discuss this at a more suitable time, if we really must,' he said in the hope they could forget continuing this conversation if he avoided her long enough. The less he had to do with her, the better, for both their sakes.

'An outsider won't know I'm not walking home from Bond Street or idling in the Park with my maid at this very moment. If you come to Ben and Charlotte's house, one of them will have to be present for the sake of propriety and I prefer to do this without a listener.'

'You trust me to behave like a gentleman, then?'

'Yes, I suppose I do,' she replied, looking surprised, and it felt like another burden on his already-braced shoulders instead of a compliment.

'Very well, let's get it over with before someone accuses us of having an assignation among the ruins,' he tried to joke, although the idea of secretly meeting her anywhere made his heart thunder and his loins tighten so shamefully he was glad it was almost twilight in here.

'At times I almost like you, Wulf FitzDevelin.'

'Don't, Isabella Alstone. I'm not a good man. Say your piece and go, before the rogue in me overcomes my bare half-share of gentleman.'

'I suspect you underestimate yourself. Anyway, that's by the by; my eldest sister and her husband wish you to know they will be very happy if your sisters agree to stay at Carnwood House. Obviously Mrs Shaw cannot uproot her whole family and stay there to chaperon us all until my sister gets back from Derbyshire, but Lady Carrowe can lend us countenance and my former engagement to your brother would be reason enough for us to share a home until you find a suitable alternative.'

'I doubt the gossips would agree with you and I've offered to have my mother and half-sisters live with me until her house is ready for them if they can't bring themselves to stay here after what happened. According to her, that would be running away and she's done too much of that already.'

'She does seem quite resolute now his lordship is no longer here to belittle her at every step,' Isabella told him, then frowned as if she'd said too much.

'Don't expect me to pretend he was anything more than a bully and a hypocrite, Isabella,' he argued impatiently.

'I won't, then, but don't call me Isabella.'

'Very well, then, Miss Alstone,' he said with a stiff bow.

'My sins reflect on my sisters,' she explained earnestly, as if she was afraid she'd hurt his feelings. If only that was all that was hurting right now, he'd be a mighty relieved man. 'After her early experience with the gossips, Miranda is oversensitive to their spite,' she went on as if she'd decided to confide in him and he really wished she wouldn't. 'I try hard not to give them any ammunition to snipe at her with and we came in here to discuss your sisters and not mine, didn't we?' she said as if he was the one who kept changing the subject.

'My mother insists she will stay here until I persuade the tenants of her late father's house in Hampstead to move out and my sisters won't go without her. Develin House could fit into this barrack twenty times over, but it's only half a century old and maybe they will find some peace at last when they live a little further from town.'

'Is that the sum of your ambition for them?'

'For now, yes. Money and rank matter less when you don't have them.'

'You don't aspire for them to be happy?'

'A society marriage won't guarantee that,' he said and forgot the barb in the tail of that clumsy comment until she coloured up, then paled as if he'd slapped her. 'Society has never opened its arms to my younger sisters and now they're penniless. If they tried to go about in polite society at the moment, they'd be fawned on for any morsel of gossip they might let drop if they are pushed hard enough,' he went on earnestly, because he really hadn't meant to take a tilt at her failed engagement to Magnus. 'I don't want that sort of attention on them, Miss Alstone, not when they've had to endure the after-effects of the Countess of Carrowe's Scandal all their lives. Maybe that's why Aline grew up impatient of sly questions and false friends and Dorrie is so protective of Theo she's more likely to land a prospective beau a facer because he's ignored her twin than simper at him as a good little deb-utante should. My sisters grew up with a father who despised them for being born female and a mother they love dearly but whose name was blasted by my existence before they were even born. Maybe half a year of publicly mourning the old devil whilst knowing he can never beat or intimidate them ever again will make them more like the usual run of society ladies. They might even be comfortable enough with strang-ers to attend one of your sisters' parties by the time the Little Season comes around again, if they happen to be invited.'

'They will be. Meantime they need friends even if they decide not to marry,' she said sagely and he sensed fellow feeling in her words and almost laughed out loud, although it really wasn't all that funny.

'And lovers if they do,' he added to tease her, since she was being absurd. She could marry who she wanted, and when the Season began, suitors would swarm around Miss Alstone like bees to honey now she was free.

'Indeed,' she said too brightly. 'Every young lady needs a choice of them.'

'Indeed,' he agreed blankly and bowed as if he was a gentleman, then held the door open for her to precede him. 'I'm glad we have had this talk, but we should postpone any more of them until my family are settled elsewhere and you are suitably chaperoned,' he said, the mental picture of her surrounded by eager beaux competing for a dance or even a smile having choked the life out of his sense of humour.

'Anywhere would be better than this,' she said

with a severe look around the dusty and water-damaged marble hall.

'Do you really think so?' he replied, surprised when there were far worse places in his experience. Apparently he thought more of her than the usual sort of fine lady, so now he was in trouble twice over—he wanted to kiss her whenever they were in the same room, but he also admired her strong character, clever mind *and* her superb figure and shining beauty. He didn't want to feel anything for her at all, but somehow he couldn't help it.

'No, of course I know there are houses more decrepit than this not even a stone's throw away from Mayfair. It was a figure of speech and I should have thought more carefully before I trotted it out,' she said with a wry grimace even more dangerous than her usual heart-shaking smile.

'Now I'm ashamed of myself for picking you up on it, but please have a care if you ever visit the Rookeries to look more closely at the poor, Miss Alstone. The places spawn crime in every form you can and can't imagine and you'd be a rich prize. Last time I was forced to rescue a lady from the stews, it didn't end well for either of us.'

'What happened?'

'She mistook me for a gallant knight dashing to the rescue. Her father wasn't quite so enchanted with me, though; he caught me smuggling her back into his house in a state of grateful fluster and disarray and jumped to all the wrong conclusions.'

'What did he do?'

'He made his footmen hold me while he liberally applied his horsewhip to my disreputable person to teach me to keep my filthy hands off my betters. Apparently he couldn't meet me as a gentleman, since I'm not one.' Wulf could feel the bitterness of the day he found out he was younger and more idealistic than he'd realised even after his rough upbringing. The burn of that past indignity threatened his guard, so he forced it into outer darkness and paid attention to getting them through the present unscathed.

'What happened when she told him the truth?'

He shrugged, not sure that the heedless and spoilt young girl ever had. 'He couldn't apologise to a bastard even if he wanted to,' he said as casually as he could, which probably meant not indifferently enough with her blue eyes focused on him as if she wanted to read his very soul. *Heaven forbid, Wulf,* his inner cynic whispered in his ear and for once he agreed with the rogue.

'And that was the start of your dark and wolfish reputation?'

'I doubt it and don't pity me, because I lustily enjoyed making his kind squirm in a very different way for some time afterwards, but being a dangerous lover to bored and duty-done *ton*-nish ladies palls after a while even for the likes of me, Miss Alstone.'

'Stop it. I don't deal in clichés, FitzDevelin, and you're trying too hard.'

'I'm trying very hard, but not about that,' he muttered under his breath and why did she have to pick that particular word? He was rigid with wanting her and the effort not to fall on her like the hungriest wolf was costing him more than she'd ever know.

'I promise not to run about the squalid areas of the largest and probably richest city in the world and need rescuing,' she went on blithely. 'Even if I did, I would never let someone else take the consequences of my folly after they put themselves out in all sorts of ways I know you're refusing to talk about. The selfish and silly girl who did that is the one who needed horsewhipping if you ask me.'

She waited expectantly for him to tell her more of the silly little story that had set him on the path to becoming the wolfish bastard the *ton* still liked to see him as, when it saw him at all. He was too busy struggling with overheated desire and this strange sensation in the pit of his stomach that might be even more dangerous to his composure if he let himself examine it closely. What could he say? Nothing civilised, so he kept quiet and that seemed to make her even more determined to defend him from her own kind and even against his own scathing opinion of a much younger Wulf FitzDevelin who still had a few dreams worth shattering.

'And I know how squalid and desperate the poorest areas are already by the way, because Lady Pemberley is my eldest sister's godmother,' she innocently went on with her counterargument. Wulf had to be glad she had no idea how dark and wolfish his thoughts were right now and tried not to let it show in his gaze. 'I expect you know as well as I do she works among the destitute and desperate whenever she can and you may be sure she takes very good care to keep me safe when we go to the slums together. So at least you will never be called upon to save me from the consequences of my own naivety. Trust Lady Pemberley for that, even if you consider me a fool simply because I was born in a rich man's bed.'

'I doubt you're a fool of any sort,' he said and why did she look as if that admission made her angrier than anything he'd managed to say to her so far?

'Then no doubt you think me a spoilt and over-privileged fine lady who likes to boast of her compassion by visiting nice, clean little children in foundling hospitals and talks about them the whole time as if they can't hear her. I almost wish you still saw me as a heartless jilt, Mr FitzDevelin,' she told him with her nose so far in the air he was surprised she didn't fall over.

'So do I,' he murmured dourly and knew she heard him, because she sniffed so loudly she sneezed from inhaling so much dust as she marched ahead of him like an offended empress.

Chapter Eight

Wulf ran up the last few stairs of the once-grand staircase at Carrowe House a week after his surprise encounter with Miss Alstone at the bottom of them and strode impatiently along the dusty corridor leading to the Dowager Countess's suite. He'd just heard that Develin House would be empty much sooner than he'd dared to hope. If he could persuade his mother to change her mind and leave this decrepit old mausoleum, she wouldn't have to endure a set of rooms so long emptied of comfort and valuables. Here worn old rugs nobody else wanted had replaced the exquisite Aubusson rugs he dimly remembered from his early childhood and the once-fine silk hangings had rotted to gossamer. He frowned at the notion they'd struggle to buy necessities for

Develin House between them. He wanted his mother to have the best of everything after enduring this dusty poverty for so long, but all he could come up with was the everyday and most of that would be second-hand.

Impatient with himself for wanting what she didn't covet for herself, he knew deep down he'd learnt what really mattered as a runaway and they all had far more than that now. Food in your belly, enough heat to stave off the chill of night and clothes to cover your nakedness could be enough if you were free. Live through today and take tomorrow when it came. He would love to get his mother and sisters out of here if he could persuade them it wasn't running away from the chill and dust and unease of Carrowe House if they moved to his mother's old home to live just a few miles away in Hampstead. If only Gresley would come, Wulf could put it about that they were leaving the place free for its new owner. But Gresley was still refusing to do his duty as the new Earl of Carrowe. Once their mother and the girls were safely at Develin House, at least he could stop worrying about them living in a rambling old ruin. Wulf and his manservant, Jem Caudle, had secured an inner core of rooms here to cut the ladies off from the rest of the house at night so Wulf could sleep now and again, but even nailed-up doors and windows and the stoutest bolts wouldn't keep out a maniac if the Earl's attacker came back. No, best get them out of here and they'd worry about new this and that once he earned enough money to buy it, or they managed to squeeze the jointure their mother was entitled to under her marriage settlement as well as the portions Magnus and the girls were due from Gresley and his nip-farthing wife. In the end Gresley would pay to keep them out of the poorhouse and avoid being lampooned by Wulf's friends.

Feeling his fingers tighten into fists again at the thought of having to ask his eldest half-brother for anything, Wulf reminded himself to save his fury for those who deserved it. His mother and sisters knew too much about angry men already, so he distracted himself by wondering if there was anything about this old ruin they would miss. Wulf decided he might miss the sheer space of it and all the history that now sat so sadly on it. Except there was space enough around his house on the Heath even for him and history was everywhere he looked in London and much of it as rotten and dilapidated as this vast old house.

He knocked on the door kept closed to keep some warmth in and called out, 'It's only me', to reassure his mother before he went in. The Dowager Lady Carrowe wasn't yet sixty and today she looked younger, despite her pallor. Her hair was still dark enough to show what a dusky-haired beauty she had been in her youth. He took a moment to admire the purity of her bone structure and fine blue-grey eyes even as he worried about the thinness that accentuated them so starkly. They might share colouring to an almost uncanny degree, but her eyes were softer and more trusting than his had ever been, despite all she'd endured at the Earl's hands.

'Oh, here you are at last, my darling, how wonderful. We've been having the most delightful coze,' she said as she hurried towards him with an instinctive grace not even the late Earl of Carrowe had managed to knock out of her.

She kissed his cheek, something she never dared do when the Earl was here to object and perhaps it was as well Gresley wasn't here to glare and fume at her for daring to kiss her bastard son either. Gresley grumbled like a bad-tempered bulldog if their mother showed the least sign of loving anyone more than him, but if he truly cared, he'd be here right now, wouldn't he?

'Hail, Wulf,' Lady Aline Haile joked and she wouldn't have done that without a defiant glare at the door when her father was alive either.

'All hail, Aline Haile,' he obliged her by fetching out their old way of defying her father behind his back and dusting it off, but his gaze had fastened on someone else. 'Good day to you, Miss Alstone,' he managed steadily enough even though his voice wanted to stutter at the vital beauty of her in this shabby setting.

'Isabella isn't here to pry,' Lady Dorothea Haile told him earnestly.

Her twin sister, Theodora, shook her head

in agreement, but she still didn't speak. Wulf cursed the old Earl under his breath for that silence. The old viper had blamed her for something he caused by shouting at her until she was too terrified to get a single word out of her mouth and Theo had not spoken since. Even her family had all but forgotten she once had a voice.

'As if she would,' Aline said scornfully. 'Isabella is our friend, Wulf, so there's no need to glower at her like a suspicious mastiff.'

'I'm sure you're right,' he said, smoothing out his frown as best he could, though it wasn't there because he thought she was here to dig out their secrets and spread them about.

Today Isabella was neat and quietly elegant, but he was struggling with a picture of her breathless and a little tousled by the wind off the distant Welsh Mountains when she rushed outside to intercept him at Cravenhill Park. Raw need to feel her lips invite and yield under his was a weakness threatening to tie knots in his tongue and his innards and it was even more impossible than usual for him to be so wound up in wanting her like this.

As he'd spent another morning with the trappings of violent death, he tried to convince himself the frustration and misery of it all must be sapping his will to resist her bright allure. He let himself imagine how it would feel to come home to her for a moment—as if every sin ever committed against him was wiped out, he concluded.

Forget it, Wulf, you've no place in her world and a sick brother, three sisters and a mother to support.

That was the slap he needed to restore him to sanity and he almost reeled under the weight of it.

'Thank you for having such touching faith in my goodwill, Mr FitzDevelin,' she said stiffly as if he wasn't a very welcome surprise to her either.

Thank goodness; if she'd smiled that sunlight-and-roses smile she kept for her true friends, he might have forgotten who was looking on and kissed her anyway. He felt the stir and shout of her proximity in his sex and insisted it behave like a gentleman for once before he fell at her feet and begged. 'How d'you do after your

long journey back to London, ma'am?' he asked
stiffly, because they were not supposed to have
met since he galloped to Herefordshire on a fool's
errand.

'Very well, I thank you, sir,' she replied and
he heard a faint trace of mockery in her voice,
as if she knew he had to be stiff as a tin solider
in order not to embarrass them all. If she knew,
then why the devil wasn't she more wary of rous-
ing his inner beast?

'I trust the roads were not too churned up after
the rain?' he asked clumsily and marvelled at
his own lack of easy small talk when it mattered most.

'I had a smooth journey, Mr FitzDevelin; it was
very nearly the most tedious trip into the country
and back that I've ever had,' she said and now
he knew she was mocking his hasty ride there,
the witchy minx.

'Then I have to thank you for bearing my
mother and sisters company so often since your
return.'

'It's always a pleasure to see *them*,' she replied,
as if the Earl's murder wasn't the sensation he

knew it was. Laying sneaky emphasis on the last word was even more provocation and thank heavens his mother and sisters didn't appear to have noticed.

Now she was eyeing her gloves and the elegant bonnet lying on an unsteady pier table nearby and Wulf supposed his arrival must have stopped her feeling joy in his favourite females' company and was doubly sorry he'd come back too early to miss her latest visit.

'Would the rest of the world thought it one as well,' Aline said with such bitterness in her voice Wulf wanted to comfort her for the hard lot life had handed her when she was born a girl to her father's bitter disappointment.

From the outset the *haut ton* had looked down their collective noses at her—maybe because she had no portion and had inherited her father's Roman nose, or perhaps because so much mud had stuck to her mother some of it rubbed off on her daughters. He had no idea how their minds worked. The fact was Aline was so busy defending their mother and little sisters from sneers and snubs nobody seemed to notice there was a clever, vibrant woman behind her haughty frown.

'I don't want them coming here to gawp, then going away to gossip about us as if they know more than the angels,' Dorrie said bitterly.

Wulf hugged her close and kissed her in a parody of a fulsome big brother until she giggled at last and ordered him to stop. 'Don't let them win, love,' he said as earnestly as he dared with Isabella listening. 'You've held your dignity so far and it would be a shame to lose it now.'

'I'm not sure I care what the wider world thinks of us any more, Wulf,' Dorrie said wearily.

'Then Theo and I will care for you, won't we, adorable Theodora?' he asked her twin with another old joke as he drew Theo close as well, made her part of the circle of love his mother and sisters always made even at the worst times. Theo didn't speak, but at least she seemed to forget to be scared for a few precious moments.

'Of course you must care, Dorothea,' Lady Carrowe told her daughter with uncharacteristic briskness.

Was this the real Gwenllian Develin, the

woman who grew out of the lovely, light-hearted girl the old Earl had courted with single-minded determination, then treated so ill she became a meek ghost of her former self? Wulf wondered why the old windbag hadn't troubled a lesser female with his mean desires and jealous rages.

'We have to mourn your father because his life was ripped violently away and nobody deserves to be murdered,' his mother said. 'After a suitable time has passed, we will be able to find you good husbands to make you happy.'

'I don't want to rely on a man for that, Mama,' Aline argued quietly. Wulf wondered if she was being brave about her limited prospects or truly meant it.

'No, indeed, there is such a slim chance of finding true love among so many unlikely candidates,' Miss Alstone said with a wry grimace that made Theo laugh shyly into his shoulder as if she had to hide her mirth so nobody could take it away.

'A chance both your sisters took,' Wulf argued while he hugged his youngest sister even closer to show her she could laugh as much as she liked now her father wasn't here to call her a grinning idiot.

'Maybe they are braver than I am, Mr FitzDevelin,' Miss Alstone said lightly.

Nothing would ever make his mother's bastard an acceptable suitor for Lady Carnwood's little sister, but he was secretly delighted she wasn't planning on entering another betrothal just yet. Tickets to cross the Atlantic were expensive and he wasn't sure the Continent would ever be far enough away if she married someone else when he still longed for her as if she was uniquely branded on his senses.

'True love comes with bravery added, my dear, but it's still an act of faith,' his mother said with a reminiscent sigh. There was silence while they considered what love had cost her and Wulf silently repeated an old promise not to risk it himself.

'I'm sorry Magnus and I couldn't make that leap, Lady Carrowe,' Isabella said as if she couldn't keep the words in even with Wulf listening.

He caught another glimpse of the striving and

burningly honest soul she usually kept hidden and cursed under his breath. She looked as if she'd wanted to love his brother so badly he could almost feel her yearning to be a wife and mother and jealousy stabbed him because she would never let herself love the likes of him.

'It's not something you feel to order, Isabella,' his mother replied with a look of concern. 'Love is a gift, not a duty to be squared up to. If you loved Magnus as more than a friend, I might be angry with you for refusing to see your betrothal through, but that depth of feeling was never there between you. To tell the truth I was relieved when you ended it, for both your sakes.'

The sadness in her voice when she spoke of true love touched Wulf even if he was the product of a love church and state said she had no right to feel. He saw the tears swim in Isabella's glorious blue eyes before she blinked as if she had no right to feel it either. Lust was tempered by tenderness for a dangerous moment, but his next sister down saved him with a denial of her own.

'Well, I'm not going to fall in love with anyone, ever,' Aline said firmly.

Wulf smiled across Theo's head to say, *Well done, little sister, neither am I.*

'If you don't, it's my fault,' his mother said sadly. Wulf wished himself a hundred miles away so he didn't have to be here as the inescapable truth of how much the Dowager Lady Carrowe had risked for love.

'Nonsense, Mama, it's nothing to do with you. We shall set up a ladies-only republic in Hampstead and make a pledge to one another never to fall in love or marry,' Dorrie joked with a frantic cheerfulness that ate into Wulf's heart like acid. She came across the room to hug Aline and Theo joined in as Wulf stepped back, glad the bond between his sisters was so strong nobody could break it, not even the late Lord Carrowe. 'You will need a passport to visit us, Wulf,' Dorrie went on, 'and even Magnus won't be allowed inside our borders without a written invitation.'

'I'm not sure if I should be insulted at the differences you make between us, Lady Dorothea,' he said in a lame attempt to go along with her.

'You should, I suspect,' Isabella whispered as she stepped past him to catch up her errant bonnet as if it was alive and on the verge of scampering away.

'Now, my dear, if you really are determined to leave us so soon, you cannot be left to wander around this mausoleum getting lost until Crumble chances upon you. I doubt he has time to escort you out and we really must finish sewing our mourning weeds,' his mother intervened before Wulf could bow and go away and brood somewhere quiet and devoid of feminine company. 'Wulf will escort you,' she went on blithely, 'and I do hope your maid won't give notice after being forced to endure our ramshackle servants' hall yet again.'

Wulf frowned and waited for Isabella to point out his mother had contradicted herself shamelessly. Apparently Miss Alstone was a frequent visitor to Carrowe House but couldn't be trusted to find her way downstairs and call for her maid to accompany her home on her own. Unlikely, he decided and wondered what game his mother was trying to play by throwing them together like this.

'If Heloise was going to resign, I'm sure she'd have done it the day I chose to return to London the very moment she finished unpacking all my luggage so she then had to pack it all up again,' Isabella joked as if she had done it on a whim.

Wulf tried to feel impatient instead of at odds with himself and a little bit glum as he waited for the Haile ladies to bid an affectionate farewell to Miss Alstone and promise to spend a day in Hanover Square. He was glad his mother and sisters had such a good friend. He just wished she wasn't Miss Isabella Alstone.

Chapter Nine

'Your mother has more courage and character than people credit,' Isabella said carefully as they made their way downstairs. Wulf was doing his stern best to escort her out in silence, as if she was his least-welcome duty in a day packed full of them, and she didn't feel like obliging him today.

'She has need of it,' he said as if he had been given a strict ration of words for the day and didn't intend to waste many on her.

He had felt the shadow the late Lord Carrowe cast over his family more than anyone, so she tried to be fair. 'I do know the late Earl wasn't a good man,' she persisted because even though this stiff and guarded conversation felt wrong it was better than stony silence. 'So there's no need to tiptoe around the truth with me.'

He looked deeply uncomfortable. 'Did he try to force himself on you? He wasn't above coercing women who didn't respond to his so-called charm and he had a vile reputation according to the kind of women the *ton* would never lower itself to listen to.'

'No,' she said coolly, refusing to be kept quiet because they both knew he shouldn't mention such women to a lady. She didn't see why she should be deaf, dumb and stupid about the harshest realities of life any longer and he wouldn't put her off that easily. 'I'm wary of ageing rakes and dark corners and it was my fortune he lusted after.'

'You think you're wary?' he asked incredulously. She felt her cheeks flush as she recalled one night when she truly threw all caution to the four winds, but that was different. 'And I know the Earl always tried to act the enlightened gentleman in polite company, so why would you even think you needed to be cautious?'

'Lord Carrowe was so harsh with your mother and sisters I'm amazed he managed to deceive so many people that he was anything other than a brute,' she said carefully.

'It wasn't like him to let the brute out when he could be overheard,' Wulf murmured as if the old man was still alive and might dash out and yell at him if he was criticised here in his own home.

She looked for signs of a small boy who lived here in constant fear of the Earl's fury in the sternly self-contained man in front of her and almost laughed out loud at her own naivety. He'd tower over the man now and all the terror would be on the other side, since the late Earl of Carrowe had been a coward as well as a bully. 'He was so hard with them I knew he was a charlatan even before…' In the nick of time she stopped herself. She had to persuade Magnus to tell his brother the truth before it fell off her tongue by accident. His family knew how to keep secrets, for goodness' sake, so why not confide in them before more damage was done?

'Even before…you found out the old jackal had a hold over Magnus that the great bumbling idiot refuses to discuss even now?' Wulf continued for her and Isabella decided her best defence was silence. 'If you could persuade him to confide in me, I'd be grateful,' he said stiffly, stopping on the stairs while they were alone in order to get as close to pleading for her help as such a proud man would ever get.

And he knew all the best places to whisper secrets here, didn't he? Such caution wrenched at her heart for the beaten and bewildered child he'd been in this house all those years ago. Still, Magnus's secrets had been so important to him they got him within a hair's breadth of marriage to the wrong woman and he had to tell his brother himself, in his own time.

'You know your brother better than anyone else does, Mr FitzDevelin, and I dare say he would have told you if you were here to tell.'

'I had to go away,' he said gruffly.

'I'm sure you did. Telling your family you weren't coming back probably wasn't wise, though, especially as you lied.'

She didn't want to remember the aching hollow at the pit of her stomach his absence had left her struggling with. When he wasn't looming over her like a sternly puzzled Roman general, she might find time to recall how desolate it felt to think she would never meet Wulf's wary winter-sky eyes again or see his firm mouth set in a sceptical line when he silently accused her of being a pampered society beauty who played with men's hearts for sport. Shock hit like a slap, then raced in her blood at the thought of never being alone with him again like this, but they were having a workaday conversation on the stairs, in a tumbledown house, with several conniving and possibly matchmaking females nearby, and that was all it was to him. She had to remember that fact and learn to live with it.

'I meant to make a new life when I left,' he said stiffly. 'I had offers to write for periodicals and newssheets and perhaps a book about my adventures. I was weary of being the Bastard Wolf and wanted to be free of him as well as my parents' sins and Lord Carrowe's malice. At least in a new world I could be my own man.'

He was already his own man, Isabella decided and wondered why he didn't know it. He still refused to meet her eyes and seemed to have no idea she secretly longed for him to admit he went because she was going to marry his brother and he couldn't endure being in the same country when she became Mrs Magnus Haile. Wulf FitzDevelin was far too guarded to do anything of the kind, though, even if it was true and she had no proof of that. Maybe a new country could give a countess's natural son a much freer and more hopeful life than hidebound and dynastic old England. She wasn't used to feeling this uncertain since she grew up and took command of her own life. It felt acutely uncomfortable and a little bit lonely.

'I soon realised I'd made a mistake; my mother and sisters need me,' he went on with a manly, defensive shrug.

'They do,' she agreed and this wasn't the time or place to want to kiss the gruff idiot again. 'Can you endure the gossip now you're back?'

'I was a fool to listen to it in the first place, and now my mother's house in Hampstead is empty, life will be much easier for her and my sisters if I can persuade them to live there with Magnus. Any help you can give me on that front would be appreciated. It may not offer the sort of gentleman-about-town appeal he's used to and Magnus has suffered a reverse of fortune as well as love.'

'It was never about money for him and we were not in love. What about you, Mr FitzDevelin?'

'I'm not in love either,' he said facetiously.

She already knew that. 'That's not what I meant and you know it. What will you do when your family are living together in Hampstead?'

'I will go my own way, Miss Alstone.'

'I know you love them too much to do that; I'm not quite the spoilt fool you think me,' she said coolly.

'You have no idea what I think of you,' he argued softly.

'Then tell me,' she demanded recklessly.

'I think you're a lovely young woman who has been indulged by a family who love you. You are stubborn and hot-headed and a little bit too convinced you know what's best for those you love. You have far more intense passions and ambitions than most ladies of quality and will blossom into a great lady when you wed the right husband and I wish you both well.'

'How kind,' she said hollowly. 'But I don't expect to marry.'

'Then I have to conclude you love Magnus after all and can't endure marrying anyone else,' he said so flatly she wondered if he found the notion painful.

'No,' she said patiently, wondering how many times she had to say so before he believed her. 'We were good friends, and if that is all you have to say, I really must be about my business, Mr FitzDevelin. I know you're busy and have little time in your life for standing about talking to outsiders like me at the best of times.'

'My mother and sisters don't consider you one of those, Miss Alstone,' he said as if he had reservations, 'but you're right; we can't stay here all day and someone has to tidy up the mess the Earl left behind.'

'And perhaps it *is* stupid of me to think I can do anything to help your mama and sisters through it,' she conceded reluctantly. 'I suppose you'd like me to stop interfering and go away?'

She might manage to stay in Hanover Square and twiddle her thumbs until Kit and Miranda arrived in town if she tried hard enough. Except she didn't exactly trip over dozens of well-wishers when she came here to keep the Haile ladies company by furtive routes and back alleys, and if she didn't come, who else would? But Wulf still seemed to seriously consider saying, *Yes, please stay away*, before he shook his head belatedly as if his sisters' and mother's needs came before his own.

'My mother and sisters need you and I can stay out of the way.'

'And you don't need anyone, least of all me?' she said, ignoring the forbidden ground under her feet.

Silence as thick and tense as the one they were suspended in while they stood in the darkness and hoped the Earl wouldn't spot them in the shadows that night at Haile Carr fell around them like a shroud. She shivered at the tension she could sense in his rigidly still body and what a devilish time she'd chosen to be shy of his ice-blue gaze because she was too afraid to imagine he was fighting a need to reach for her when she wanted to feel his hands on her so urgently she was shaking. She grasped her own behind her back to stop herself from reaching up to smooth his frown away. If she was alone in this need, she had to accept it and walk away. It was a foolish dream. When he'd left England for a new life without even saying goodbye to her, she had all but sleepwalked into marrying Magnus because she didn't want to wake up and face the truth about all three of them, but she was awake now. Barely possible chances made her heart race as he stared down at her as if he'd never seen the likes of her before, and if she could be unique for him, nothing else would matter.

'I was born on the wrong side of the blanket, Miss Alstone,' he said bleakly and made her ache for that innocent babe even while she wanted to stamp her foot at him for thinking she'd care.

'None of us have a say in when and where that happens,' she managed to say in a rather rusty voice he could interpret how he liked, but if she wasn't careful, she'd cry for what might have been and that would be a disaster for both of them.

'True, but you were born in your father's bed.

Best if you let me speculate who mine was alone,' he said and refused to even meet her eyes this time. She had to hope it was because he thought they would give too much away. Hope was the last thing left in Pandora's box when all the cares of the world escaped it after all, and since she'd spent half a year trying to crush it, she knew it was almost indestructible.

'You don't know who he was, then?' she asked cautiously.

'My mother won't say and apparently the man she loved died before I was born, so he isn't here for me to suspect. Since she was wed to a man who only ever loved himself, I can't blame her for finding consolation and affection elsewhere, but our marriage laws are cruel, aren't they, Miss Alstone?'

Isabella felt as if every muscle she had was stiff at the thought she might have been irrevocably tied to his brother in a week or two and never a shred of real love to bind them for life between them. It felt as if she'd stood on the edge of a chasm and stepped back just in time. Because? Because marrying your best friend when he loved another woman was a mistake and Wulf was right, the law was cruel.

'At least when I ran away, her husband couldn't use me to try to break her any more,' Wulf said hoarsely, as if talking about that time made it feel too real again.

'You went for her sake?' Her heart stumbled at the thought of him doing so when he was far too young to be so brutally alone.

He was so male and self-sufficient now it was nearly impossible to picture him as a helpless boy a grown man had ranted at and beat whenever he felt like it. Isabella wondered if Lady Carrowe had thought her lover worth the price their son paid and almost ran back to ask. No, that was the ultimate impertinent question and she wasn't prepared to strip her own heart bare to find a good enough reason for asking it quite yet.

'It doesn't matter now,' he said with would-be cynicism, as if he'd consigned his feelings to a dark cupboard many years ago and wanted them to stop there. 'And don't convince yourself the gossips are wrong about me, Miss Alstone, because I truly hated the Earl and I'm a bastard in more ways than one.'

'You clearly have a talent for melodrama, sir. Perhaps you'll grow out of it now the chief cause has gone.'

He hesitated in mid-glower and laughed instead. The surprisingly joyous sound of his deep chuckle seemed to lighten the shadows of even this poor old house and his genuine smile made her knees wobble.

'I have lived on my wits since I was a boy, so maybe you should excuse me.'

'And perhaps that's why you haven't found out what you're truly capable of yet.'

'Have you read something I wrote, then, Isabella?' he asked softly. 'And does that make you less indifferent to me than you pretend or just curious?

She blushed. 'Yes, and the latter,' she admitted as casually as she could with his eyes watchful and almost amused on her as if he knew differently.

'What did you think?' he asked, not quite managing to be indifferent.

'That you take a reader to places they might never see and show them what really happens there. You write vividly and passionately about matters that ought to worry your readers a lot more than they do, but you still hold something of yourself back. Perhaps it would cost you too much to test your talent to the limit. The Earl did so little to deserve your attention in life that you'd do better to live up to your own standards than defy his.'

His ice-blue eyes were intent and even a little defiant now and she wanted to shiver with something beyond coldness as she met them as steadfastly as she could. He nodded as if acknowledging she was right. 'I'm glad he wasn't my father and even more so that he didn't bother to pretend he might be.'

'And I like your mother's maiden name better than his. In your shoes I'd be proud to own it and never mind the rest.'

'Maybe you would, but Wulf is easier on the tongue and you have a fine name when you're not being ma'am,' he said with his tongue firmly in his cheek.

'I do believe you just called me a little madam.'

'No, how could I be so crass, Belle?' he parried and the teasing glint in his eyes when he named her that way warmed them so much she heard herself sigh like a besotted schoolroom miss.

'My brother used to call me that,' she said with a catch in her voice she thought she'd managed to train out of it.

'I'll settle for Isabella, then, if we're ever this strictly alone again,' he told her as if trying to tiptoe around a grief that was part of her and she was touched he cared enough to try.

'No, don't; I like it. My brother Jack would have liked you. You're honest and trustworthy, unlike the snake his school sent to escort him home when he grew ill. Jack would have refused to share a carriage with Nevin Braxton if he'd been well enough to push him out of it.'

'That's the name of the viper who pretended to wed your eldest sister when he was already secretly married to your cousin, isn't it?' he asked gently.

She was glad he didn't pretend not to know about the scandals in her own family closet. 'Yes, and a worm of the first order he was, too. We Alstones aren't really calm and civilised folk at all, Wulf. That devil's spawn did everything he could to ruin my sister's life when she was only seventeen and I find that unforgivable.'

'Clearly,' he agreed, meeting her eyes full on and how wonderful it felt to be understood. Apparently he agreed she had every right to hate the couple who did their best to make the Alstone sisters' lives a misery when they were too young and unprotected to fight back.

Heady warmth fizzed through her like a slow-burning firework. He understood her and hadn't backed away as if she was unnatural and wicked to hate those two so much even today, when she was old enough to at least try to forgive and forget the terrible chaos Nevin Braxton and Cousin Celia wrought on her young life. Instead of condemnation in his eyes, there was warmth and fellow feeling and something a lot more exhilarating. Isabella's heart raced with excitement and something even headier she wasn't quite ready to put a name to even in her own head yet.

She did know no other man made her feel as

if the world had faded away and they were the only people left in it. She had longed to feel like this again since the moment she left the terrace at Haile Carr, feeling as if a crucial part of her had had to be lopped off so she could do it without breaking down and refusing to take another step away from him and what might have been. Now she could stare into his supposedly icy-blue eyes again and stop pretending she didn't want to be scorched by his heat so close she could feel him breathe. She was free to be foolish this time and reckless enough not to want to be wise.

'You don't think me hard and unnatural because I can't forgive them, then?'

'I think they don't matter, they don't deserve to. I also think every inch of you is beautiful and never mind how nature made you. Your temper and thorny pride and all those other reasons you're about to come out with to put me off are all part of you, Belle Isabella,' he said so softly she had to stretch up to hear.

'And I think you should hurry up and kiss me, Wulf,' she said even more softly and licked her lips very deliberately. Wasn't she brazen?

His hands on her as he urged her even closer were urgent and far more than mere touch. It felt like a merging of him and her, a familiar presence in her heart that she knew as well as she did her own. She struggled to find words or a way to tell him how he made her feel and couldn't. He was here and reaching for whatever this was at last and that had to be enough. He mouthed her name against her lips; his tongue licked the edges of it as if he had to know the fullness of them from the outside in and she felt a long sigh run through her body like overheated magic. He was gentle against the half-open question of it as she gasped and breathed him in, desperate for Wulf-warmed air. Then his mouth was teasing against her lips so she would part them further and she couldn't say anything at all.

Here he is again. A familiar, strange and longed-for rush of heady wanting shot through her as he groaned something silently urgent against her mouth. Her fingers trembled as she reached up to feel every bit of him they could get to in the shortest time possible. *Ah, here*; smooth, firm skin over a wilful jaw; the tension of raw passion on his high cheekbones; the feel of long, unfairly luxuriant lashes against the sensitive pads of her fingers as he closed his eyes to the outside world and plundered her mouth as if he could never saturate himself in enough of her, would always come back for more, so he could sip and demand and beg for another taste, more kisses, more Isabella, more of anything she was willing to give, utterly unable to hold back from him.

So she pulled his head further down, further into her, fully engaged her mouth against his in a demand they echo the roaring need for more, for everything, for all of him. She wriggled against his arms in an attempt to get him to give the last bit of himself he didn't want her to know about, locked together by passion and the most urgent wanting she could ever imagine feeling if they both lived for ever. She coveted him so wildly now it drove her on with hot need, sharp, goading and demanding. Was it too much to want a man like this? It could be, perhaps it should be. She could feel her pride prickling warily in the far distance, knew the edge of danger in being so close to this uniquely wonderful man in every way. And why couldn't he ignore it as well and be the same sort of wanting, needing idiot she was?

She keened something inarticulate and needy against his mouth as he still seemed to hold back. She was so close to the edge she wanted to jump straight off and be damned to any tomorrows. Even his breath was short and deep now, almost a groan as his body leapt against hers, despite his gallant attempt not to let her know it. He did want her desperately, though; his sex needed her even if his mind didn't want to let it. She savoured the fact, sipped it from his opened mouth as he stifled a moan of frustration against her lips. How wanton a lady's hands could be as she wilfully tried to undo his manly scruples. A little whisper of sanity said he was right, this wasn't the place or time for such a naughty exploration. She tipped her head back so he could work his hot mouth down her throat and she could tangle his crow-dark curls with her fingers and feel the shape of him, learn the secrets of his muscle-corded neck, finely made ears and the sensitive line of his jaw while he drove her to the edge of madness by licking the pulse at the base of her neck, as if he was in awe of the frantic beating of her heart under his ravenous mouth and wanted to explore and incite it even more.

His hands shifted to keep her at his mercy when she wriggled her frustration. She wanted his hands to be busy undoing her. She longed to be utterly open with him as she'd never wanted to be with another man in her entire life. She couldn't even begin to imagine wanting any other man except this one so hugely. Shock trembled on the edges of this sweet, relentless, driven need inside her.

Here she was, swamped in raw, relentless need and a curiosity it felt impossible to fight was pushing her ever closer to the edge of that chasm. An opening up inside her that felt more than physical wanted to invite him in: *Take all I have and give me every way of being between a man and a woman; show me everything.* She must have whispered something almost as untamed as that in his ear while she was round there to make him groan, then try to stifle it against her skin before he gave them away, spellbound together in this vast, deserted stairwell. He trailed kisses back along the pathway he'd burnt down her throat and up to sip at her mouth as if he couldn't quite bring himself to part from her, but he was still going to. She silently cursed his formidable self-control, hated his ability to detach himself from what their senses and their bodies wanted so much all her scruples were flown. His will was stronger than hers. His experience so far ahead he knew where they might get up to if they dared and had decided, no, they would not dare. It had felt so precious and unique for her to long to be his lover like this and now he was drawing away? Distancing himself, she accused silently. She met his eyes with a challenge and dared him to risk her anyway.

'We can't,' he whispered raggedly and at least that meant he was less cool than he wanted to be while he was busy shutting down the real Wulf FitzDevelin as if she'd imagined him. 'Not here—not like this,' he added as he met her eyes again and let her see more than he probably wanted her to.

'Why not?' she whispered as if it was halfway between a threat and a promise. Was he protecting himself from the myth no lady could love the Countess of Carrowe's bastard? Or maybe he didn't want to love her more than he didn't want to love any other woman. If she wasn't hurting so much at the idea he was backing away from her more than any other female, she might wonder if she was insane to want to take the last tumble into love with such a stubborn, complex and utterly infuriating man.

'You're not getting away that easily,' she threatened half-jokingly, seeing the promise of true intimacy if only he'd believe in it in his wary eyes. Warmth threatened the cool of his ice-blue irises as he looked down at her and almost smiled. She knew if he ever let himself love her, he'd do it more fully and deeply than any other man could. If only she was the woman he could love and trust, he would make her feel extraordinary for the rest of their lives, she thought wistfully. 'I'm not letting you get away with running to avoid me this time, FitzDevelin,' she threatened softly. 'I'll chase after you if you go anywhere near a port, and if you get aboard one ship, I'll simply board the next one.'

He ignored her attempts to joke and managed to put enough distance between them to watch her reluctantly make herself as neat and smoothed down as she ought to be after calling on his mother. She deliberately didn't mention the fact his own dark hair looked as if he'd been out in a gale after her amorous attention. Was that because she half-wanted them to be found out? Maybe—perhaps she secretly wanted his mother and sisters to know he meant more to her than a polite almost-gentleman who could escort her downstairs as coolly and calmly as if she really was only a nodding acquaintance.

'You should let me go,' he said bleakly, eyes back to the arctic wastes he used to set the world at a distance, as if she was a brief madness he'd recklessly allowed himself and now regretted.

'Never tell an Alstone what to do, Mr Wulf. We tend to do the opposite simply to prove we can,' she half-warned and half-threatened.

'If you refuse to be careful for your own sake, then do it for my mother's and learn from her example,' he said soberly. 'She thought she could take an impossible lover and look where that got her.'

'You, it got her you. I think your parents loved to very good effect, even if you don't,' she said brazenly.

At last he smiled reluctantly, as if her refusal to be brushed off had to amuse him because it flew so wildly in the face of common sense. 'I believe I've just been deeply flattered, Belle.'

'So do I, Wulf, although you've done little enough to deserve it.'

He quirked an eyebrow at her to challenge that denial and stood back to survey her as if she was a novelty he couldn't quite believe he was seeing. 'Be careful where you light wildfires, Miss Alstone,' he warned soberly. 'They smoulder for days before they set whole forests ablaze, hot enough to terrify the damned back into hell.'

'There you are again; melodramatic to a fault. I was right about you, Mr FitzDevelin.'

'Wulf,' he corrected sharply, as if it mattered that she thought of him as he truly was and it felt like a small victory. 'And I'm still illegitimate and have three sisters, a mother and an elder brother to set up before I can afford a wife.'

'I don't need supporting.'

'And that's supposed to make me feel better?'

The offended pride in his deep voice was evident, but he had no idea how determined she was when she really wanted something, or how dirtily an Alstone could fight when they wanted to win badly enough. Perhaps he should take a closer look at her ruthless piratical ancestors if he thought she was about to go away and give up on him simply because he thought she ought to.

'No, it's supposed to make you realise most of your scruples about offering for me are irrelevant.'

'They will be real enough if we're caught here like this and whispers start doing the rounds about us. Can you even imagine how many of your relatives and friends will line up to challenge me if they find out what we were doing just now? Oh, no, that's right,' he said as he stood further away to look back at her, 'I forgot; I'm not worthy of a sword or a pistol, am I? So will it be an ambush in the dark and a good whipping or two in order to teach me not to tilt at windmills?'

'Not on my account. I'm quite capable of standing up for what I want and I'm not sure I like being called a windmill.'

'Don't make a joke of it, Isabella,' he said rather painfully. 'I know you're an independent woman of means who thinks she knows her own mind, but I won't let you be ostracised and mocked for the sake of a by-blow other ladies used to toy with in secret. You might think you could dare to be a pariah and a laughing stock with such a lover, but I won't let you risk it,' he said grimly and she could see from the stubborn set of his mouth he believed it.

'Do you really think I care what the scandal-mongers think of me?'

'You might not, but I do.'

Chapter Ten

'Is that you, Miss Isabella?' Heloise asked uncertainly from the dusty hallway below. 'Are you all right?'

Isabella felt her heartbeat start to race at a gallop and told herself of course her personal maid hadn't heard anything they had said or done up here. When they found time to speak, they spoke softly and Wulf would have known if anyone was listening because his ears seemed to be uniquely honed for trouble whenever he was in this poor old house. There was no need for her to jump guiltily as if they'd been caught plotting a scandal between upstairs and down, but if he wasn't prepared to own up to what they were, she would have to be guilty about it as well.

'I'm not quite sure,' she murmured.

'If you don't know, nobody else will,' Wulf mocked softly, then bowed stiffly and ghosted back up his half of the stairs as if he'd never come this far down them to swap secrets and kisses with her.

'Perhaps I imagined him,' Isabella whispered wistfully to herself, then spoke up to reassure her maid all was well and now the sun had come out it wouldn't be such a hardship to walk back to Hanover Square after all, would it?

Heloise sniffed so loudly Isabella heard her even up here and smiled ruefully at her own reflection in a dusty and badly speckled mirror on the half-landing. She felt so flat and alone now Wulf had withdrawn his vital presence, but she still looked as if someone had lit a good chandelier's worth of candles inside her. So she took a moment to remind herself he hadn't even whispered a word of love to salt all that drivel about gossip and duty for her. Apparently even if he did love her he wouldn't marry her and risk a lifetime of being more important than the polite world to her, so she really had no reason to look kissed and sleepily on fire as well as more alive than she'd felt in six long months while he was away.

'I suppose we can let ourselves out through the front door, since the latest flood of callers seem to have given up and gone away,' she said to her maid as she finally reached ground level and hoped Heloise wouldn't notice her latest employer was nowhere near as calm and carefree as she sounded behind a hastily donned bonnet.

'I'll look outside before you walk out there, then, Miss Alstone,' Heloise said doubtfully, peering through the dusty glass of a Judas opening from another age. 'I knew it was a reckless notion. A lady has just arrived and from the look of the horses she's come a fair way.'

'What sort of lady?' Isabella asked warily, picturing one of the formidable matrons who had tried so hard to bluff their way through these doors the last few days after staying away for twenty-seven years after the Countess of Carrowe was publicly disgraced by her own husband. Cursing Wulf for leaving her to deal with his family's visitors as if they were nothing to do with him, she wished she had stolen out of the back door as usual now and not decided to pin her colours to the front door of Carrowe House whether Wulf wanted them there or not.

'She looks a few years older than you, Miss Isabella, and a quietly dressed, decent sort of lady.'

'Not the kind who would come here solely to collect gossip about her ladyship and the Miss Hailes and spread it abroad?'

'She's gone to a lot of trouble if that's all she's here for.'

'Then we might as well open the door and see what she wants, since we are on our way out and Lady Carrowe's staff are otherwise engaged.'

'Aye, both of them,' Heloise murmured and stepped back so Isabella was the one to let whoever was out there into another lady's house as if she had a right to.

'Oh, hello,' Isabella greeted the lady on the doorstep as if she'd had no idea she was there when she opened the door.

'Hello; do you know if Lady Carrowe is at home?' the stranger asked as if she'd travelled too far and too fast to bother swapping polite formalities with a stranger.

Feeling dismissed and chilled by the cool and wary look the newcomer was sending her from a pair of wide blue eyes gentlemen probably found irresistibly vulnerable, Isabella shrugged. 'That depends quite a lot on who you are,' she said and stood in the way so this stranger couldn't simply march inside uninvited.

'Obviously she was at home to you and I've never set eyes on you before, so she is sure to welcome me,' the woman said with an arrogance Isabella suspected was mostly for show, but it felt quite real when you were on the wrong side of it.

'So you say,' she challenged back. She had a strong suspicion who this was and, if she was right, she'd decided not to like Lady Delphine Drace the moment Magnus confessed the real reason why he proposed marriage to her on his father's orders and the appalling dilemma this woman had left him in. Isabella might have put an end to the engagement with a secret sigh of relief, but this woman had hurt a friend and could have helped trap her and Magnus in a chilly marriage where both of them secretly longed for lovers they couldn't have.

'Delphine! Oh, it's so good to see you again at long last. But why on earth are you standing on the doorstep arguing with Miss Alstone? Mama and the girls will be so pleased to see you and Wulf's here as well,' Aline said, beginning at the top of the stairs and chattering all the way down as if she couldn't get here fast enough to hug the wretched woman. Isabella stepped out of Lady Delphine's path and wondered if she should get ready to break Aline's fall, but she'd underestimated the energy behind her friend's normally contained manner. Aline managed not to crash into the newel post before she launched herself at the newcomer to hug her as if she thought everything would be all right now the wretched woman was here at long last.

'Lady Delphine; what the deuce?' Wulf's deep voice called as he strode hastily down from his vantage point at the top of the stairs and whatever room he'd retreated to so he could pretend he had no idea why Miss Alstone was still here. Then he grabbed the newcomer and hugged her in turn and Isabella wasn't jealous in the least. No, not at all. He wouldn't hug the woman like that if he knew what she'd done to his brother, though.

'Thank heavens you're here at long last,' he said easily to the woman and Isabella's fists tightened so much she had to relax them before her nails ate holes in her soft leather gloves. 'Mama and the girls have missed you sorely,' he added and jealousy twisted viciously in Isabella's gut until she had to get away or shout something hot and furious at the woman for being at the heart of this family after what she'd done.

'Come, Heloise,' she murmured and hustled her maid away in order to avoid being formally introduced to the reason why there had been so many bumps in her own road lately. Lady Delphine Drace was the very last female she wanted to meet when she was still trying to deal with the consequences of the silly woman's actions, or lack of them.

'Magnus, oh, my darling. It's lovely to see you again, but you shouldn't have made the journey back here until you were feeling a lot better than you look right now,' Lady Carrowe scolded Wulf's brother later the same day.

She stood back to view her second son at arm's length and Wulf knew she was trying her hardest not to cry. Gus probably did as well. There was barely a sign of the once light-hearted and sociable Honourable Mr Haile in his brother's thin face and shadowed eyes, but Gus's smile made a brave attempt at resurrecting him.

'Now, do make your mind up, Mama,' he said. 'Either you want me here or you don't and how could I stay at Cravenhill Park cosseting myself like an ageing spinster when I knew you needed me here?'

'I've been stuck here longing to come to you and spoil you shamelessly, but I knew the gossips would trouble you all the more if I persuaded Wulf and the girls we should travel to Herefordshire to look after you. Maybe I should have because Lady Shuttleworth ought not to have let you travel when you look as if a strong wind might blow you over.'

Gus shot Wulf a reproachful look as if he should not have even told their mother about his collapse, but what else would excuse his absence when his father had been horribly murdered? 'Perhaps I'll ape my little brother a little late in the day and run away from home,' Magnus said lightly and made their mother laugh.

Wulf thought even this sad old house couldn't quite kill the sound of his mother's spirit reviving after years of forced penance, but Gus deliberately refused to meet his eyes to agree he could see the change in her as well. Wulf felt impatient with his brother's old habit of being visibly put out when his life wasn't going as easily as he thought it should. *You'd have thought he'd have got over it after the turmoil and upset he's been through lately, wouldn't you?* Wulf told an invisible listener in his head who looked very much like Isabella. He was in even more trouble than he'd thought if he was holding inner debates with her instead of himself.

'I might come with you,' Lady Carrowe told Gus with a smile.

'I did offer my house if you want to do that; it's a bit small, but we could manage if the girls don't mind sharing a room,' Wulf said.

'No, my love. I'm not bringing trouble down on you in your place of sanctuary. If we came to you, we would be sure to be accused of hiding away and I won't have that. I'm done with that, but if we went to Haile Carr with our goods and chattels, your brother would be obliged to let me live in the Dower House, if only because it would look bad if he didn't,' their mother went on, trying to make the best of things. 'Now he and Constance have the Big House they can't claim they need it themselves.'

Wulf had often wondered why his mother seemed to like Gresley almost as little as he did himself. Apparently she didn't feel duty-bound to hide her feelings towards her eldest son now his father was dead and he was a hundred miles away and hadn't come as soon as he heard the old Earl was murdered. Wulf puzzled over the old enigma of a doting mother who loved all her children except one and couldn't solve it this time either. Even Lady Mary Junget, the Dowager Countess's first child and eldest daughter, received a rapturous welcome when she came up to town. Lady Carrowe would sit with her fractious elder daughter for hours, patiently soothing her into a more hopeful state of mind and doing her best to get her to realise she was lucky to have a faithful, if rather dull, husband and a tribe of healthy children. Yet for her firstborn son their mother would give a wary nod of greeting and the blank, almost defensive smile she usually kept for her husband.

'I do hope we won't have to go there to beg for shelter,' she added, confirming Wulf's idea it would be a great sacrifice to ask for the home she had every right to as mother of a current earl and widow of the last one.

'We won't beg for anything, Mama,' Magnus said, looking a lot more like his cool and self-confident old self as his expression said the idea of having to plead for what was theirs by right revolted him.

Wulf thought he might have to swallow his pride if Gresley proved too mean to give up his mother's jointure, Magnus's own patrimony and the girl's small fortunes without a fight. 'If Gresley holds off claiming this place a few more days, you can all go to Hampstead and not have to,' he said soothingly because Gus had been ill and would find out the harsh realities of his new life soon enough. 'As it was once your home and your father left it to you for life, living there as soon as Gresley deigns to come to town and take possession of this wreck won't be interpreted as running away from your obligations as Dowager Lady Carrowe.'

'I forget I'm one of those now. I shall have to practise a disapproving frown in the mirror,' she said and Wulf thought those self-appointed guardians of the rules of polite society would have more of a battle than they thought if they tried to put her back in the corner her husband ordered her into when Wulf was born.

'Please don't, but will you agree to move out of this ruinous old barrack for the girls and Magnus's sake if you won't do it for your own, Mama? We can soon have Develin House replastered and repainted and you and the girls can fuss over Gus as much as you please and use his health as an excuse to seek clear air and open spaces for the poor old breakdown to recuperate in.'

'Thank you for that, dear brother,' Magnus said

with a long-suffering sigh Wulf thought largely put on.

He had to discover what was troubling his brother and he believed Isabella now—it wasn't her refusal to wed him that had brought Gus so low he couldn't throw off the lethargy that fever he'd had after Christmas left him struggling against.

'Develin House has always felt like home to me and this *is* Gresley's house now. I suppose he can do what he likes with it if we don't need it and Hampstead isn't that far away,' his mother said as if her resolution to stay here and defy the gossips was weakening now she could see Gus needed to get away from this vast and smoky city to recover his strength.

'Well, I won't be sad to go,' Aline said brightly. 'This poor old house has needed knocking down and starting again for the last fifty years.'

'Probably more, my love,' her mother said with a rueful glance at cracked plaster, rotted panelling and the faded runners and crumbling brocade curtains in what had once been a Restoration Lady Carrowe's luxurious parlour. 'Yes, let's go to Hampstead,' she finally agreed and Wulf felt his burdens lighten a little as he calculated how much easier it would be to keep them safe from stray maniacs in a much smaller, more modern house.

Magnus was home and Aline and their last housemaid had done the best they could with the food available to at least make a gesture at killing the fatted calf. Wulf felt he must stay with them all tonight although he'd prefer to be at home alone, with maybe a bottle and a warm fire to sit and brood by. Then he'd be free to think about Isabella instead of worrying about his brother and what sort of life he could have when he recovered. Wulf refused to entertain the notion stubborn, funny and compassionate Magnus Haile would give up on life as if it didn't matter. Yet if he went home, something told him Gus would be the one sitting up with a brandy bottle and that wasn't a way out he was prepared to allow either. Stay he must, then, and he'd better try to take part in this muted family reunion instead of sitting here brooding about a woman he couldn't have.

Except his mind would keep wandering back to this afternoon and his latest attempt to pretend he wasn't in thrall to Isabella.

And be honest with yourself, at least, Wulf. You've longed for her like a love-sick puppy ever since that night at Haile Carr. One passionate and stealthy kiss could be written off as an accident, twice is a habit. You have a burning need for a lady you can't have and isn't it lucky no one knows about it except her?

He couldn't snuff out the thought of Isabella warm and real in his arms a few hours ago. Even while he ate dutifully, listened to his family and occasionally joined in their banter, he couldn't stop wondering what she was doing and feeling right now. Here the Earl of Carrowe had been missing from his wife and daughters' lives for so long his death hadn't touched them as deeply as the murder of a better father would have done. Thinking about the man lying horribly and pitiably dead a few rooms away one dreadful morning a few weeks ago was enough to put Wulf off his cheese pie and whatever greens were cheapest at the market when it was closing. Isabella was a much more inviting subject and thinking about her seemed inevitable, so he might as well indulge himself and forget the old devil for an evening.

The Isabella underneath that glamorous protective shell of hers was frighteningly alluring as well as so complex he wondered if she'd stop surprising him even if they had a lifetime to explore each other. The resolute version of her he first met in the ramshackle estate office down the hall was even more unforgettable than the glamorous and lovely society lady who coolly ordered him to go away at Cravenhill Park a few weeks ago. His inner fool might whisper that the real Isabella saw past his scandalous birth and lack of fortune, but all he had was a modest account at Coutts and his pen. The account and his career both suffered from him crossing the Atlantic twice to try to forget a woman he couldn't have. And that reminded him he should be working on the account of his travels he'd promised to have with a printer as soon as possible to earn some of it back again.

Even if Isabella would have him as the most disreputable husband she could choose to infuriate her family with, he refused to be a kept man. Living off his wealthy wife wasn't for him. Not knowing quite how to be a man while he wasted his life trying to keep up with her and all her social obligations sounded like a nightmare to a man who had learnt to rely on himself very young. Maybe he should make her a formal proposal so one of her brothers-in-law could shoot him for daring to ask and he wouldn't have to worry about impossible things any more.

Idiot, he told himself as he tried to retune his ears to the conversation and face reality. Even when the Earl had beat him to the edge of sanity or locked him in the dark until he was so terrified and hungry that he'd agree to do anything he was told to, the escape of self-destruction had never occurred to him. Hatred had driven him to succeed, to spite a brute in the skin of a civilised man. No, he wouldn't let it be *because* of the old Earl he'd made anything of himself but *despite* him. And perhaps it was time to do it for a better reason. A picture of the best reason there was hit him like a brick in the face and finally shocked him back to the present, because he wanted Isabella in his life so badly, but he still couldn't have her.

He was distracted from his thoughts by Delphine Drace entering the room after her long rest from the journey. The tense silence when Magnus stood up and stared at her as if he'd received a mortal blow wrenched Wulf's attention away from Isabella and made him question another lot of assumptions.

Delphine was staring back at his brother and Wulf had to wonder at the tension between them. Delphine must have thought she was safe from seeing Magnus when rumour said he was ill and over a hundred miles away from Carrowe House. Wulf wondered fiercely what she'd done to hurt his beloved brother so badly that Magnus would flinch at the sight of her.

'Magnus, I thought you were fixed at Lord Shuttleworth's country seat until you were better,' she said at last and it sounded like an accusation.

'I was,' Gus said, looking as if he found it hard to string more than two words together in her presence without cursing.

'Yet here you are,' she added hollowly.

As a boy Wulf had been jealous of the bond between Gus and the girl he was so close to when they were in the country, where Wulf wasn't often permitted to go. After Wulf ran away from home, Lady Delphine Bowers had been Gus's playmate and partner in crime more than ever. Wulf used to wonder sulkily if his brother had missed him at all. Then they all grew up; Gus went to Oxford and Lady Delphine was tidied up, polished and turned into a young lady to make her debut in polite society. Then she met Sir Edgar Drace and Wulf hadn't given her much thought until she turned up on the doorstep earlier today. He'd felt pleased she was being a faithful enough friend of his family to turn up even this late in the day and thought no more of it.

'I couldn't stay away from my home and family at a time like this, Lady Drace,' Magnus was replying stiffly. 'As soon as I was well enough I insisted on coming back. Lord Shuttleworth was kind enough to send his coachman and two grooms to make sure I didn't topple out of his travelling coach halfway here.'

'You were very ill, then?' she asked.

Wulf recognised something yearning and bitter in her eyes when she stared at his half-brother, because he felt that ache when he watched Isabella when he thought nobody was looking. What was keeping them apart? Magnus was legitimate and the woman he yearned for a widow. He recalled Isabella's hints that he needed to talk to Gus about the reason why their marriage didn't take place and cursed under his breath. If Delphine and Gus were in love, then why the hell had Gus asked Isabella to marry him? And who else was knotted up in the mess they'd made?

His brother had a lot of questions to answer and it was high time Wulf asked them and refused to let Gus slide out of telling him the truth.

Chapter Eleven

'Are you quite sure you wish to dine with us tonight, Isabella?'

'Of course, Charlotte; you keep such interesting company I'd be a fool to stay away when I will have to endure so much of the other sort once the new social Season is in full swing and all the debutantes are busy giggling in corners.'

'Do stop being so old and sophisticated, my love, but you must know how endlessly Ben and his friends like to argue over their pet projects by now,' Charlotte said with a shrug that almost convinced Isabella she was worried her guests would rattle on about steam engines and lathes and celestial bodies and Isabella would be bored.

'Lucky I'm not the empty-headed society female some people think me. I find the talk around your table on such nights fascinating and I don't *think* I've ever sat about fanning myself and trying to grab the limelight at any of your entertainments so far. I could always stay in my room if you'd rather not risk me putting on a public display of fashionable boredom.'

'That's not what I mean and you know it. Even if you were bored to the edge of mania, your company manners are far too good for you to let it show. I was the one who had to drill them into you and Kate after your wicked aunt left you to raise yourselves like a pair of wild ponies abandoned on a mountainside.'

'Then if you can trust my manners, why don't you trust me to be as richly entertained by your clever friends as I usually am?'

Charlotte frowned at her own feet as if to avoid Isabella's gaze, so her friend was seriously worried but didn't want to admit it. Silence stretched uneasily between them for once. 'It's not you I don't trust,' she said uneasily at last.

'Then who *don't* you have so much faith in?'

'Whom,' Charlotte corrected half-heartedly and looked wistfully at her baby daughter's cradle, as if she wished the little mite would wake up furious just this once.

'Whom don't you trust, then?' Isabella asked with exaggerated patience.

'It's not that I don't trust him exactly.'

'Am I supposed to know whom you mean?' Isabella said shortly.

'I know *you*, Isabella. There's a capacity for deep feeling in you I don't think even you know about and it's a pity you engaged yourself to marry Magnus Haile without loving him with every fibre of your being, but I'm so glad you saw sense and refused to wed him.'

Charlotte met Isabella's eyes so steadfastly she suspected her friend had been trying not to say what she thought since she first read about her engagement in the *Morning Post*. And hadn't she found endless reasons not to call on Charlotte and Ben before she left for Haile Carr so she couldn't tell them about her engagement? As she thought back, that said so much about her secret doubts she was surprised she hadn't questioned it at the time. Maybe Wulf was the shock she had needed to make her wonder if the life Miss Isabella Alstone had built was as flawless as she'd managed to convince herself it would be once she married a good man.

'And what's that got to do with the price of fish?' she asked brusquely. 'Or a dinner you and Ben arranged for a few friends before I came to stay?'

'You don't know all our friends,' Charlotte said glumly and shifted in her comfortably padded chair as if she might have sat on a pin.

'Is one of them a murderer or a thief, then?' Isabella heard herself joke lamely and how could she even say that in jest after the Earl's terrible death? Charlotte had caught her off guard with that jibe about thinking she could control her feelings when she knew how impossible that was now.

'No, criminals are such bad *ton*.'

Isabella chuckled at her friend's imitation of one of the *grandes dames* expressing their views as if they were all that mattered, but she knew a red herring when she smelt it. 'So, no criminals—who don't you want me to meet at your dinner table tonight, Charlotte dear?'

'It might be better for both of you if you don't meet right now.'

'I'm even more intrigued about whom you think I'm going to be rude to.'

'Not rude precisely,' Charlotte said carefully.

'What, then?'

'Intrigued and pretending not to be.' Charlotte's words came out in a rush, as if she'd been trying to hold them back, but truthfulness wouldn't allow it.

'You will have to be plainer to convince me it's a good idea to stay away when you have rashly invited me to live here until Miranda and Kit are back.'

'If you must have it, Wulf FitzDevelin accepted our invitation to dine before his recent family drama unfolded. We can't tell him not to come because you're staying with us, Isabella. He's too sensitive about his illegitimate birth as it is and we've been trying to set this meeting of minds up since he got back from America.'

'Ah, I see,' Isabella said carefully and wished she wasn't blushing. 'You think I can't be civil after what happened, or didn't happen, between me and his brother?'

'I'm sure you'll be crushingly polite as only you know how.'

Isabella felt herself flush again under her former governess's steady gaze and almost admitted she sometimes used an excess of good manners to defend herself against the more curious and malicious among the *haut ton*.

'I have met Mr FitzDevelin more than once at Carrowe House since I came back to London in such a hurry, Charlotte, and I won't hide the fact I visit the Hailes behind society's back from you. You know I can't turn mine on people I grew very fond of when we all thought they would be my family by marriage. Mr FitzDevelin and I even manage to be polite to one another most of the time, despite my lack of common civility.'

'Now I've offended you.'

'No, but I admit to being a little hurt you think I'd snub him in public.'

'Under all that polish you're still the same ruthlessly outspoken little madam I first met, aren't you?' Charlotte said with a grimace. For a moment she seemed ready to abandon the subject and leave things be, but that was too much to hope for. 'No, it won't do, Isabella. I can't let you pretend I'm mistaken and ought to keep my worries to myself. You're attracted to the wrong brother, aren't you?'

'What on earth have I done to deserve that outrageous slur, Charlotte?' Isabella tried not to let her voice squeak as she fought to control her shock that her best friend had worked out her darkest secret. 'I jilted his eligible, handsome and amusing elder brother whom he loves. Mr FitzDevelin wouldn't want me if I was sent to him wrapped in silver gilt and tied up with pure gold ribbons.'

'Attraction and mutual need don't follow rules, Isabella. If they did, I'd be a governess or school-marm and Ben would be who knows what by now.'

'This isn't love and yours was.'

'Ben was born a bastard and felt it in every inch of his giant, gallant, daft frame, but I'll never regret marrying him. I love him as I could never love another man if I had to live without him for a millennium.'

'I know that, but why are you telling me?'

'Because it's wonderful to love such a prickly bear of a man and find out he loves you back.'

'Oh, no, don't tell me you're matchmaking now. A minute or so ago you were trying to keep us from meeting at your dinner table tonight and what I feel for Mr FitzDevelin isn't love, or anything close to it. Don't get carried away and start building castles in Spain.'

'How do you know?'

'How do I know what?'

'That he doesn't love you?'

'Because I've seen far too much of love matches, thanks to you and my sisters, to mistake this for love,' Isabella said and crossed her fingers under her skirts. It might *not* be love, and even if it was, it wouldn't lead to a happy ending.

'I suppose you're old enough to know your own mind.'

'I do; I'm not in love with Mr FitzDevelin.'

'I don't think you'd dare admit it if he was the man from all those wild dreams you never admitted having, but you can't reason away love and I suspect at least half of you doesn't want to.'

That was too close to the bone. Isabella wondered what she needed to say or do to persuade her friend to let the notion she and Wulf were more than nodding acquaintances go. 'Mr Fitz-Develin doesn't even like me.'

'Then since you're so definite about not loving him, I'll try to treat you as fellow guests attending the same simple meal. It could be a struggle, since you usually leave the room or close the conversation if his name is mentioned, but I'll try.'

'There's nothing simple about your dinners,' Isabella said lightly, 'but if you and Ben can't get your odd ideas about Mr FitzDevelin out of your stubborn heads, I might as well have my supper in the nursery or go to Carnwood House.'

'With the knocker off the door and most of the staff in Derbyshire with Kit and Miranda? I'll cancel the whole affair before you spend a glum evening with a maid of all work, the bootboy and a taciturn footman for company.'

'I'll stay, then, but rid yourself of the notion I

like Mr FitzDevelin more than any other nodding acquaintance. Kit would laugh himself hoarse if the poor man galloped to Wychwood in order to demand my hand in marriage and so would I.'

'Would you now? I wonder,' Charlotte said as if she had her own ideas about how funny it might be.

'Yes, Mr FitzDevelin would be horrified to hear you talk so.'

'Would he? Poor Dev,' her friend said softly.

'If ever I've met a man capable of looking after himself, it's Mr FitzDevelin.'

'Wouldn't that make him your perfect man? He might elbow past that fine control you pride yourself on before you knew he was doing it.'

'Oh, be quiet, Charlotte. Waste your breath on one of your children or save it for Ben, but please write me off as a hopeless case and leave me be.' Isabella stuck her nose in the air and went upstairs to pick out her most modestly stunning gown in the hope of making Wulf suffer for being the cause of the last half-hour of relentless interrogation, even if he didn't know it was his fault.

Chapter Twelve

She should have been prepared for the shock of Wulf FitzDevelin looking handsome as the devil in a dark evening coat and immaculate linen after her conversation with Charlotte earlier. Isabella shot a sidelong glance at the man when she thought nobody else would notice. Tonight he seemed quite happy to ignore the clever conversation and free flow of ideas around the table for the fine eyes of the lady seated next to him. Part of her hoped he was throwing up a smoke-screen to mask his interest in her instead of the eagerly wicked Mrs Fonthill. This could be his clumsy way of protecting her from the curiosity of her friends.

Charlotte had placed them opposite one another at the dinner table and Isabella dearly wished she didn't have to watch him flirt with someone else every time she looked up from her dinner. The bit of her that wasn't reasonable hoped Wulf knew her every move as acutely as she knew his. That Isabella was bitingly jealous every time she caught him smiling at the overblown creature, or openly admiring her cunningly displayed bosom. If he was acting, he was so good it looked as if he wouldn't notice if Miss Alstone took to dancing stark naked among the entrées in an attempt to wrench his attention away from the woman at his side. She glared down at her plate because her eyes were oddly misty for some reason she didn't want to think about. Perhaps she'd caught a cold from the children. At least that would give her an excuse to retire early from this delicious but somehow rather awful dinner and that seemed a very alluring idea right now.

It was the thought of all those experienced and eager women he once confessed he'd made love to that had made her faith in him threaten to melt away. She tried to tell herself Wulf was only pretending to run true to form for her sake, but the image of one or two of the ladies she knew considered their duty to their husbands done and a young and handsome lover their just reward for bearing all those sons played over and over in her mind and made the whole evening hideous before it had hardly begun.

Wulf was so fascinated by his dining companion he didn't seem to notice Isabella sneaking sidelong glances at him when she wasn't trying hard to be polite to the gentlemen on either side of her. She couldn't enjoy the company of all these clever, enterprising and interesting people because Wulf was behaving like a moonled idiot with an overblown female who ought to know better. She felt insulted he'd been the same with her in secret and suddenly began to doubt his sincerity during their shadowy encounters. She ought to dismiss him from her thoughts as if he was no more than a stupid fly buzzing around another woman as if he'd never heard of Miss Isabella Alstone. Yet the other men in the room faded to watercolour next to him. She had to clench her nails into her palm until it hurt in order not to leap out of her chair and rant at him for ignoring her after their latest snatched kiss in the gloom.

For an awful moment she also wanted to stab a pin in the woman he was so engrossed with. She longed to be the cool and aloof Miss Alstone she was before she met him. No good; that version of her packed her bags and left six months ago—on the night she met Wulf FitzDevelin. The night Isabella was shocked, intrigued and sensually excited by every last handsome, bitter, faithless inch of him between one breath and the next. How could she be intrigued by a man who was blatantly flirting with another woman while she watched from the sidelines, even if it was a pretence? She shouldn't hate the woman he was ogling, but sympathise with her. Mrs Fonthill was falling for the same sensual promises in his ice-blue eyes Isabella had.

Blaming the object of his flattery instead of the man who fixed his eyes on her as if *she* was the one female in the world he wanted only yesterday was wrong. Wulf didn't belong to her because of a few stupid kisses they should never have snatched. So of course she wasn't jealous or vindictive; she was disgusted by the lures a married woman could cast with her husband sitting nearby. By now the rich curves of the woman's generous breasts was holding Wulf's attention like iron to a magnet and reasonable Isabella was giving up. He did nothing to discourage Mrs Fonthill's possessive little touches and blatantly seductive glances under her skilfully darkened lashes. Little doubt these two would have a more satisfying end to their evening than he'd ever allowed her, but if the lady deserved censure because she was married, what about him?

He deserved her contempt, she decided. When he woke up next to a tawdry and overripe bedmate tomorrow morning, he'd get his just deserts. Isabella imagined the lady's sleek brows and lashes without the lampblack she used to darken them. It could end up smeared across Mrs Fonthill's suspiciously blushing cheeks if she didn't wash it all off before she lured him into her bed. Next Isabella considered the lady's elaborately looped and bejewelled hair and decided her luxurious locks could be padded out with false curls as well. She let them fall down on the smeared and ruffled pillows to shock Wulf in the morning, too, and it would serve him right for not seeing past the very obvious lures of a woman who wouldn't admit to being a day over thirty in a court of law.

She was quite enjoying her vengeful fantasy now and was almost charming to her immediate neighbour for a few minutes as satisfying images of Wulf reaping the price of his sins ran through her head like a bad play. How dare he use another woman to deny the attraction that sang between them even as they said a stiffly polite good evening to each other?

Stop right there, Isabella, she silently corrected herself. *This is the lesson you badly needed to learn and never mind the one he'll get in the morning. These are his true colours.*

Except she didn't want them to be; she didn't want him to lie in another woman's arms tonight and soar to whatever heights lovers achieved in the witchy darkness.

'No, he *can't* be the lover I long for and can't have. I won't let him be,' she whispered under her breath, horrified when Ben picked up her tension if not her words and followed the direction of her eyes. He had the cheek to grin as if he thought it was a fine joke she was watching Wulf with hungry eyes while he flirted with another woman.

Feeling out of sorts with herself and almost everyone else, she remembered Charlotte's warning: Mrs Fonthill was bored by talk of arts and natural science and the inventions her husband doted on. Apparently the lady had a generous dowry and it was her money that had set the Fonthill Works on its feet and kept his innovations going until the markets realised they had need of them. Now he was successful in his own right, the lady had lost interest. In fairness she *had* thrown herself at Wulf and maybe the gallant great fool was too kind under all that hawkish male beauty and aloofness to humiliate a lonely and frustrated woman in public. If it wasn't Wulf's sleeve the woman was clutching, Isabella might pity her for being married to a man who cared more about steam-powered engines than his rich wife.

She shuddered at the thought of how Magnus

might have come to view her after a few decades of marriage. He was far too much of a gentleman to treat a lady he wed for money so shabbily. Isabella shuddered at the thought of the life they would have had together if she hadn't found the courage to call off their wedding. At least Wulf was born of love and not duty—he endured a rough and bitter upbringing because of it, but he never had to doubt his heart and instincts as his half-sisters and brothers did because of the man who fathered them.

Now she was thinking about his brother to try to blot Wulf out of her mind and that wasn't working out very well, was it? She clung to it in the hope she could do better. Magnus's life had been pulled out of shape by being the Earl of Carrowe's second son, a spare in case his elder brother failed the succession. Magnus was sent to Eton and Oxford and thrown on the *ton* with too small an income to be fully part of it, but no space for a bigger dream. It was a wonder he had grown up so good-humoured and blasé about his role, she mused while the ladies quit the dining room at Charlotte's signal.

With any luck, she might manage to forget this silly fascination with Wulf's every move and glance if she thought about his half-brother long enough. Mrs Fonthill had peeled herself away from Wulf with open reluctance and at the last possible moment as the ladies followed Charlotte to the drawing room. Isabella willed her fingers not to clench into claws and made a murmured excuse about checking on the children. If she stayed, she'd lose her temper and say what she thought of Mrs Fonthill flaunting her lush bosom to attract a man's attention. To truly deserve a Wulf FitzDevelin in her bed she'd need more than a full figure and a lusty imagination.

The children were asleep for once and the night nursery disappointingly calm. Since Isabella couldn't face watching Wulf flirt with another woman any longer, she decided to stay away. Charlotte could twit her in the morning if she liked after she'd sworn she could be indifferent to Wulf for a whole evening, but she couldn't do it now. Isabella rang for Heloise and told her she had a headache and would try to sleep it away. Her maid would convey a message to Charlotte before she decided there must be a crisis in the nursery and came up to find out what it was and never mind her guests.

Ever since she found out Wulf would be here tonight Isabella had been secretly elated. This would be their first out-in-the-open, social meeting. As a very real headache throbbed in her temples she blinked back tears for the lonely feel of an evening when the man she longed for spent all his time with someone else. Knowing she had lied to Heloise and couldn't sleep if she tried, she waited a few moments to make sure her maid had gone away, then wrapped herself in her warmest shawl against the spring chill and went out to pace the spacious garden alone. At least out there she could breathe fresh air and have room to be properly alone. She longed for cool clear air off the Pennines and the freedom of the hills above Wychwood that she had tramped so often as a girl. Perhaps if she could get back there, she wouldn't hurt so much. She tried to tell herself it was only her pride that hurt, but she knew it was a lie.

She paced past the French windows towards

the airy family garden Charlotte and Ben had made. Pausing for a moment, she yielded to temptation and looked back into the drawing room. Instead of bending over Mrs Fonthill as if he couldn't take his eyes off her, Wulf was staring out of the windows, as if he knew she was out here by instinct, but that was impossible, wasn't it? Far easier for her to see him than for him to look out with the light from the candles that were making the darkness deeper than ever behind her. She eased back a little and held her breath until he looked away and turned to answer someone's question, or perhaps slant his latest *inamorata* an easy smile. Isabella wandered deeper into the wide gardens that were the main reason Charlotte and Ben took this house, allowing their growing family as much freedom as town children ever had.

It was far too early in the year for the roses to be in flower yet, but the pale glimmer of a late primrose or the tall and glossy pale pink tulips the gardener had carefully placed wherever the boys didn't run were lighter marks in the darkness. The moon didn't look anywhere near as big or bright here in sooty London. She compared it to that night last summer at Haile Carr and found it wanting in so many ways—no heat, no heady and exotic perfume and, worst of all, no Wulf. No comparison at all, then. Drat the man. Without him this was night-time in a pleasant enough garden where she could find a little peace after a noisy and disappointing evening, but essentially it was as blank and lonely as all the other nights since.

She shivered; time to live with what was instead of yearning for everything Wulf wouldn't allow himself to be. So she wandered a little further into the walks and even smiled briefly when she spotted a new den the children had built in the wilder bit here at the back of the gardens. She moved on despite a childish urge to crawl inside and cry for a bit, then curl up safely until morning. There was a neat bench almost tempting her to be still in the faint moonlight, but she didn't sit. If she wanted to be still, she would be inside, tucked up in bed while the most determined guests lingered over the fading sparkle of ideas and a last glass of brandy. This far from the front of the house and the mews, she had no idea if most of the carriages had already rattled home with their sleepy occupants drunk on ideas or Ben's fine cognac. She didn't care anyway, she assured herself and wondered if Mrs Fonthill was brazen enough to take her newest lover up in hers and leave her husband here to be called for later.

'Fool,' she muttered and paced restlessly along narrow paths and back on herself because it was a largish garden for London, but not by Wychwood's vast proportions or Edmund's rolling acres. Either would do now, except she had a whole London Season to get through before she could get to real, wide countryside and truly fresh air. She heard a faint click and a hint of movement off to her right and stopped in her tracks to consider if she ought to run or shout for help first. Neither, instinct told her as a tall and very masculine shadow loomed out of the back of the garden, but what the devil was he doing here?

'How dare you?' she whispered not quite loudly enough to be heard by anyone close enough to find them, as if they'd had an assignation planned all along.

'I'm hardly going to lose a fine reputation or a good name if I'm caught, so why not?' he murmured.

'No, and wouldn't it be a shame if you had to cultivate one of those?' she sniped back, but he was too busy frowning down at her as if he had every right to be here quizzing her to rise to her goad.

'I hurt you,' he told her huskily, and did he think she didn't know?

'I doubt it,' she snapped and wished she could think of the perfect response to his abrupt words now instead of having it occur to her long after he'd gone.

'Charlotte Shaw was watching us so closely I thought a light flirtation with another woman would stop her speculating about me and you.'

'Why?'

'Because Ben Shaw would kill me if he thought I had designs on you, if he didn't send for your brothers-in-law to do it for him.'

'What a faint-heart you are, Mr Wulf.'

'No, I'm a realist,' he said grimly and looked so certain and stern about it in the faint moonlight it might take gunpowder to shake his stubborn belief he had no right to be involved with a lady of birth and fortune.

'You're an idiot,' she told him severely. 'And if that's all you came to tell me, you can go away again.'

'I haven't finished.'

'Well, I have and I have a headache.'

'So I understand, but you looked so lonely out here, Isabella,' he said as if that explained why he came back to keep her company.

'You must have eyes like a wolf as well as their bad reputation, then. How did you get in here so easily?'

'I was taught to pick locks by a very fine craftsman,' he said modestly.

'And you think that's a good thing for a gentleman to know?'

'I think it's the sort of thing wolves like me are expected to know and there's no harm in being predictable when it gets me where I want to go.'

'There's no story in here, Wulf; nor a Mrs

Fonthill to make it worthwhile for the Wulf Fitz-Develin to creep about in the shadows. If you think Ben's safe is easy to crack, you should have brought your friend and half the contents of the Woolwich Arsenal with you because you're wrong.'

'I'm not a thief,' he told her as if she'd tweaked his pride.

'You obviously consort with one.'

'He's reformed, I hope,' he said impatiently and there was just enough moonlight to see him frown as if he wasn't quite sure about that and it worried him.

She didn't want to find that admirable, so she turned away from the sight of him, the shadowed, lurking-in-darkness and barely visible man he seemed to think was all she deserved. 'You should go now before someone sees you.'

'Who could?'

'Whom,' she corrected him snippily and was almost ashamed of herself until she recalled Mrs Fonthill's low-cut gown and hungry eyes.

'You should open a school,' he teased softly and how she wanted to be gently teased into a better humour and perhaps more, but she was so tired of peering through the night or the dust heavy shade of Carrowe House at him like this that she wasn't going to be as easily distracted this time.

'I should go inside and refuse to speak to you until you're prepared to own up to me in public,' she told him bleakly and felt him wince.

'Put the shoe on the other foot, Miss Alstone. You can't want a bastard like me attracting attention to you in public when you were betrothed to my half-brother until very recently. If I was considered pitch before that and the murder, I'm a whole lake of it now.'

'I make it a rule only to kiss men who admit to knowing me whenever and wherever we meet.'

Maybe she had been cursed to fall in love with the wrong brother and none of the neat endings she had mapped out at the start led to the right place. There—that was the snap of reality she needed to meet his accusing look with cool reserve even if he probably couldn't see it. She *couldn't* love him. And what right did he have to question her when he'd spent the entire evening wooing a potential mistress?

Isabella swept down the nearest path to the house in a swirl of expensive silk and finest lawn petticoats, Wulf trailing slowly behind her. Yes, this was the gown she chose with both her sisters last autumn, wasn't it? When she was trying so hard to believe this man was nothing to her and it didn't matter if he *had* left England never to return. Sensing she wasn't quite her usual self after a scandalous meeting under the stars she couldn't tell them about, Kate and Miranda had carried her off to their favourite silk merchant to pick something fine and frivolous and hoped it would help whatever was troubling her when she was engaged to marry a fine and handsome gentleman and ought to be dancing on air. So it wasn't so much a quietly fashionable gown as a hug from her beloved sisters, a reminder she was loved. A contrast to Mrs Fonthill's blatantly low-cut gown and brutally corseted waist and there was that nasty little clutch of jealousy in her belly again. It made her feel sick and uneasy and he shouldn't have come after her, she decided crossly and glared back at him again.

'They would be gentlemen, then, wouldn't they?' he said cynically and she wanted to slap him, except there was a hint of jealousy in his voice that made her silly heart race although she'd forbidden it to.

'Not if they tried to kiss me in the dark to find out if I would kiss them back. And who are you, Wulf, if you're *not* a gentleman?' she said relentlessly.

'A man who doesn't know who his father is,' he said as if that was all he'd ever be and this time hot tears prickled at her eyes. She told herself it was her fury at his intransigence that put them there.

'A man who doesn't know who he is for the lack of one?' she said and turned to face him. He was so heartbreakingly handsome and so determined to be the big, bad wolf, yet he'd got in here past Ben's careful defences, and all the reckless risks he'd have run if he was caught, because he thought he'd hurt her. 'That's not enough to sum you up now, Wulfric FitzDevelin—you've made yourself and never mind who your father was.'

'Aye, I've made myself into a fool,' he said as if he was joking.

He'd stepped closer still as if he had to convince her by proximity alone he was unsuitable to even be seen with Miss Alstone by the clear light of day. Instead he was pure, or perhaps impure, temptation and more so than ever when he was being so ridiculously modest.

Her fingers shook with the effort of not reaching for him as she tried to smooth an imaginary crease from the skirt of her gown. 'You've made me into one as well and more than once,' she admitted huskily and what sort of an idiot was she to remind them of that when she ought to be raging at him for his sins, but the root of his dalliance with Mrs Fonthill was in his stupid blindness about himself as a man she wanted and had let herself fall in love with somewhere along the line. How could she go on being furious with him when his stubborn conviction he was too much of a rogue to deserve her was part of the reason she loved him in the first place?

'Oh, the deuce; why did you have to bring that up now?' he muttered crossly.

'You have so many questions and not enough answers,' she replied lightly and would have walked away if he hadn't hooked his arm round her waist as if it belonged there.

She tried to imagine she hadn't longed to be in his arms, but couldn't dig up the right sort of petty little insults it would take to make him let her go. She'd wanted him mercilessly since he walked into Charlotte's drawing room looking so darkly dangerous and determined to ignore her. She did her best to stiffen in his arms and think of winter to cool her ardour. 'Take your hands off me, you lecher,' she whispered not quite fiercely enough, 'and that's a polite term for Mrs Fonthill's lover, by the way. I'm sure you know more impolite ones than I do. Choose one and wear it, Mr FitzDevelin, because you earned it tonight.'

'I'm such a dirty dog and you want me, so I might as well add to my sins.'

Isabella hardly heard her own gasp when he pulled her even closer and kissed her fiercely before she could think of a protest. Well, no, that was a lie. She *thought* of several, but he wasn't going to leave her any breath to speak anyway, so she drew his head down so she could kiss him back. It was such lusty pleasure to be in his arms and she shouldn't even know such delights existed until she was a respectably married woman. Except she did. It was like being adrift in the most exotic and lovely country she could ever imagine visiting and coming home all at the same time. Her heart was beating so fast and light now she wondered if it was thundering in his ears as loudly as it was in hers. His mouth was ravenous on hers as if he'd been starving for her and at least there was no hint of Fonthill's perfume or another woman's easy hunger on his lips. Wulf FitzDevelin wanted Isabella Alstone. She wriggled triumphantly and heard him groan at the feel of her restless body moving against his before he slid an even more passionate kiss across her willing mouth and stilled her with pure heat.

'Isabella,' he half-protested and half-praised her when he finally managed to lift his head and murmur her name.

'Wulf,' she muttered back and he kissed her again as if he had to imprint the taste and scent and touch of her on his memory. Sadness pinched at her even as the urgent heat of him spoke of long hot nights and lazy summer days of loving without boundaries and she knew it was a lie. Only he could take her there and he was far too much of a gentleman to risk it, the great fool. It was a joyous sort of pain, this outrageous need of him that gnawed at her in a way she couldn't find words to tell herself about, let alone him. She felt the jet buttons of his waistcoat bite into the soft skin of her torso through gossamer layers of silk, boned satin and lace, and stretched sensually against him to let him know she wanted it all gone. She wanted him naked; just him and her. With nothing between them but salty skin and lovers' whispers of praise and encouragement.

'I want you so much; I want it all,' she murmured with lips that felt numb. Their mouths were made for loving and not talking right now.

'No, Belle, we can't,' he muttered low and gruff as the injured wolf he looked like when he raised his head as if every fraction of an inch he made himself put between them hurt in some vital way.

'Not here and not now, I know that; but tell me where and when and I'll come to you.' She offered all of herself, rashly, completely and with such exhilarating feelings inside that all the lies they'd told each other since they met that first night melted away. 'I will,' she argued with a frantic nod as his eyes told her he'd already made up his mind not to let her.

He shook his head as if he couldn't quite believe his ears weren't making up lies about her. 'No, you won't,' he said firmly, getting his inner warrior on to the parade ground with unseemly haste. 'Stop it, Isabella. You can't ruin yourself with a bastard like me, however willing you are.'

'Willing?' she said as if it was poison on her tongue, which it felt like as she watched him be all the things she loved him for but almost hated right now. He could say what he liked about being a bastard; it was his damned honour and his pride standing between them—like twin statues of virtue and nobility she wanted to smash to tiny pieces and dance on. 'You think

I'm only *willing*?' she demanded. She was desperate for them to love one another right now, not passively willing to let him have his wicked way with her as if she was some milksop out of a bad play.

'Yes, in every way there is,' he said as grittily as if he'd been turned to stone despite the warm wonder of his body so firm and masculine against hers.

He couldn't quite draw completely away from her to leave her achingly lonely in the shadows again, though, could he? He wasn't going to let them be lovers and what else could they be out here in the little hours and the darkness if he meant to be noble? So he was distancing himself from her as if he was about to board another ship bound for New York, but this was different. Now she knew Wulf longed for her as acutely as she did for him. Although she would be being loved to the last degree of heat-soaked pleasure right now if they were equals in that, wouldn't she?

'Is that all you think I am?' she asked in a voice that sounded as if all the blood and life in her was soaking into the cold stone pavers under her feet while he stepped round her with a polite *excuse me*.

'Yes,' he said stiffly, as if he really wanted to be a thousand miles away now, 'that's all.'

'Liar,' she hissed at him. He flinched; his eyes closed to deny it and he shook his head as if he desperately wanted to mean it. 'You want me every bit as much as I want you,' she went on fiercely. 'You want me, Wulf; denying it won't make it go away. You've done that for more than half a year now and it hasn't worked, has it?'

'Do you want me to admit I need you as urgently as my father did my mother?' he said harshly, as if who he was explained everything. Why were they back with that tired excuse?

'Or as much as she wanted him,' she challenged. 'Knowing her, as I have come to since I engaged myself to marry the wrong brother, I can see your mother must have loved your father more than life itself to take such a risk with you,' she ended more gently. He didn't think anyone could love him so much; she could swear it until she was blue in the face and he'd never believe her. 'She loves you so very dearly, Wulf,' she said softly, feeling her whole future swung on making him see he was lovable and worth the risk she would take if she let herself love him for life. Something told her she had already made that giant step without leaving herself a way back. 'Since she loved your father passionately enough to break her marriage vows, she must have loved him nearly as dearly as she does their son.'

'Then why didn't she fight for us? Why not leave the Earl and proclaim me and my father boldly from the rooftops? She's a Develin, for heaven's sake, she could have thumbed her nose at the world and her father would have sighed and tut-tutted for a while, then shrugged and taken us in and made the best of a bad lot.'

'What would have happened to your elder brothers and sister? However much she loved you and your father, she couldn't walk away knowing what Lord Carrowe would do to them when she wasn't there to protect them from his fury.'

'So she chose to live not even half a life for their sake, with no power or influence to alter what I was made to do? Don't you think they would have been better off without her, given the Earl's never-ending need to punish her for daring to take a lover, and I can't believe she ever loved *him*.'

'Neither can I, but she's not the sort of woman to marry solely for advantage, so she must have felt something for him,' Isabella argued and wondered why she was defending Lady Carrowe when she'd never found the courage to do it herself.

'If she ever did, it was long gone by the time I arrived. She must have hated him for keeping me under her nose to beat every time he thought she was tempted to stray again. I wish she'd told him so every time he did it rather than close down and grit her teeth as if she deserved whatever filth he threw at her.'

He said it as if only by hating her husband could his mother be halfway right not to have rescued him. Isabella frowned and thought harder about the lady's reactions to a man she had come to hate too much herself to see things clearly until now. 'I think she pitied him,' she said slowly as the truth dawned.

'How could she pity such a hyena, Isabella?'

'For being one, I suppose.'

'She's a saint, then, but I'm not and never will be.'

'No,' she agreed and couldn't stop herself from giving his tense face a loving pat to console him for everything he'd endured, 'but somehow I still like you quite immoderately.'

'Don't,' he argued gruffly, putting his hands about her waist as if he was about to push her away before she got past more of his defences. 'Don't forgive me for anything I've done, Isabella. It's hard enough to walk away from you as it is.'

'Then don't do it, Wulf. Accept me as I am, as we are, equals before God.'

'You're Miss Alstone and I'm Lady Carrowe's bastard and once upon a time I would have gone home with that lonely rich woman while her husband was busy with his steam-powered engines. I would have scooped up her frustration and loneliness and enjoyed her body until I went on my way, whistling with the dawn.'

'And even that horrible image won't convince me you're as rackety as you think. You cling to a method of measuring the world out in grudging parcels, Mr FitzDevelin. Luckily I don't think so little of myself or the rest of the world, so why must you?'

'Because that man made me this way,' he said as if she'd driven the truth out of him and ought to be ashamed of herself. 'I'm a nameless fool with nothing but my pen between me and the devil. I have my mother, three half-sisters and Magnus to keep and can't afford the luxury of a Miss Alstone in my bed. Your noble brothers-in-law would kill me and quite right, too; then where would my family be?'

Now he'd said it he stood and glared at her with such furious longing in his eyes she wished she could laugh and dismiss his scruples as petty and unimportant. All she had could be his as well, if that was the only thing keeping them apart. Wealth and grand houses would feel less than nothing without him. She wanted to rage and stamp her feet and demand he put her and the life they could have together before this stubborn folly, but she knew him too well by now to batter her poor heart against his stony pride again tonight. Tomorrow or the next day maybe, but tonight he'd worn her down and her head was aching again.

'I might be worth it,' she joked rather lamely, the hardness of tears threatening at the back of her throat as she acknowledged a harsh truth and felt infinitely weary at long last. If he didn't love her enough to grasp what they could be together, there wasn't much point in humiliating herself again.

'I'll never risk making a bastard with you, Isabella.'

'Then marry me instead,' she offered rashly, feeling the rightness of it slide into her mind as if it had always been waiting to be recognised as the glowing piece of good sense it truly was. 'Your family would be safe and with Kit and the rest of my family behind us you wouldn't need to worry about them again.'

'I would be a kept man. A tame fool dressed up to impress your friends. Dragged to fashionable parties and soirées to be pointed out as a rich woman's folly. No, thank you, Miss Alstone; I'd rather be laughed at as an example of my mother's idiocy than mocked as my wife's.'

So this was how it felt when the tears you were struggling with faded away because your sorrow was too big to cry away. No wonder Edmund left London for three years when Kate turned his love down again and again as if it was of no importance. Suddenly she longed for her brother-in-law's wise counsel, wanted the comfort of Kate's loyal and loving arms around her and for both of them to tell her they loved her, even if Wulfric FitzDevelin couldn't, or wouldn't. He'd never admit he felt more than simple lust for her even if he longed for her every hour of life God allotted him. He'd got it so firmly lodged in his silly head he could only do her harm there was no point in him even considering loving her.

'Good evening to you, then, sir. I can't make small talk with you here in the middle of the night any longer, so I suggest you truly scurry off home and forget you ever saw me out here.'

'How can I do that when I've hurt you again?'

'Have you, Mr FitzDevelin? Ah well, such things will happen to reckless ladies of fortune who take risks with the likes of you. I wish you goodnight,' she said lightly and dodged past him and marched back to the house as if she really did.

Chapter Thirteen

'How can you wish me anything of the sort, Belle?' Wulf murmured. 'How can you be that kind and how do you think I'll ever sleep softly again without you in my bed?'

He thrust a distracted hand through his hair and briefly thought he must look as if he'd been out in a gale with sooty locks all awry and neck-cloth disarrayed by her exploring hands. He touched the mess she'd made of careful grooming and his body turned against him as he ran over places she'd been, as if some of her must linger there to be savoured and treasured. He'd said no and made her walk away when she felt as if she could be his whole world; everything that would make his life feel so rich and generous it would never matter who was born in what bed when they were together. Except it did. He would always feel ashamed of being dependent on his wife and hadn't he once taken a long hard look at his mother's marriage and sworn never to make such ball-and-chain promises himself? Marriage had trapped the last Earl and Countess of Carrowe in a lifelong cycle of jealousy, frustration and contempt on one side and fear and a weary sort of pity for a man who turned out so much less than he could have been on the other.

Wulf was less than Isabella Alstone. Less hopeful, less joyous and a lot less of a gentleman than she deserved him to be. Even without his own shortcomings his lack of a real name would drag her down if she shared it with him. Imagining how their children would be teased for his own lack of a father, he shuddered at the memory of pinches, name-calling and spite when he was included in some childhood party he'd done his best to forget for Magnus's sake. They had never talked about his brother's clutch of schoolboy friends who met up to create havoc together in the holidays again after that hellish day. Poor Gus felt guilty for not turning his back on his friends and being recklessly loyal to his half-brother ever since and that was what torn loyalties and being a bastard really meant. Isabella had no idea how it felt or how she would feel if he was stupid enough to expose her to it, so he wasn't going to let her find out, especially if he loved her. He wasn't quite ready to admit that disaster just yet, but he was afraid he might if he looked harder.

An argumentative inner voice whispered he could refuse to take a penny of her fortune, spend the odd holiday on one of her grand estates at his own expense and go on working hard at his chosen profession to prove the gossips wrong when they said he married her for money. And were they all blind? What fool would marry Isabella Alstone for her money? She was everything a man could fantasise about in a woman and a lot more he'd never dared to dream about before he met her. To own the everyday privilege of making love to her exclusively for the rest of their natural lives was something a man might sell his very soul for, if he had one. The Countess of Carrowe's natural son could only bring her conflict and unhappiness; her world would reject and revile them as a pair of fools who'd regret what they did when the novelty of playing against the rules wore off.

So where was he with his catalogue of reasons why not? If only he lived another life, then he could pride himself on being an independent man and just about manage to ignore the differences in birth and fortune between them. In this one he would have to take from her and he'd rather risk the sheer terror of his family having nothing much to live on if Gresley refused to honour his commitments. The so-called polite world would mock Isabella if she married him when she could have wed Magnus and taken Wulf as a lover once she was done with securing the Haile succession. Not that they had much left to succeed to; the old Earl had spent everything he could and Gresley was the only one with a penny to his name.

The very thought of Isabella in Magnus's bed made his fists clench so hard his knuckles went white even now. He'd had to put the width of the Atlantic between him and this terrible image of her and Gus wed and busily securing that succession together. He'd been tortured there and back by the idea he'd got far too close to something exceptional with his brother's wife-to-be that night at Haile Carr. Now he felt a blinding, unreasoning rage threaten to suck him under at the very thought of any other man laying a finger on Isabella with more than the most innocent reverence in his mind and he loved his brother. He was a mess, he decided, and cursed viciously under his breath.

Even that finger would probably be too much for him. The burn and thunder of blind fury running through him at the very thought made him clench his fists and he had to remind himself where he was and that he wasn't supposed to be here. His inner fool wanted Isabella to be a coolly reserved and faintly amused great lady with every man she ever came across for the rest of her life except him. He wanted her so desperately and in every way there was that it hurt. Temptation roared at him to forget scruples and burgle every bedchamber in that innocently sleeping house yonder until he found hers. Then he'd stop and adore every last inch of her until Ben came and pounded him into a pulp. They'd snatch satisfaction for however brief a time they were allowed before some busybody realised nobody could get through Miss Isabella's locked door to find the intruder. They could love gloriously at least once. Given his size and temper, Ben would roar and rage at the sight of any man taking advantage of Isabella, even if she'd asked him to do it, and Wulf would not be able to defend himself or his actions, because he still wouldn't marry her.

Yet the need to feel her under him, around him, with him as they made love soared so wildly he smashed his fist into the nearest tree trunk. He tried to bless the agony he'd inflicted on himself as it jagged through him like hot metal so sickness bloomed in his belly instead of lust. Once he'd stopped being sick and sorry for himself, he had to get out of here as stealthily as he got in and then forget why he came. Isabella had looked so alone and lonely in the darkness out here when he'd glanced up from flirting with another woman to show the world Wulf FitzDevelin was on the prowl again, snapping up bored wives their husbands were foolish enough to leave untended. He was as bad as ever, so no need to speculate about the odd wolfish glance he cast at the unattainable Miss Alstone he couldn't quite suppress. Now all he had to do was walk a few miles across dark and dangerous London to try to sleep in his own home, since he couldn't endure Carrowe House tonight and pretend nothing was amiss. Maybe he could honour his overdue appointment with the brandy bottle to take away the taste of using one disappointed woman to hide his interest in another.

'Wulf, Wulf! Don't just lie there; wake up,' Magnus demanded, but what right did he have to interfere?

Wulf had to grope his way up from a very peculiar dream and felt a hard jag of pain in his misused right hand when Magnus shook his shoulder. He cursed and kept his eyes closed as he tried to come to terms with life in a newly tarnished world he was going to have to get used to. He didn't want to emerge from his coward's cocoon of drunken sleep and even inside his chilly stupor it didn't feel much like morning. Gus wouldn't be shaking him as if he ought to be wide awake if it wasn't time to face the world, though, so it must be, mustn't it?

He groaned, remembered Isabella marching away from him last night and refusing to shed a single tear although he'd seen the shine of them in her eyes. Perhaps he preferred the nightmare he'd just emerged from of Mrs Fonthill pursuing him around the Shaws' drawing room like Diana the Huntress with hounds in full cry as her husband obliviously built some sort of shiny machine and laughed very loudly. Odd, but at least the memory of it distracted him. If he'd ever felt the need to chase animals about the countryside on horseback, he'd give it up here and now. 'Dratted woman,' he murmured and felt his brother's attention waver from whatever he'd woken him up to talk about.

'Never mind her, whoever she is. You need to read this or, given the state you're in, perhaps I'll read it to you as you're probably seeing double.'

'You woke me up to *read* to me?' Wulf asked

and opened bleary eyes to stare at Gus, too shocked he'd run mad to be furious with him.

'You'll understand when you hear, or perhaps you'd like to wake up to find half of London on the doorstep and you with no idea why they're here?'

'Half of London don't know I've got one, let alone where it is,' Wulf argued grumpily, but he yawned and tried to find enough attention for whatever Gus thought he should know.

'They will find it now,' his brother said grimly.

'Why? What have I done?'

'Not you; him.'

'Oh, *him*,' Wulf replied hollowly, knowing Gus must mean the Earl, since that was the 'him' who had blighted both their childhoods. 'You'd have thought we'd be safe now he's on the other side of the grave. Still, at least he's no kin of mine.'

'I shouldn't be so sure,' he thought he heard his brother mutter under his breath, but his ears were too drunk and sleep-shot to listen properly.

'What does he want?' Wulf said grumpily as he heard the first stirrings of the dawn chorus begin outside his bedroom window and knew he'd only just slept and any moment all that brandy would sour his head and stomach. 'I'm awake as I'll ever be at this hour.'

'You'd best get up and dress first,' Magnus warned, eyeing the wild spectacle Wulf knew he presented.

'Come on, Gus, tell me what he said or did and get it over with,' he said and felt a suspicious shiver ice its way down his spine, as if the old snake had managed to slither into his room somehow, but that was impossible now.

'Just read it, Wulf,' his brother said wearily and he might as well.

Charlotte had the *Morning Post* in her hands and was staring at the wall opposite as if it had suddenly become fascinating.

'What is it, Charlotte? Not bad news about someone close to us, I hope,' Isabella asked.

'No, nothing like that. I thought it was an advertisement slipped inside when they delivered the papers when I first saw it, but it's worse than that.'

'Then what is it,' Isabella demanded.

This morning her head hurt and her eyes ached and she was surprised her friends hadn't noticed how out of sorts she was when she made herself join them at the breakfast table as if nothing much had happened last night. She ached when she thought about that interlude in the garden, yet hugged it to her like a miser. Wulf parcelled out their time together in such meagre little portions she might have to make a few minutes last a lifetime if she couldn't convince him what an idiot he was being.

'It's described as a special notice,' Charlotte said. 'I suppose they didn't know what else to call it, since the man is already dead.'

'Do tell us who you're talking about, my love, before Isabella throws her breakfast at you," Ben said.

'You don't want to know what it says, then?'

'If you would like to tell me, then I promise to listen,' he told his wife with a grin he knew perfectly well was infuriating.

'Harrumph,' Isabella coughed as politely as she could. 'The special notice?' she said airily when they both looked at her as if arguing was far more interesting than anything the outside world could offer them.

'Oh, yes, you would be interested, wouldn't you?'

'I don't know, since you haven't told me what it says yet,' Isabella replied with what she considered exemplary patience.

'It begins with a list of the late Earl of Carrowe's names and titles.'

'Lord Carrowe?' Isabella gasped.

'I shall not read them out. He should have had his mind on higher things when he wrote this and not listed all the reasons he could find to feel self-important. Oh, my! Oh, my goodness. This is quite dreadful and horribly unseemly. The printers should have refused to put it into print and I should have read all the way through before I teased you.'

Isabella began to dread what the late Earl of Carrowe's last twist of the knife would turn out to be. 'Go on,' she said hoarsely.

'He goes on: "I, the most noble Earl of Carrowe et cetera, aver and attest that my wife, Gwenllian Augusta Develin-Haile, Countess of Carrowe, has borne me three legitimate sons during her lifetime, despite her treasonous infidelity with another man between the birth of my second and third sons. Sealed proof of Wulfric Develin-Haile's true birth as my son, as well as a record of the death of his mother's lover a twelvemonth before his advent, is lodged with my lawyer and the relevant authorities at the House of Lords, lest it should prove necessary to assert his right-ful place among my heirs and their successors. My wife is a weak, sinful and easily led woman, but Wulfric Develin-Haile is truly and legally my son. I commend my soul to God as a wronged and much injured husband. No doubt He will judge my wife both before and after she follows me to the grave and at least there she must lie beside me for all eternity and truly repent her sins of adultery and betrayal.'"

Isabella sat silent and horrified as the echo of Charlotte's recital of those cold and unrepentant words died and the world changed around her. At last she shook her head, because she couldn't find the right words to say how furious and sad and stunned she was on Wulf's behalf. The old

Earl's self-serving wickedness was now public knowledge and she hated to think how the Haile family felt this morning, but what about Wulf? He was an innocent victim of his father's cruelty. When Lord Carrowe set out to punish and vilify his wife all those years ago, he did it by rejecting and abusing his own son and her heart bled for the bewildered little boy he once was. For the first time in her life she felt as if that cliché was true as she rubbed a hand over it to make the ache seem smaller. The selfish, brutal and wilfully cruel waste of it was breathtaking.

'Oh, how could he do such a monstrous thing?' she whispered numbly.

'Poor Lady Carrowe, this will hit her so hard. I can hardly bear to think how she must be feeling this morning,' Charlotte said after a shocked silence.

'And poor Dev,' Ben added.

'Around every breakfast table in every house *this* is delivered to of a morning people will read this wickedness,' Isabella said, pointing at the printed sheet she so badly wanted to burn, except to do any good it would have to be the original, wouldn't it? And it was far too late. 'They will read it to anyone willing to listen in their turn and his life and all his father's shameless spite will be a sensation over the teacups for the world to wonder at for their amusement.'

'He will hate the Earl even more now,' Charlotte said.

'How can he not? That evil old man was a stone-hearted basilisk and I pity Wulf's eldest brother for having to wear the title in turn,' Isabella said in a flinty voice and met Charlotte's eyes even knowing there was bitter fury in her own and she was giving far too much away. All she wanted was to be with Wulf, to make him realise it didn't matter; none of it made a ha'penny worth of difference. He could have anyone he liked as his father, even the one he was cursed with at birth, and she would still love him and he still couldn't stop her doing it.

'Don't expect me to argue with you, my love, but I think you need to sit down and take a sip of your coffee,' Charlotte said as if she was afraid Isabella might break if she didn't. 'There's no point being ill for the sake of a man who used his own son as a weapon to beat his wife with.'

'Aye, breathe in, Isabella,' Ben ordered sharply.

At least the urgency in his deep voice broke through the watery unreality she had almost got lost in and Isabella gasped as if he'd slapped her. Air rushed into her lungs and she swayed as the reality of this cheerful, intimate family room re-formed. She was back from the edge of fainting for the first time in her life and the world she'd come back to was a different place.

'I'll be perfectly fine in a moment,' she said and took a few sips of coffee to prove it.

'Good, you gave us quite a shock by reacting as if the old viper has taken a potshot at you instead of his wife and son. I'm sorry not to have seen how serious it was when I first lit upon it,' Charlotte said with a bewildered flick of the hand at the sheet of newsprint lying on the floor where she'd dropped it when she started to her feet to catch Isabella if she really lost her senses.

'As well I was with you when I heard this instead of getting it from a chance-met acquaintance eager to spread the latest delicious morsel of scandal.'

'Since you reacted as if he took a shot at you instead of his son I have to agree,' Ben said.

'My feelings are my problem,' Isabella challenged his giant stature and fierce protectiveness. 'The last thing I want is you standing over Wulf glowering at him or dashing off to make Kit to do it instead. I know my own mind, so until Wulf Fitz-whoever-he-is-now makes up his mind how he feels about me and the world, I expect you to respect my judgement and leave him be.'

'You do like a challenge, don't you?' Charlotte put in mildly enough and Wulf was right, her friend did seem to have strong suspicions about their feelings for one another, whatever he actually felt.

'The tittle-tattlers will be nigh breathless with self-importance when they hurry out to spread this folly abroad,' Ben warned. She could see he wasn't happy about her choices, but he'd sat back in his chair to brood about them, so she supposed he must have listened.

'Never mind about them; the Countess and her

daughters are my friends and I want to help if I can,' Isabella said.

'Best get them somewhere quiet where nobody knows who they are and make certain it remains that way,' Ben replied.

'No, they must stay where they are and pretend they knew all along. That way it might seem like a wearisome matter they all got tired of long ago. They need to shrug it off as if they're surprised the world took Lord Carrowe's word against his wife in the first place and it's always been obvious he was lying,' Charlotte argued.

'So there's nothing we can do?' Isabella asked, feeling useless.

'We could invite the girls to stay with us for a few days, Izzie, but I don't know if they will agree to come. They seem devoted to their brother and will probably want to stay at Carrowe House to show the world they were never ashamed of him in the first place, so why would they run away now?'

'I'm sure it would help him to know his sisters have at least the offer of a safe place to get away if they choose to,' Ben said gently.

It didn't feel like enough and even the thought of Wulf's shock, bitterness and betrayal when he read his father's chilling statement made Isabella clench her fists. She desperately wanted to be there for him, not his sisters. She cared about them, but she would be able to offer Wulf comfort when nobody else could. The man who sired him had only owned up to him because he thought the precious Haile succession might be in danger one day. There was no love in it; not even a single word of remorse or acknowledgement the old Earl was a sinner and a monster in life and intended to carry on being one after death with this hurtful, self-justifying piece of bluster. And of course it was true. Her heart sank even further than when he left her standing like an idiot on the terrace at Haile Carr, feeling as if she'd been struck by a natural wonder and the world would never look the same again. The feeling she had about him the instant their eyes met had sat uneasily on an Alstone sister who swore never to want a man as urgently as she wanted Wulf FitzDevelin. She didn't take the time to look deeper into his dark looks and the silver-blue eyes he inherited from his mother sharpened and edited by wary cynicism so they were uniquely his back then.

He was the man she tried so hard to wish she'd never met—bastard Wulf who defied her to think him less than his brothers because he was born in the wrong bed. A man who stood proud and challenging after that moment of true shock when Magnus spoke and he realised exactly who he'd kissed under the hot August stars; a man who dared her to suddenly find him unworthy of her heat and desire because he was her fiancé's half-brother. That last part of it blinded her with shame, but she should have looked harder, should have known there was nothing simple about him or his family. He carried his mother's stamp so distinctively his father must have seen it at his birth and realised he could take revenge on his wife in the cruellest way possible. That wicked old man knew his lies wouldn't be challenged by a Haile nose or their dark brown eyes. Even now she was finding excuses for her refusal to see past an accident of birth by arguing the Countess should have fought for her son.

Nature gave her husband the perfect cover for his ill intent, but she could have challenged him. And how could the bitter, jealous monster the late Earl had become disown his own son simply to punish Lady Carrowe for daring to love a better man? Knowing Wulf's mother, her lover would have been a better man; she wouldn't have loved him if he wasn't.

Isabella tried hard to see past her hatred of the old Earl. Maybe there was the faint shadow of a better man under his misplaced pride and selfishness once upon a time. At least that would account for the Countess marrying him in the first place. Their children had so much talent and character it would be a freak of nature if every scrap came from their mother. Most did, of course, but the man who wrote this terrible admission of what he'd done to his son also sired at least five good and clever people. She couldn't claim to know the new Earl, or Lady Carrowe's elder daughter—they were older than the Hailes she knew and rather aloof. Yet all the Hailes she did know had a deep integrity and humanity that made their father's folly seem even worse. Perhaps they showed the world what their father might have been before he wasted his promise so terribly it was all gone by the time he denounced his third son as a bastard.

'If the Earl had proof his wife's lover was dead a year before his son came into the world, she could have used it to defend herself and her baby against his wicked lies,' she said at last.

Ben nodded his agreement; 'Common justice argues she was wrong not to, but who knows what he did to keep her quiet?'

'It's not about justice, it's about control,' Charlotte said with a shudder and Isabella remembered her friend knew all about that from the wrong side. 'The great and noble can say what they like,' Charlotte went on, 'because the world listens to those with a title. The rest of us endure their arrogance and pretend it doesn't hurt us.'

'But it still does. I'd never ignore or slight you, my Amazon Queen, whoever told me I ought to,' Ben said and met his tall and vital wife's eyes with love and passion and a fierce protectiveness in his own.

'Sometimes you two make me realise how

lucky I am in my family,' Isabella said because there wasn't much point pretending she wasn't here.

'Then sometimes we should be quiet. We're more than fortunate in the one we've made together, as well as in the love of Ben's natural father, his stepmama and his two little half-brothers.'

'It was a shame my first half-brother didn't turn out so well, but Charlotte is right, Izzie, we are blessed.'

'And at least none of us had to own up to a father like Lord Carrowe,' Isabella said and almost managed to make it a joke. Yet the bite of that self-serving announcement still hurt her on Wulf's behalf. She had to blink back tears of fury and the sort of pity he'd hate.

Wulf was the man she loved, if only he loved her back. There was a slender chance he might have let himself to begin with, but now he'd think he was cursed tenfold. At war with himself for being his father's son, he'd step back from any woman who might want him as the third son of an earl now. Wulf was so much his own man she mentally raged at him before he could even say it. As if his birth made the slightest difference to her. She loved him and would go on doing so when he didn't offer for her now he was legitimate and a suitably noble match for the late Earl of Carnwood's youngest granddaughter. He was a stubborn idiot who thought he knew what was best for her and somehow that made her love him even more, so she was clearly a hopeless case.

'I must find Heloise,' she said numbly, 'My new gowns are ready to be fitted, so I might as well go to the dressmakers' while they're quiet. The polite world will soon flock to London and the seamstresses will be so busy they might rush the alterations.' It was the best excuse she could come up with on the spur of the moment, but luckily Charlotte didn't have time to sit about waiting for seamstresses to hem a gown or alter a sleeve and she didn't suggest coming along.

'Are you sure you're well enough to stand still for hours while they tweak your new gowns until they're perfect, Izzie?' she said.

'I might as well be busy and at least Heloise will be happy in the temples of fashion.'

'To make up for all the hours she's spent sitting waiting for you at Carrowe House of late?' Charlotte said as if warning Isabella even the most discreet lady's maid might not keep those hours to herself much longer.

Chapter Fourteen

Sending Heloise to the workrooms of the most exclusive Bond Street dressmaker with a minute map of measurements and a list of required alterations wasn't devious, it was necessary, Isabella told herself. She ghosted down the side roads and alleys that would get her and the taciturn footman Miranda and Kit had left in London round to the back of Carrowe House without being seen. Yet again there would be clusters of interested idlers outside the front, watching liveried footmen hammer on the vast doors with calling cards while their masters and mistresses watched from carriages and expected the Hailes to naively let them in.

She knew this visit was ill-timed and probably wrong, but she still needed to see Wulf. The late

Earl's appalling announcement cut to the very foundations of who he was and she cared about the man Wulf made himself and never mind the Earl's nasty little games. He could call himself what he liked, he was Wulf and that was all that mattered to her. He wouldn't want to hear her say so right now and might not believe a word she said, but that didn't mean she didn't have to say it.

'Ah, I thought Jem or his mother must be back earlier than expected,' Magnus told her when he cracked open the kitchen door, then reluctantly held it wide enough for Isabella and her stern protector to slip in before he closed and barred it against invaders again. 'They went out marketing for us, since the girls can't show their faces for fear of being mobbed by the curious.'

Isabella knew Jem was the name of Wulf's manservant, or friend or whatever the lad and his mother were. She suspected they could have met when Wulf was a wild boy alone on the streets, since he treated them more like family than servants. Even hardened by the Earl's mistreatment Wulf must have been an innocent in that underworld. She was glad he'd found at least two friends, although Jem must have been little more than a baby back then. Isabella thought it unlikely an eager tabby or sneaky recorder of other people's misery would get a word out of them about Wulf or his family or indeed anything much at all.

'Gregory is large and strong and very close-mouthed, aren't you, Gregory?' Isabella said and her companion nodded to prove it. 'He will hold this door against all comers for as long as you need him to, but you'd best give him a good description of both the Caudles, Mr Haile, or he won't let them in either.'

'I suppose I would be better employed elsewhere,' Magnus said as if even today he didn't have the strength to argue and she obviously wasn't going to leave. He knew her well enough not to accuse her of idle curiosity and she desperately hoped Wulf agreed with him.

'Then I shall accompany you upstairs,' she said and waited as patiently as she could while Magnus gave Gregory a detailed account of Jem and his mother. They left Gregory glaring at the closed door with the suspicious determination of a medieval retainer relishing the prospect of seeing off an invading army.

'He doesn't get out much,' she said when they were out of earshot, 'and I had to see Wulf.

'He's not feeling sociable,' he warned and led her through the labyrinth of kitchens and store-rooms and up to once-grand reception rooms.

'I expect you're right, but I still need to see him.'

'It's been a heavy blow; he's not quite himself.'

'That's not his fault, though, is it? You have to tell him what your father did last summer, Magnus. He won't feel he can trust anyone if he has to find out from someone else.'

'He's got enough to cope with right now.'

'Honestly, you Hailes are stubborn as mules. I should have known you were full brothers the moment I met him.'

'We're like the old Earl?' he said, looking revolted.

'No, you're both good men and very like each other under the skin.'

'Wulf is definitely a good man, but I'm not so

sure about me,' he said with something like his old rueful and charming smile.

'Weren't you supposed to make sure nobody got in to gawp at us, Gus?'

The fury in Wulf's voice said he was already in a fine temper after reading his father's iniquitous notice and now he was jealous as well. 'Wulf,' she greeted him flatly.

'Miss Alstone, how delightfully unexpected,' he replied with mocking politeness and an exaggeratedly elegant bow.

'I suspect you are castaway, Mr FitzDevelin, so I shall come back when you're sober enough to know a hawk from a handsaw.'

'I'm not sure it's polite to call my brother a handsaw and please don't trouble yourself. Mr FitzDevelin will not be at home. He never was at home here and he certainly isn't now.'

'Oh, for goodness sake, stop feeling sorry for yourself,' she said impatiently.

'If I waited for you to do it, I'd die of old age,' he grumbled half-heartedly.

'You don't need any help with that,' she argued and maybe he needed a nice refreshing argument to make him drag his head out of the nearest brandy bottle.

'I'm drunk,' he informed her grumpily.

'And that excuses you from being anything else, does it? When did they write that into the rules for gentlemen, Mr Haile?'

'Don't ask Magnus how I should be; he doesn't know how I feel.'

'I wasn't asking him.'

'Oh, the devil. I'm him, aren't I?'

'The devil? Not quite yet…' Isabella hesitated to call him that by his true name again and compromised on '…sir.'

'Give me a few more hours and another bottle and I'll be halfway to hell, so I'll be sure to give him your regards,' Wulf said and Isabella almost wished she'd left him to escape into a bottle for a few more hours.

'You are Mr Haile, though, Wulf,' Magnus pointed out helpfully.

'Thank you, I've just found out that mad old fool was my father after all and you're expecting me to be happy about it?'

'He was my father all my life, why should you get off so lightly?'

'Oh, Gus,' Wulf said and lurched a little as he strode down the remaining stairs to hug his brother so fiercely Magnus nearly toppled over in his weakened state. 'How the hell have you lived with knowing it all this time? He's put the devils that ran him into me as well now with that cursed announcement of his.'

'You live with it by not letting him do it, Little Brother Wulf. By trying everything you can think of to make yourself a better man,' Magnus said steadily.

There was the truly kind, honourable and determined man Magnus was before life and love and his father tried so hard to break him. 'Your brother is right,' Isabella intervened when Wulf opened his mouth to argue.

'And if you think he's so wonderful, why didn't you marry him?' he growled and glared at them both.

'Mind your own business,' she told him loftily.

'You are my business,' he said fiercely, 'and he's my brother.'

'He's got a point, Isabella. Best not to repeat ourselves, but we could always try again,' Magnus said so lightly she wondered if he knew he was tugging a tiger by the tail. 'We could elope.'

For a moment Isabella was horrified by the idea he might be serious. 'I think you're forgetting the last six months and the fact we both have interests elsewhere,' she said carefully, because this probably wasn't the right moment for the confession she'd urged on Magnus earlier.

'Ah, yes, they're quite difficult to ignore, aren't they?' Magnus said sadly and she almost wished she'd held her tongue.

'What interests?' Wulf barked.

'You really are a very stupid man,' she told him haughtily, so frustrated he didn't realise what he was to her she almost wished she hadn't come.

'Not stupid enough to be interesting because I'm the third son of a lord,' he sneered.

'Oh, I don't know; you're not very interesting in your own right at the moment, are you?' she said with a contemptuous glance at his wildly disordered sable hair and unshaven chin.

'No, but I was the bastard I thought I was last night and today I'm only one in spirit,' he said.

'I'm sure you're too hard on yourself.'

'Oh, go away,' he told her as if her company was suddenly too much to endure. Yet she caught sight of his reluctant half-smile when he turned away from her with a gesture of pretend revulsion. 'If I wanted my ears assaulted by the opinions of strangers, I could open the front door and hear them in droves.'

'I'm not a stranger.'

'By the opinions of a lady I happen to have met before and who refuses to mind her own business and leave me be when I beg her to, then,' he corrected himself with exaggerated patience and almost a grin of complicity, but she wasn't ready to be complicit or meekly go away as he bid.

'A lady who won't let you ignore and slight her because you're not who you thought you were and I won't be making any more furtive assignations with you so you can pretend I'm virtually a stranger when you happen to meet me in company, Mr Wulf Whoever-you-want-to-call-yourself-now. And if you ever kiss me again, you can do it in daylight with half the world looking on or not bother because I'm done with hiding in dark corners with you, whatever name you settle on,' she told him brusquely and turned on her heel to leave because this seemed like a good place to start.

It would give him something to think about other than his obnoxious father and she *was* tired of hiding in corners. If he felt anything real for her, he could follow her into the light and prove it to both of them. She couldn't stop herself looking back when she reached the door to the kitchens, where Gregory was stoically waiting for her. Wulf's eyes were blank with shock after her reference to their trysts in front of Magnus, so at least her ultimatum had given his thoughts a new turn.

She finally noticed Lady Carrowe and her younger daughters looking on with eager attention when she wrenched her gaze from him long enough to see them on the last half-landing. She'd been so engrossed in how Wulf felt about her she hadn't even noticed them creep downstairs. At least she didn't need to explain the situation to his family next time they met and she refused to let him pretend he hardly knew her. She nodded to say she meant every word and didn't care if they knew about those kisses because she refused to be ashamed. Even so she hoped they weren't too shocked and knew she considered them true friends whatever happened from now on.

'I wish you all a good morning,' she said and swept out because there were times when there really wasn't anything else to say and this felt like one of them.

Chapter Fifteen

'**W**ell, that's certainly told you, Wulf,' Magnus said with the once-familiar careless grin he ought to be pleased to see back on his brother's face, Wulf realised rather numbly.

'Don't you think you should go after her?' Aline put in as she seemed to snap out of the trance she'd gone into after hearing Isabella's impossible invitation to kiss her in front of them all or leave her alone in future.

'And do what?' he said wearily.

'Well, kiss her again, I suppose.'

'I thought you didn't approve of such mawkish nonsense.'

'I don't, but I suppose you two must enjoy it, since it sounds as if you've been doing it quite a lot,' Aline said with a puzzled shake of the head as if she couldn't quite imagine how any-one could, but each to their own.

'She had no business telling anyone,' Wulf managed with a defensive frown and wished everyone would go away until he'd got over the self-inflicted pain beating in his head like a war drum now she was gone and he was in no fit state to run after her. He'd probably be arrested for bothering a lady in his present state and he still wasn't sure he was as ready to throw cau-tion to the winds as she thought he ought to be. After all, his caution was for her, wasn't it? He might be the Honourable Wulfric Haile now, but he felt like a shabby sort of a gentleman and he still couldn't offer her much more than himself. What sort of prize was he for a beautiful, clever lady of character like Isabella?

'It sounds as if Isabella had every right to drag whatever you've been up to out into the light, my son,' his mother told him severely and Wulf groaned and put a hand to his aching forehead and rubbed as if that might make it all go away— as if anything could now Isabella had made that reckless, ruthless and ridiculously brave ultimatum in front of them all.

'Fresh air is what you need most right now, Little Brother,' Magnus told him sagely. 'Well, that and a shave. Oh, and probably a bath as well because you might as well begin clean and tidy. After all that I know just the place where you can hire a fast horse and you'll get as much fresh air as you can handle on the road to chase away that headache,' he added helpfully and grinned despite Wulf's best frown to tell him what he thought of his misplaced humour.

Dorrie exchanged a puzzled look with her twin. Theo mouthed something at her and she gasped, then nodded as if she was fool not to have got the meaning of Magnus's ridiculous insinuation straight away. 'Oh, yes, Derbyshire; of course,' she said wisely and as if that clinched things. He wasn't going to gallop all the way to Wychwood on a wild goose chase when the Earl of Carnwood was likely to set the dogs on him when he got there, third son of an earl or not.

'I'm going home,' Wulf said dourly, then stamped out the back way because he didn't care what his family or Isabella said about the value of openness, he wasn't risking the front one in this state. He might hit somebody if they got in his way and that would never do, now would it? 'And there's plenty of fresh air to be had at my house on the Heath, thank you very much, loving family of mine,' he muttered under his breath as he slipped through back alleys in Isabella's wake. 'Women!' he confided in a startled groom from the next-door mews, then stamped off into bustling, busy London to walk off some of his temper and most of his headache and try very hard not to think about anything at all.

'Gres! Well, I never. We thought you'd quite forgotten the way to London,' his next brother-in-line greeted the new Earl of Carrowe not very enthusiastically as soon as he'd managed to shoulder his way past the crowd of still-hopeful onlookers outside Carrowe House a few days after his father's startling announcement from beyond the grave that Wulf was his get after all.

'I tried to, Magnus; believe me, I tried,' Gresley said wearily as soon as he was safe inside the house and out of earshot of those interested spectators.

'I wager he's actually telling the truth, for once,' Wulf muttered from where he stood in the shadiest corner of the hall, watching the family reunion with a cynical eye.

In a way it was his fault his family were still being besieged by the curious, so it felt like his duty to pretend to work here instead of at home today and take his turn at keeping the curious at bay. It wasn't as if he'd got much done since the latest set of bombshells blew his life apart, so no matter if Gresley's arrival shot any chance of concentrating on the article he was supposed to be writing out of the water.

His mother shook her head reproachfully as she picked up on his cynical comment. She had been doing that a lot since Isabella made her startling statement, then marched out of the house to leave him to deal with his family's feelings as well as his own. With a last look to say *If you can't be pleasant, be quiet*, Lady Carrowe stepped forward to receive her eldest son's dutiful kiss on the cheek. 'You should have sent word you were coming, my dear, so we could put on a better welcome,' she rebuked and hugged Gresley before stepping back to survey his travel-worn appearance with a frown.

'This house would have to be knocked down and rebuilt before there's much of a one to be had here,' he responded gloomily.

Most of his family had had to endure all this dust and decay day in and day out, so why couldn't Gresley hear how crass that comment sounded? He lacked the imagination to put himself in someone else's shoes, Wulf decided and perhaps that was the real reason he seemed most like his father out of all of them. How odd to be one of seven instead of one of one and Wulf wasn't sure how he was going to like being Gresley and Mary's little brother.

'It is a wreck, isn't it? And quite beyond repair, even if you actually wanted to repair it,' Aline said almost triumphantly, gazing around the dusty and worn marble hall with affection. 'Thank goodness the state of it usually keeps the *ton* at bay without us even having to try very hard to fend them off and it would have been good to have some help with that, by the way.'

'I was busy,' Gresley blustered.

'You said that when we begged you to come here to deal with the coroner and magistrates and lawyers,' Aline challenged impatiently.

Wulf stayed silent so he wouldn't rage uselessly at his eldest brother because Gresley was so like his father it was almost uncanny. Later, when Gresley was rested and fed after his journey, they would have to discuss Wulf's dealings with the magistrates and constables, but there wasn't a great deal to tell. Even Sir Hugh Kenton hadn't been able to find a clue to who the murderer was or how he got into this leaky old house and out again without being seen by a living soul. Carrowe House, with only two elderly servants and so many rotten old rooms even the family had forgotten about, was the ideal place to slip into, murder a man who expected his family to respect his privacy at all times, then slip out again without being noticed. How anyone wasn't noticed wandering about this great city covered in blood was beyond Wulf, but there was no trail of it to give them a direction to look in. Had the man been devilishly lucky or simply devilish? Best not add the supernatural to the list of things to worry about when there was quite enough on it to keep him awake at nights already. Wulf thought there must have been more than one person with the Earl when he died—one to murder him in what looked very like hot blood and the other cool enough to make sure they didn't leave a trail for anyone to follow. Sir Hugh had told him to keep that idea to himself because the less the villains knew about their ideas for catching them the better.

Wulf was glad he'd persuaded the Caudles to move in and paid a couple of heavies to watch the place from the outside every night. He resolved to hammer shut another set of doors and windows to keep his mother and sisters doubly safe for however much longer they insisted on staying here. He had already made an inner core of rooms as secure as possible without rebuilding the place from the ground up. It was locking the stable door after the horse bolted, he admitted to himself, but the very thought of whoever killed the Earl coming back kept him awake at nights even when this endless longing for Isabella in his bed didn't. The villain could have murdered them all or done other unthinkable things without anyone outside the house hearing a thing. His own wild ride to Herefordshire on a wasted errand left only Gus between their mother and sisters and a murderer. Wulf shuddered at the idea of his brother confronting a desperate man when he was in such a weakened state after his illness. He was furious with himself for being more than a hundred miles away when they needed him most, so how could Gresley leave them to face the world without him when their father was murdered here? He was supposed to be the head of the family, for goodness' sake.

'Fell off my horse,' Gresley finally admitted sheepishly, as if owning up to that was worse than patricide. 'Sprained my ankle and looked like the loser in a prize fight for a fortnight.'

'You didn't want to come here and help Mama cope with our father's death and all that followed because you looked a little the worse for wear?'

'No, Magnus, I didn't. I didn't want to now, but Connie insisted. Well, at least she and her father and the grandees from the Home Office did. Connie says I can't ignore what amounts to a royal order to come here and sort things out and I had to admit she was right to get any peace at all.'

'A royal order?' Lady Carrowe asked in a hollow voice.

'Yes, apparently the fuss caused by that nonsensical letter the Earl left behind him was the final straw for the King. He can't intervene openly for fear of stirring up even more public outrage against him. The Earl was one of his friends and the least said about that the soonest mended, so the King's cronies sent a messenger to tell me that while they are ready to write Papa's murder off as an unlucky encounter with a burglar, they can't close their eyes to his tangled private affairs any longer and insist on knowing the truth of his untimely ending. They sent for some bloodhound the Crown employs to deal with matters they want sorted out discreetly, then quietly lost as only the Home Office can lose things. First they've got to find him, however, as they carelessly sent him abroad on another matter. In the meantime I have to take an interest in this old wreck of a house and say bland and soothing things to calm everyone's nerves.'

'Oh, dear. Well, never mind, we'll soon be off to Hampstead and you can hardly be expected to stay here on your own,' Lady Carrowe said soothingly.

Wulf marvelled how skewed things were when his mother thought that would make Gresley feel better. Since he was looking resentful and defensive and troubled all at the same time, someone had clearly put the fear of God into him. Wulf secretly admired the forcefulness of whoever made Gresley face reality, and if this hunter they set such store by was half as good at his job, the murderer had better watch his step.

'The King is worried his reputation might suffer because Father was a friend of his? As if he could be more unpopular if he'd set out to make his people hate him,' Aline said scornfully.

Wulf nodded, although he shouldn't encourage her to be so outspoken. Aline might yet find a man brave or reckless enough to marry her, but she'd have to mind her tongue if her hero wasn't to run away screaming.

'It took royal intervention to get you here?' Magnus prompted, very likely to stop Gresley scolding Aline and set off a furious argument.

'Revolution,' Gresley added sagely. 'The King is afraid of the mob.'

'I can't see why our private disasters would stir them up,' Wulf said as he stepped out of the shadows as his true self for the first time.

'It's not private, though, is it? The old fool made a sensation of us all with that notice on top of everything else.' Gresley refused to meet his eyes, but the fact he'd replied was an admission Wulf had a right to take part in this conversation and he'd always tried to ignore his very existence until today.

'Frederick wasn't to know he would die violently,' their mother defended her late husband half-heartedly.

'Then he should have done,' Wulf muttered darkly. He saw his eldest brother's lips twitch as if he wanted to agree, but apparently that was going too far.

'Lucky you were too far off to be accused of his murder,' Gresley grumbled instead. 'If anyone had reason to do the old dog to death, it's you.' That was probably the only apology Wulf would ever get from his elder brother for years of pretending he didn't exist.

'None of my children are capable of murder,' Lady Carrowe said firmly.

Wulf wondered why Gresley flinched when their mother was asserting his innocence as well.

'Someone is,' Gresley said heavily.

Wulf almost wished the men of power had left well alone, but the longer the Earl's death was a mystery the more gossip and suspicion would do the rounds. Someone had the sin of murder on their head, but he still wasn't quite sure he really wanted to know who it was.

'I'd better sleep here, I suppose,' Gresley said as if to change the subject. 'It's more comfortable at White's, but Connie says it will look bad if I don't put up here. At least when the formalities are over and the will is read, I can go back to Yorkshire and you'll all be happier in Hampstead away from this.'

'It is your house now, so you must do as you please,' their mother told him.

'Let's all get our hammers out, then,' Gresley joked and Wulf chuckled, then noticed Gresley was staring at their mother as if he longed for more than she could give him. How had he missed that need for so long?

'Not until the upholsterers are quite finished with Develin House, if you please, boys,' she said.

'No, that would be unseemly,' Gresley said and he was his usual stiff and insensitive self again, so maybe Wulf had imagined it. 'When you are ready to move out, then, Mama,' he added and went off to hurry his valet and grooms.

Again Wulf had an odd feeling of kinship with his eldest brother he'd love to crush to powder and wondered if he'd ever get a firm hold on who he really was. He wasn't who he thought, but how could he be an earl's third son when the old man had denied him at birth? Add the burning regret and hunger and sheer bloody-minded stubbornness roiling away inside him since he'd refused to chase after Isabella and accept her terms and it was little wonder he hadn't slept properly for days. If only she would break through the wall he'd built round his privacy and demand he marry her again, he could give in and pretend he wasn't too much of a coward to admit he couldn't live without her. Well, he could live, the last half-year proved that, but it wouldn't really be living, would it? Existing was the best he could look forward to.

Meeting Isabella opened him up to a whole world of feelings he hadn't wanted to know about, but had he got so used to living in the shadows he couldn't see the sun? It hurt to feel, so he hadn't let himself. Until he met her and her breathtaking beauty and energy and sheer love of life demolished the walls he'd built round his inner Wulf as a boy. What he was going to do about all these untidy, unsafe emotions he wasn't sure right now, but her ultimatum meant he couldn't go on trying to pretend he didn't have them much longer. But if he couldn't bring himself to beg her to marry him when he was Wulf

FitzDevelin, how could he now he was the legitimate son of a lord? A lord he cursed every time he closed his eyes, then woke to the memory of who he really was stark in his mind.

It felt as if something loathsome lived inside him and he didn't think he was going to be anywhere near as good at overcoming their dark heritage as Magnus had proved himself to be. Wulf couldn't get his mother to talk about it either, apart from a sad shake of the head and an assertion she had always known exactly who he was. She gave birth to him, so of course she knew that, but why hadn't she challenged the Earl? Wulf FitzDevelin was an illusion, the only certainty he'd had as a child was that his parents must have loved each other for his mother to risk so much making him. Even that certainty had gone and he felt like a chair with a leg missing and bound for the bonfire. If he loved a woman as unique as Isabella Alstone, wouldn't an unsuitable, unsavoury character like him do better to stay away from her and not risk letting her down? To marry him she would have to take so many reckless risks it seemed impossible to ask her for them when he looked at how little he had to offer in return.

'Now Gresley is finally here, will you at least tell *me* why you let the Earl disown me at birth before he wheedles it out of you?' he murmured to his mother when the others had returned to the least cavernous reception room available and were waiting to see what Gresley would do next.

'He was closer to his father than the rest of you, so he might know Frederick's reasons for what he did better than I do, but I will tell you some of mine,' she said as if choosing her words so they couldn't trip her up later. She gestured towards the old estate office he had inflicted on Isabella after she returned from the country. More secrets to hide; more lies to tell—she was quite right about him, wasn't she?

'Anything that would help me make sense of who I really am would do,' he said rather desperately and hoped he could concentrate on what might be a very important conversation for him in spite of the memories of Isabella here, so vividly beautiful and alive against the shabby hopelessness of this used-up room. He was beyond being angry with his mother anyway. She'd paid such a heavy price for not arguing against her husband's lies. Wulf always thought he was the outward proof love was more important than anything else in his mother's life, even him. As a boy, that made the bond between them seem more special than the one between her and the others and now he felt as if he didn't know her at all.

'Your father did it to control me, and as having him as their father did his other sons so much harm, I thought at least one of you could be your own man if he stuck to his lie and disowned you.'

At first it sounded like a flimsy excuse for being so spineless, but Gresley and Magnus really had been pushed into a mould the Earl thought would make perfect Haile men of them. Magnus's determination not to be the arrogant and thankless man his father wanted saved him from being made in the Earl's image. Would *he* have had the strength of mind and heart to do as Gus did? Or would he have been even more wild and defiant to prove he was his own man and maybe even downright dangerous, considering the bad blood in his veins? Standing here thinking about how hard he'd tried not to love Isabella in this very room, he wondered if his mother wasn't almost right to have stopped him being the Dishonourable Wulfric Haile at birth.

'I had to be my own boy first,' he reminded her all the same. 'The world didn't even wait for me to turn my back before it sneered at Lady Carrowe's Shame.'

'I was wrong to stay silent then and later when he beat and bullied you to show me I couldn't stop him treating you exactly as he chose. He had already told his silly story by then and I doubt anyone would have believed me if I'd argued with him when you were old enough to be hurt by his lies and it was already too late.'

'So your lover was a fantasy of his as well?'

'No, he was very real. I loved him so deeply and desperately, but I had children and already knew what a devil your father could be. I couldn't leave them in his hands to run away with the man I longed to be with so deeply it almost broke me.'

She watched him with a challenge in the cool blue eyes he was the only one of her children to inherit, as if she thought he'd say she was wrong to look at another man when she was married to the Earl of Carrowe as well as all the other things she might have been wrong about after her lover accepted his marching orders.

'You mean you didn't…?'

'Yes, that's exactly what I mean. I wished I had when your father denounced me and called you a bastard anyway. I could have offered you a truly noble parent if I'd only taken my true love as my lover, Wulf. I regret not being able to do that for you, although I expect the Earl would have tried to throw another man's son on the parish. I would have stopped him, of course, but he would still have tried and thought he could get away with it.'

'He was mad enough to have killed us both and said it was your fault.'

'Oh, my love, don't condemn yourself to a lifetime of waiting to go insane. Your father wasn't mad. He was appallingly spoilt from the day he was born as his parents' only child and heir. They were very much to blame for making him weak and querulous and quite unable to control his temper, but he was as sane as the next lord. No, that's a bad example; he was a lot more sane than one or two of them.'

'True,' he agreed, realising Isabella had been right, his mother really was the strong one of the pair, despite the Earl's physical strength and self-righteous anger and all the bluster that went with it.

'I wouldn't turn real love away if I had my life to live again,' she told him. 'Living without it cost us both too much.'

Chapter Sixteen

'Why did Isabella jilt you, Gus?' Wulf asked his brother as casually as he could manage when they were strolling in unfashionable Green Park to try to build Magnus's strength back up a little at a time.

'Why would I tell you that?' his brother said after such a long time Wulf was wondering if he'd heard.

'I need to know,' he replied, fighting the instinct to say it didn't matter.

'Why?'

'Is that all you're going to say?'

'Until you give me a better reason, yes.'

'She told me to ask you,' Wulf admitted gruffly.

'Really? You did a lot of lurking in corners before she called a halt, didn't you?'

'I don't think there's a law against it,' Wulf said defensively.

'You remind me of yourself as a sulky boy, Little Brother,' Magnus said and leaned against a tree with some of the careless ease and confidence he used to exude.

'You remind me of yourself as a not-much-older insufferable know-it-all.'

Wulf *had* to know why his brother's betrothal ended abruptly. Secretly he had rejoiced to hear it was all over between Magnus and Isabella, of course, but he realised he would have had to sail away and not come back again if the wedding had gone ahead. Funny, his heart had never told his head how much it didn't want the wedding to happen while he had sat in a cramped cabin week after endless week willing the ship to return to England faster than wind and sail could get it there.

'Ah, but I'm not the one with the burning desire to root through my brother's private affairs,' Magnus said with some of the old steel back under his cool society manners.

Wulf would normally have rejoiced that his

brother was acting more himself, but right now he needed answers more than confirmation his brother's spirits were beginning to revive. 'I haven't got any for you to find,' he replied gruffly.

'Isabella has my sympathy; I never realised you were a slow top.'

'You were in the way. How could I barge past you and pounce on her like the wolf the Earl named me for?' There, now he'd admitted he wanted Isabella and Gus smiled as if that was exactly what he'd been waiting to hear.

'I didn't even know you'd met Isabella until you galloped off to Cravenhill Park to confront her on my behalf, you blundering great idiot.'

'We met on the night of your betrothal ball.'

'You were there after all, then? Despite saying you weren't going all the way to Haile Carr to be thrown out.' Magnus raised his eyebrows in that infuriating fashionable habit he had before he fell to earth.

'You're my brother,' Wulf said tersely.

'I looked for you, Wulf, and made a point of telling Gres and the Earl if they tried to humiliate you I'd call off the wedding. I needed your support more than you'll ever know and you stayed away and before I knew it you'd left for the New World. I felt more alone standing on that quayside watching you sail away than I've ever felt in my life.'

'I'm sorry, Gus. I let you down as well.'

'As well as who?'

'Whom, Big Brother, whom.'

'Do you want to live to get much older, Wulf?'

'Tell me why you asked the most beautiful female I have ever laid eyes on to marry you when you don't appear to love her and she doesn't love you.'

'Ah, now that sounds like a very personal interest indeed. Why does she want you to know?'

Wulf paced the just-about-green grass because he couldn't stand still. He hadn't managed to say it to Isabella yet, so how could he admit it to Gus? 'You're right, it's very personal,' he said tersely.

'How personal?'

'Too much—I have nothing to offer her. My name stinks even more since the Earl made things worse by making a show out of hating Mama so much he disowned his own son to punish her for looking at another man. No wonder the King wants to forget he ever had a friend whose marriage was an even bigger mess than his own turned out to be.'

'I don't think that's possible, but Isabella won't care about what the world thinks if she loves you.'

'How do you know?'

'Because I know her better than you do from the sound of things. I also know you'd like to hit me, despite the fact I'm not up to brawling with you right now.'

'Ah well, we always knew I wasn't a gentleman.'

'No, you believed what our father told you; the rest of us knew he was wrong,' Magnus said and turned away to pace in his turn. 'I don't want you to despise me,' he admitted at last.

'You let me out of cupboards the Earl locked me in when we were boys and fed me when he forbade it. You even took his blows when you could and taught me to ride and drive up and down the local mews and got me to swim in the Serpentine because he wouldn't take me to the country with the rest of you because I liked it and that would never do. If we live to be a hundred and quarrel like fishwives for the rest of our days, I couldn't turn my back on you, Gus.'

'I felt guilty because when the Earl took his anger out on you he didn't have so much of it left for me.'

'Gresley probably felt guilty about that as well, but he didn't help me. You could always tell me what I want to know now and we'll call it even.'

'Clever, but I suppose I owe it to Isabella to tell you the truth, even if I do lose your esteem,' Magnus said as if truly he believed he could.

Wulf would turn a blind eye even if his brother confessed to murdering the Earl, but Isabella was right, he needed to know the secret haunting his brother. 'Just tell me and we'll deal with it,' he urged.

'We can't, nobody can,' Magnus said with a sigh that sounded as if it came from his boots. 'But you still need to know, so I suppose I should tell you. It really began when Sir Edgar Drace died.'

'I *knew* Lady Delphine was at the bottom of it somehow,' Wulf said, remembering that night at Carrowe House when tension felt so tight between Magnus and Lady Delphine he almost expected to hear something snap.

'Don't interrupt if you want to hear more. I'd rather not tell this tale at all, so it's up to you.'

'Consider me silent as the grave.'

'Don't, you have no idea how often I wished Drace in one.'

'He wasn't much of an asset to the human race,' Wulf said. 'I had to report his fury at the poor for the sin of being poor too often to mistake him for one of those.'

'Ah, but it wasn't for the sake of suffering humanity I wanted him dead, Wulf. Drace made Delphi give up riding and she must not dance or drive or do any of the things I know she loved to do before he married her. He wouldn't even allow her to visit Mama and the girls when he took her to stay with her parents for a few days. I hardly saw her, but when I called one day, she was wearing long sleeves and even they couldn't quite cover up the bruises. When I challenged her about them, she told me the law allows a man to chastise his wife as long as he doesn't kill her. He was a Member of Parliament and the magistrates might have looked the other way even if he killed her in a rage, so I did what she wanted and stayed away, but I hated him for being such a bully.'

'As well you weren't anywhere near when he broke his neck, then.'

'I rode all night to find her as soon as I heard he was dead,' Magnus admitted, 'and I didn't even stop to wonder why until I got there. She was so thin I could nearly count her bones through her skin, Wulf. She was nothing like the harum-scarum Delphi I used to run wild with all summer and missed when I was back at school. The plain truth is I love her, Wulf. All those years the real reason I hated Drace was because he got to her before I could.'

'He and the Earl will be company for one another in hell,' Wulf said and couldn't find a single spark of outrage in his heart for his brother's guilty secret so far.

'Don't make light of it. I should have found a way to make him stop beating and humiliating Delphi. I should have stopped the Earl doing the same to you as well, so don't ever call me a good man again,' Magnus said bitterly.

Wulf could see him shaking with the effort of sharing his dark truth and even for Isabella's sake he couldn't put his brother through more pain. 'Never mind, Gus, Isabella and I will find a way past it,' he said.

'You both deserve the truth.'

'I doubt I do.'

'Then you need to hear my story, so you don't hurt her like Delphi hurt me.'

Wulf was shocked by the idea he could turn bright and vibrant Miss Alstone into a pale shadow of herself. The thought horrified him.

'What on earth did Lady Delphine do to you, then?'

'She took me as her lover for every stolen moment we could snatch together in a summerhouse on a neighbouring estate unlived in for years, accepted my rampant adoration and all the pent-up love I'd only just admitted to myself, and enjoyed it as if that was what she was born for. She embraced her own sensuality and threw herself into being adored and I thought I'd found heaven on earth for six whole glorious weeks of bliss. I stayed at an inn a few miles away, but my horse could have found his way there blindfolded by the end of them.'

'What happened?'

'She told me it was over. It had been a pleasure to find out what the sins of the flesh really felt like and she thanked me politely, as if I'd given her a pretty fan or a lace handkerchief. And, oh, no, of course she didn't love me and never had. I was a convenient lover when she needed to feel warm and wicked after all those years of cold and propriety with Drace. Now I'd taught her all I knew she had her eye on her next lover who, by the way, had far more money and power than I'd ever have.'

'Bitch,' Wulf gritted out and meant it.

'No,' Magnus argued. 'Count, Wulf. Count backwards and use your brains.'

Wulf shook his head to clear it and saw what Magnus meant. 'Her *daughter*?'

'She's mine,' Magnus agreed as if more words would undo him.

'Delphine's passed her off as Drace's and I doubt that's much of a favour in the long-term,' Wulf said with the snicker of his own supposedly illegitimate birth in the back of his mind.

'She's the image of me, poor little mite. Nobody could look at her and me side by side and mistake her for Drace's get. That's why Delphine brought her child to London when she came to visit us, then made her maid stay nearby with the baby instead of openly bringing my daughter to Carrowe House, where we Hailes couldn't fail to recognise one of our own.'

'So why haven't you married her and claimed the baby as yours anyway?'

'Delphi won't say yes. Delphi's woman sent me a letter begging me to visit her mistress a couple of months after Delphi gave me my marching orders. I delayed because I knew it would hurt to see her decked out in the spoils of her next love affair. By then she was visibly with child and had to admit it was mine because there was no chance the baby was Drace's, never much chance he was capable of siring one at all actually.'

'A boy would have taken his title and estates, though.'

'She promised to admit the child wasn't her husband's if she birthed a boy because she couldn't live with the imposture if her child took so much from the true heir. Thanks to her parents' insistence their private fortune was settled on her and any children when she married that apology for a gentleman, she didn't need his money, but my little girl saved her the trouble of confessing what she sees as her sins.'

'You've seen the child?'

'Yes, and loved her the moment I laid eyes on her, Wulf. I can't claim her because her mother won't let me. I've tried everything to convince Delphi to marry me, but she refuses to even consider it.'

'She's a fool, Gus,' Wulf told him.

'No, I'm the fool. If only I'd stayed away for a few months after Drace's death, she would have had to marry me when I got her with child as there would be no question of it being his in law. Delphi's rejection was bad enough, then Father found out and she still wouldn't marry me. That would be to admit what we did when her husband's body was hardly cold in his grave and she couldn't brave the censure of the polite world for being so wicked and actually enjoying herself for once in her life. She thinks she can pretend we didn't do anything of the kind, that her daughter will grow to look more like her as she gets older. According to Delphi, a baby's brown eyes can turn green or blue and her hair will pale into something less like mine. She will grow up a baronet's posthumous daughter unless we put doubts in people's heads by marrying each other.'

'She's an idiot and doesn't deserve you.'

'Drace had to beat and abuse her to make himself want a woman enough to even try to get her with child, Wulf. Then I threw myself at her like a greedy boy before she had hardly even taken in the fact her prison door was open. The longer it goes on the worse the puzzle and any scandal gets when we're found out. I suppose I'm not much of a catch anyway.'

'You would make yourself one if she said yes,' Wulf told his brother. 'You might have been raised a gentleman, but you'd work for love if only she would let you.'

'Well, she won't, not even when the Earl decided to blackmail me with our lovely little secret. If I didn't marry a fortune and hand it to him, he said he would tell the world Lady Drace's daughter is my bastard.'

'So you offered for Isabella?' Wulf whispered as if saying it out loud might break them both.

'I should have let him do his worst.'

'He would have done it. He would have ruined the woman you love out of pique if you didn't do as he bid you.'

'Yes,' Magnus admitted bleakly. 'So I let Isabella be the ransom.'

'Did she know?'

'Not then. When I asked her to marry me, you can imagine how relieved I was when she said no. Then she came back to me with a scheme to pay the old devil part of her dowry on condition Aline, Dorrie and Theo lived with us. I hadn't told her about Delphi and our affair, of course, but Isabella saw through the old man's surface charm and insisted he assign guardianship of Dorrie and Theo to me before he'd get a penny of her dowry. Isabella insisted she didn't want to be in love and a rational marriage would suit her very well. I suppose she could see how unhappy the girls were at Carrowe House under the Earl's thumb, too, and we were such good friends, Wulf. And once I'd offered for her, how could I withdraw? So we agreed to wed and I believe that must be where you came in.'

'You nearly married her.'

'I expect we would have come to our senses sooner or later.'

'Don't lie, you would have wed Isabella because you couldn't marry Lady Delphine and no woman deserves that.'

'Isabella least of all?'

Wulf glared at the tree Magnus was leaning against as if he needed it to hold him up. 'I love her,' he confessed at last.

'Shouldn't you be telling her instead of me?'

'Yes,' Wulf grumbled. 'How did she find out about Lady Delphine?'

'Another letter.'

'Lady Delphine's maid seems to be on your side.'

'Not noticeably.'

'Then why interfere?'

'Because of the child and maybe she wants her mistress to be happy and cared for despite herself as well. Perhaps I never deserved to be happy after what it did, but you deserve Isabella.'

'I don't, but living without her is worse than offering for her so she can turn me down.'

'You'll always regret not taking a chance, but how are you planning to make this grudging proposal?'

'You're not the only Haile who can offer an elopement to a lady.'

'However you offer for her be sure you make her happy, Wulf. I might have to kill you if you don't. If Carnwood or Shuttleworth or your friend Kenton don't get there first, of course.'

'She has to say yes first,' Wulf said gloomily.

Chapter Seventeen

A whole weary week had passed since she humiliated herself in front of Wulf and most of his family at Carrowe House. Isabella counted off the days and decided her reckless throw of the dice had been a failure and she didn't know what else to do. Maybe she was going to have to drag herself through the new social Season without him after all. Even the idea of pretending she couldn't imagine anything more delightful than hot rooms, sharp-eyed critics and too much warm lemonade made her feel slightly sick, so the reality was bound to be even worse.

'I hope you really are planning to have your new gowns fitted this time, Isabella,' Charlotte said with a frown when she saw Isabella's outdoor clothes and her best bonnet waiting to be set on her perfectly arranged locks.

'Heloise won't let me escape twice.'

'Good, you're going to need every one of them for the new Season now you're unattached again,' Charlotte said cheerfully and carried her still-teething baby daughter back into the sitting room as if there was no more to be said.

'I'll be glad to go home, too,' Isabella muttered at the closed door and only just managed not to stick her tongue out. 'Come, Heloise, if you had kept a still tongue in your head, I wouldn't have to do this, so don't try to creep upstairs as if you never even heard the word *mantua-maker* and don't dote upon every aspect of fashion.'

'Your gloves, Miss Alstone,' Heloise said and held them out reproachfully.

'Thank you,' Isabella said, slipping them on and trying not to remember a hot night at Haile Carr when she'd used her evening gloves to fan her hot cheeks. She turned briskly for the door.

'Your bonnet, Miss Alstone.' Heloise caught her up with a look of deep shock that any lady would go out without one.

'Confound my bonnet,' she said and jammed it on as she ran down the steps.

'Never damn a bonnet like that one, Miss Alstone; it's probably sacrilege,' Wulf said as she reached the bottom and realised he was waiting there for her. He took off his silk hat and bowed gracefully, then offered her his arm as if they had trivial social encounters of this sort every day.

'What are you doing here?'

'Well, that's not very polite. You should send your mistress off to learn better manners somewhere very refined indeed, Heloise,' he told her maid and the wretched woman tittered and got ready to follow them as if she thought the whole event run-of-the-mill as well.

'Never mind my manners, you are not the type of man to wear clothes like that or stroll about Mayfair as if you have all the time in the world and not a lot to do with it.'

'I do today. I am busy walking the beautiful Miss Alstone to an engagement, or at least I would be if you could start moving instead of standing there glaring at me as if I've just said something outrageous.'

'But why?

'Why not?' he countered as if it was quite normal for him to come here looking like that, offer her his arm and expect her to meekly go with him. He looked even more dark and dangerous than usual in the elegant day attire of a gentleman he wore with his own unique flair. And now she was supposed to stroll along by his side as if the very sight of him in full daylight didn't make her knees wobble?

'You did say no more hiding in dark corners,' he pointed out helpfully, and what else could she do but take his arm with that demand in her mind to say this was her fault?

'True, but I can't believe you listened.'

'Neither can I,' he said with a rueful smile that made it even more difficult to stroll along at his side as if they were polite acquaintances. 'I haven't been very good at it so far, have I?'

This was her own fault. She had asked for him to admit he wanted her company in full daylight as well as the intimate darkness they usually met in, but the best thing about the dark was that it *was* intimate. They could feel each other move with slavish fascination and nobody could hear or see them and whisper about them behind their backs. Out here, strolling along the broad streets and squares of fashionable Mayfair, it felt far too exposed and public. She was even more conscious of his lithe body as they walked side by side because she couldn't reach out and touch him. It would cause a scandal if she did any of the things she longed to do right now. So of course she only wanted to do them all the more.

'No, but I'm so glad you decided to this time,' she said and smiled because he had listened to her for once and come out of the darkness.

If she had to endure not doing any of the things they had been doing in the shadows since the night they met, it was worth it to walk at his side and show the world she knew and appreciated the youngest Haile brother no matter his parentage. Knew him and was so proud to walk side by side with him on a beautiful spring morning she didn't want to say goodbye when they reached the dressmakers'. They couldn't linger and stare into each other's eyes here, though, because this was how things were when you were out in the open, under the critical gaze of the fashionable ladies and gentlemen strolling up and down the most fashionable of streets. He bowed in farewell and raised one eyebrow at her as if he knew about all that heat and breathlessness and wanting she was trembling on the edge of.

'Mrs Shaw believes we might happen to meet in the park at the fashionable hour tomorrow. Apparently her new barouche has plenty of room for a chance-met acquaintance if I get there quickly enough to oust all the other ones who will be queuing up to claim a ride around the park with the beautiful Miss Alstone,' he said so calmly she had to wonder if she was the only one burning up with need.

'Shouldn't we make our own assignations?'

'We aren't very good at arranging them in the open, though, are we?'

'No,' she had to admit and this was the new reality she had wanted, so she supposed she had best get used to it.

Driving in the park together, walking to museums and art galleries, sharing Charlotte's box at the theatre with half a dozen others, and even a small and exclusive evening party for a few hundred of the hostess's closest friends where Wulf made what he called his 'debut in polite society' was very well, but Isabella enjoyed the day they spent at Develin House with his family, inspecting works done and planning what would fit where, so much more. Isabella had changed so much since this time last year she hardly recognised herself as the same woman when she looked back. The old Isabella was prepared to settle for less than her sisters had. She didn't believe in love, so for her love would never exist because she had reasoned it away. Marriage to a good friend for the sake of a family and rescuing his sisters from a dire situation seemed so sensible why turn Magnus down when he asked her to marry him? This Isabella who lived in the now cringed at the idea of her then self blithely ignoring all the passion and need inside her and for what? For the sake of building a safe little box to put her life in, then forget how small she had to make herself in order to fit inside it.

At least today they had been allowed to drive back from Hampstead in Ben Shaw's pared-down racing curricle alone but for the tiger—the groom dressed in striped livery—as long as they stayed in sight of the others following them in Charlotte's barouche. The diminutive tiger was so busy clinging on and watching Wulf's driving with an eagle eye to listen to them, so it was almost like being alone. All these proper social meetings had left Isabella feeling desperate for half an hour's unregulated conversation with the Honourable Wulfric Haile.

'You do know I don't need all the trappings of fashionable life to be happy, don't you, Wulf?' she asked and watched the hazy, smoky city grow ever closer in the evening sunlight as she tried to pretend his answer wasn't vitally important.

'You don't need to meet your family and friends and talk and shop and maybe even gossip a little now and again?' he asked as if he wasn't quite so sure about that.

'I do need *them*, but not half the peerage and a few hundred of their hangers-on along with them. When I said I wanted to meet you in the light of day, I didn't mean you should change into someone else to make it happen.'

'I'm not; I'm finding out who I am and who I'm not. You said you needed us to know each other by daylight and I'm Wulf Haile as well as Dev and FitzDevelin now, so we need to find out who he is between us. The me I am at heart sometimes ends up shut in a room for days until I get a chapter or a book or even a page just how I want it and I doubt I'm very easy to live with.'

'You think finding out about the man you really are behind all the dash and devilment will frighten me off, don't you? You should know that I am quite capable of amusing myself, then. Don't lump me with the spoilt little socialites who need constant attention and flattery if they're not going to turn into a Mrs Fonthill or another of your bored lady friends the moment a husband finds something serious to do with himself. Perhaps I'm more like you than you think as well, because I'm only just getting to know myself as well and I owe a lot of that to you, Wulf.'

'I thought you were pretty much perfect as you

were the night we met,' he said as if he meant it and she had to be flattered even if it wasn't true.

'No, I was lonely and uncertain of what I wanted that night and even a touch terrified by what I'd done in agreeing to wed Magnus. I thought I could never be in love because I didn't *want* to be; it wasn't to be trusted and I thought good sense, a few mutual interests and plenty of friendship and respect made a better basis for marriage than some fleeting passion that would melt away as soon as desire faded. I was so wrong, Wulf, about that and so many other things. I have never been perfect and never will be, but I'm not prepared to accept second-best ever again or be second-best for someone else.'

'How could you be?'

'Ask your brother,' she said with a wry smile.

'I already have and you were right, I did need to know his sad story.'

'And now you do know it, what's next?' she asked as they reached the city and her heart sank at the idea of parting from him again until their next frustrating encounter in front of too many people.

'Will you marry me, Isabella?' he asked, an anxious glance betraying how much her answer mattered to him.

'Why?'

'Well, not because of my lack of fortune, noxious reputation and dubious charm obviously. So it would have to be because I love you. I can't promise you much, but I can promise you'll never be second-best for me, Belle.'

'You love me?'

'I wouldn't have dressed up like a dandy or made my debut in polite society if I didn't.'

'You don't sound very happy about it.'

'I would be if I wasn't waiting for an answer and even more desperate for you than ever in so many different ways.'

'Of course I will, you idiot. I thought you were never going to ask.'

'And I can't believe you said yes,' he said on a huge sigh of relief and a look of pure joy that made her love him even more. 'Don't make me wait long, Belle. I think I might burst into flames out of sheer frustrated desire if you don't marry me very soon.'

'Your brother promised me an elopement, but I suppose one Haile brother will do as well as another,' she joked and joy was so real in her heart now. Then there was that wicked ache deeper down and it felt utterly wonderful to be alive and by his side, even if they did have to wait a few more days for much more.

'This is one thing I intend to do a hundred times better than Magnus and I've got off to a fine start by loving you with every fibre of my being. I'm so glad he's an idiot.'

'No, he's a good friend, but that's all. I used to wonder why I wasn't in love with him now and again during the years after I met him during my first Season. He's a fine and handsome man and I truly hope he'll find love again and this time with a woman who has enough courage to love him back whatever anyone has to say about them being together, but he's not you, Wulf. That's why I could never quite persuade myself to fall in love with him. It's why I misbehaved so scandalously with you in the dark that first night at Haile Carr. You're you and he's simply my friend Magnus.'

'Well, that's a relief, then. We won't have to emigrate after all.'

'Do you really want to live in a new country?'

'Only the one you're in, love; if you want to explore one, I do as well.'

'Not just now I don't; we have far too much to do here to go skipping across the Atlantic Ocean and back because you feel like a change again. Maybe when your sisters are happy and your mother is quite settled and your brother is himself again we could think about an adventure or two.' Isabella considered that list and couldn't leave off the biggest reason they had to stay because they had to begin as they went on and be honest with one another from now on. 'And then there's your father's murderer to be tracked down and punished before someone else gets the blame.'

'Are you sure you want to share in our notoriety, Isabella?' he asked as if she might throw his love aside even now because she lacked the courage to recognise it for the huge gift it was.

'I want your closeness and our love and laughter, all the shared jokes and sharp corners and loyalty, Wulf, and the Earl truly doesn't matter any more. His murder is important because your family will only be free of him when it's solved, but his petty jealousy and self-indulgence and meanness are dead and done with and I love you and want to share everything that makes you as you are for the rest of our lives.'

'Good, then if you still want to elope, I can be free next Tuesday.'

'I need a gown,' she said in a panic all of a sudden because it was only five days away and she couldn't marry him with the trousseau she had made when she was going to marry his brother.

'I'm not sure I agree with that statement,' he said wolfishly and she laughed joyously and, as they were back at Ben and Charlotte's now, he threw the reins to the tiger and lifted her down from the precarious vehicle as if she was little more than a featherweight.

'I'm certainly not marrying you naked, you wolf,' she murmured as he slid her down his rigidly eager body and made sure she knew he wanted her so urgently the days ahead already felt like an eternity.

'You can wed me in a suit of armour if you want to, just make sure you do.'

'I will,' she promised and kissed him boldly on the mouth in front of Ben's grooms and anyone else who happened to be looking because this was the man she loved and the world would just have to get used to it.

Chapter Eighteen

Wulf neatly turned Ben's curricle into a lane that looked as if it didn't go anywhere very much. Isabella wondered if the wheels would ever be the same again and how they would get up and down this road in the winter. Right now the prospect of being marooned here with her new husband seemed very appealing, so she supposed they were right about there being a silver lining to every cloud.

'A fine catch I am, bringing you home in another man's carriage,' Wulf said as if he was still worrying about the differences in their respective fortunes and how she would feel about being isolated by mud and perhaps even snow up here come winter. She thought she'd managed to convince him money didn't matter to her as long as they were together, but she would manage it in the end now they had proved to one another that love could overcome far bigger odds than they had set it so far.

'You're my fish and I'm proud of you,' she joked but wondered fleetingly if Ben's gleaming paintwork could survive wide hedges and a narrow lane unscathed much longer, despite Wulf's skill with such a dashing equipage. The lane began to climb more steeply and the tiger Ben insisted on sending along looked as if he had doubts about maintaining his dignity if he fell off the back of his master's fine carriage.

A short way up and the road improved and widened a little to welcome visitors brave enough to get this far. Isabella was a countrywoman at heart, so it certainly didn't frighten her to be this far away from other people. She wondered how Wulf's devoted manservant and his mother would rub along with Heloise, though, and was surprised the woman agreed to stay now Isabella Haile was determined to be as unfashionable as possible most of the time.

'Oh, now I see why you love this place so

much,' Isabella exclaimed with a gasp at the wide expanse of open heath and woodland spread out in front of them like one of the most beautiful landscape paintings she could ever imagine seeing. 'You feel you could set out to explore the whole world from up here and why wouldn't you love it?' she murmured.

'Welcome to my home, then, ours now, until you find us one that suits you better,' Wulf said and helped Isabella down before leading her towards the back of the substantial cottage, leaving the tiger and Jem Caudle, the manservant, to deal with the horses and luggage. 'Once upon a time I came here to get away from people, but since I met you, any time we spent apart felt lonely. For more than half a year now I've longed to have you here where nobody much even knows there is a house at all and we can be private together.'

'You spent a goodly proportion of that time sailing the oceans to get as far away from me as possible,' she said coolly.

'What else could I do when you were going to be Magnus's wife?'

'Stay here and convince me not to be so silly, I suppose.'

'He's my brother.'

'True, but I'm your wife,' Isabella argued and the sound of that word, so new and precious she wanted to dance and do all sorts of other things not nearly as suitable for the outdoors at this time of year, made her forget to be angry with him for leaving.

'I know,' he said huskily.

'And you're my husband.'

'You talk too much, Wife,' he whispered against her lips.

'Silence me, then.'

'No, I like you noisy,' he said with a wolfish grin.

He tugged her closer and kissed her until her eyes crossed and her head was spinning as if he'd realigned the planets and even gravity couldn't be relied on any more. One of his hands was running over her neat derrière as if it had every right to be there. It did now and she didn't want it to stop. She wanted to be inside as fast as possible so that they could do all sorts of lovely things to each other as soon as possible behind closed doors.

'I love you, Wulf,' she said dreamily and the future she had secretly longed for looked back at her from his extraordinary silver-blue eyes, making her feel truly beautiful for the first time in her life.

'And I love you, Isabella,' he said as if they were making another set of vows. His voice had gone even more husky as she made a wickedly inquisitive exploration of his leanly muscular torso and it reminded her of the hot summer night when she met her fate on a shadowed terrace and nearly forgot herself in so many ways she ought to blush.

'Will it be dark soon?' she asked, the feeling she might melt from the inside out if they couldn't love one another making her long for the night ahead.

'Not soon enough,' he said, 'but you did say you were tired of lurking in the shadows with me, didn't you?'

'I did,' she whispered. 'I think it might rain,' she lied with a rapid glance at the clear blue sky.

'And it would never do for us to get wet on the first day of our honeymoon, would it?'

Isabella could feel shivers of pure need running through him as if he was a greyhound ready for the chase. He shaped her waist with broad, strong hands, bringing her hard up against his eager body, and she felt all her senses bloom and seek out every facet of him they could discover with all these finely made, wretchedly inconvenient clothes on. He felt hot and heady and totally male under her exploring hands and her knees were being unreliable again. She wanted these hotly passionate kisses more than ever, but the lovely, feverish delight of waiting for tonight, anticipating how it might feel or where they might go together before the night was done was something to savour, to feel her way through with his eager assistance because it mattered so much it shouldn't be rushed, especially on their wedding night.

'You're such a calm and peaceable man we'll never quarrel,' she lied with a witchy, knowing smile that invited him to share the joke as they hurried through the almost wild gardens towards the front door somebody had left invitingly open before tactfully disappearing.

'If you wanted one of those, you'd be on your way up the Great North Road with my brother bound for Gretna instead of married to me.'

'He's a true gentleman, but I do believe we can be silly and besotted and smug about each other without his help right now.'

'I wasn't raised to be such a gentleman as my brother, though, Isabella. I'll try to be better in future, but it's probably too late for gentility to take.'

'I love you as you are and you look like a perfect gentleman to me.'

'Then try behaving a bit more like a lady at least until we get upstairs,' he reproached her playfully, trying to put a little space between them so they didn't end up making love for the first time on the stairs.

'And I do like doing things I shouldn't with you,' she murmured provocatively as they had to stop and kiss each other again before they remembered to go up another step.

'We're married now,' he said sternly and he

looked so manly and ruffled and trying not to be the wild lover under all that gentlemanly restraint that she laughed, causing him to look deeply offended and let her go.

'Then it's our duty to do all the things we weren't supposed to on the night we met, but with extra naughtiness added for interest. We can be lovers even if we are married, and if that doesn't work, we'll just pretend we're not.'

'Everything works with you,' he said shortly. 'A bit too well,' he added and she giggled because she was free to express all the emotions she'd had to keep bottled up for far too long. With him she could be the woman she was always meant to be, the one who'd stepped out from behind Miss Alstone's elegantly restrained protective cover the night they met and goaded her with wild fantasies of Wulf FitzDevelin as her lover from that moment on.

'Oh, my Wulf, you're such a good man, but could you stop being stern and gentlemanly and protective now and remember I'm your very willing wife?'

'Isn't that all the more reason to be most of

368 *A Wedding for the Scandalous Heiress*

those things now I'm your husband?' he said and the heat and hunger she could feel coming off him echoed the heat and hope inside her.

'No, not here and not now,' she said and shaped his tense jaw with tender urgency, hoping he'd lose that formidable control of his very soon and ravish her so thoroughly she forgot her own name and where she was.

'I am far less of gentleman than your husband ought to be,' he said far too seriously.

'You're the only one I want,' she said and stood on tiptoe against him so he could tell how much she did.

'You don't hold back when you give your everything, do you?'

'No, but I love you and you love me—that's the promise of a lifetime I believed I wasn't worthy of until I met you.'

'And you think I'm a wonder for you? What do you think you are for a mongrel wolf like me, love?'

'Oh, Wulf, I do love you,' she responded fatuously, but luckily he seemed to like it because he looked down at her and grinned as if he couldn't help himself.

'You do, don't you?' he said as if he'd only just let it truly sink in.

'I do; you are handsome and clever and creative and daring and I love you so much it almost hurts.'

'You are a dream I didn't dare dream and now I've got you chained to me for life I'm never going to stop having it, night after night.'

'Good, don't! And I think you're very good with words.'

'Words are the last thing on my mind right now,' he told her gruffly and gave up on getting her to their bedroom the usual way, lifting her off her feet, then impressing her mightily by running up the remainder of the stairs and into the charming old room she caught a glimpse of before he dropped her on the bed and joined her without even taking his elegant and gentlemanly wedding shoes off his feet.

'You'll get blacking on the sheets and Mrs Caudle will never forgive us.'

Wulf said something rude and toed the shoes

off even as he did something very hasty to Isabella's elegant spencer jacket and let her up long enough to shrug that off before starting work on her fine silk gown himself.

'Careful, it's my wedding dress,' she chided breathlessly. 'Let me,' she urged and pushed his hands aside to undo the laces herself and push the fine fabric over her shoulders without ripping it because she knew she would treasure this gown all her life and she didn't want it damaged even though she wanted it gone as much as he did.

'Do I have to feel the same way about all this starch and silliness, love?'

'Not if you don't want to, but you look quite magnificent to me,' she said as she sat back on the wide old bed and admired him as he struggled with buttons and ties and she watched and appreciated the show from under heavy-lidded eyes.

'Did you know they make you wear a corset to get the right waist to fit this ridiculous nip-waisted coat and the right sort of trousers? The tailors call it a vest, but the damned thing has bones in it.'

'Now you know how we women feel, but it's all right; I can see from here you don't need one, so there's no need to convince me there isn't a spare inch on you anywhere, my Wulf. Thank you for enduring it for my sake, but we looked wonderful on our wedding day, didn't we?'

'We did, Belle, and now it's time for the best part of the whole day,' he told her huskily and ripped off the soft cravat that went with his fashionable finery before he knelt on the bed next to her and put all his best sensual efforts into getting her out of the rest of hers in the least possible time.

'It's a good job I didn't want to wear my underpinnings again,' she chided as he watched her with hungry, warm eyes and now it was her turn to feel a fine tremor run through her like wildfire.

'Your nether garments were quite charming, Mrs Haile, but right now I prefer you naked.'

'How are yours, Wulf?' she countered and

tugged at the ties of his shirt to find out for herself.

'I'm not as pretty,' he told her.

'Let me see,' she said as she worried at the hem of his shirt until he gave in and pulled the thing over his head with a ragged sigh. 'More,' she ordered implacably and the silly, unnecessary 'vest' was soon gone and they were on to his undershirt. 'I preferred it when gentlemen like you wore those sleek cutaway coats and tight pantaloons, but I suppose it got ladies who couldn't have the likes of you in their beds too excited, so they invented trousers and nipped-in coats to stop them fainting with frustration.'

'You talk too much,' he murmured and she realised he could be right.

'That's because I want you too much,' she countered and then she was silenced and greedy and eager all in one incoherent package at the sight of him, all muscles and smooth male skin and tension. 'You're magnificent,' she said at last and breathed out because she was going to faint if she didn't.

'And you're simply breathtaking, my love,'

he countered and took a ragged breath of his own as he ran his ravenous gaze over her softer curves and eagerly voluptuous breasts announcing she really did want him desperately with almost painful need.

'Touch me, Wulf. Kiss me,' she urged because she needed him to do something about this merciless hunger before it burnt her up completely.

'How can I not? I'll break if I don't have you now, my darling,' he breathed and now his hands were fire and power and gentle reverence all at once, and his mouth? Oh, as for his mouth… Isabella ran out of words and sank into a world of instinct and feeling and love with a delicious, delighted sigh.

'If I'd known love was like this, I would have tracked you down and badgered you to teach me everything about it a great deal sooner,' Isabella murmured as she lay back against her husband's shoulder, still learning every detail of him under her skin where it kissed against his and giving a delighted little wriggle at the idea of her best adventure yet.

'Be still, you wanton. We really ought to thank Magnus for getting me to Haile Carr and close enough to meet you for the first time. I wasn't exactly welcome in the best drawing rooms of the *ton* then, so we might never have met at all if not for him.'

'I hope you're not planning to lurk in the dark waiting for immodest ladies to fall on you like a she-wolf ever again,' she teased him, relishing how stunningly new and wondrous it felt to be his wife in every way. All the glorious days and weeks and years of learning even more about wedded bliss ahead of them left her utterly speechless and transported by sensual wonder, already anticipating the next time they could fly somewhere stunning and wordless together.

'Not unless it's with you,' he said and the intent heat in his ice-blue eyes said that could be arranged.

'Good,' she said militantly and rolled over to prop herself up on her elbows and stare down at him because why wouldn't she now she had the right to and he was so much worth the looking at. 'I hope you're not expecting any offspring of ours to be pattern cards because you're sure to be disappointed.'

'We're not exactly those ourselves, so it would be asking far too much,' he murmured and stopped her reply with fierce, joyous desire, then sat up and shifted in the wild nest they'd made out of the once-immaculate sheets and blankets. 'For the rest of tonight we'll have to pretend to be, though,' he added dourly and leapt out of bed to put more wood on the fire as if that was the only way he could keep his hands off her.

'Why?' she said as he leapt back into their joint warmth because this was April and an English spring and he was a human and not a wolf after all. She turned up her face for another kiss because whatever he was she loved him almost as desperately as she had before he showed her how much more there was to loving than she'd ever suspected.

'I want you…' he began, then raised his head.

She tried not to be disappointed he wasn't demonstrating how much at this very minute. She was greedy for her first and only lover now she'd finally got him into bed. 'I know,' she said smugly.

'Behave yourself, Mrs Haile. I'm not making love to you again tonight.'

'Why not?'

'Because it will hurt. No, stop that; you're not getting your own way this time.'

'I can't believe you're being so stuffy, and to think I believed you were so dark and dangerous when we first met and now you're being such a fine gentleman I could spit.'

'Put it this way, if we make love now, you won't want to do it again for days. Contain yourself and there's always tomorrow.'

'I suppose we could just cuddle, if it wasn't so cold.'

'Princess,' he accused her, then got out of bed again to snatch a shawl for her to wrap herself in. Isabella was glad Heloise had been over here to unpack her most treasured possessions before the maid enjoyed a nice little holiday at Develin House, ruthlessly reorganising the Haile ladies' wardrobes.

'With a body like that you can call me what

you like, my Wulf,' she said with everything she wasn't supposed to want explicit in her heavy-lidded eyes as he slipped back into the warm nest of bedclothes beside her.

'And there I was, thinking you loved me for my mind,' he said easily and pulled her back into his arms, holding her wrapped in soft cashmere next to him to shield her from the arousal that had made her realise what a truly gentle man she'd married.

'I do, but it's not my fault if you come with added manliness, spice and sensuality. All that just makes me a very lucky woman, I suppose.'

'True,' he said modestly and reached for the finest wine and hothouse strawberries Magnus had somehow managed to present them with as a wedding-night luxury they hadn't had time to appreciate until now.

'What are we going to do about the girls?' Isabella whispered.

'Let them work out what they want, Belle. They have had too many years of being controlled and told what to do for us to start interfering now.'

'Then do you think Magnus would like to be my estate manager, since we're not going to be spending much time on them?'

'My wife the heiress,' he said with a wry smile of resignation.

'Just your wife, Wulf, that's all. We can put my fortune into trust for our children if you like because I'm a writer's wife now and we don't need it.'

'That depends how many you're planning to have, but I'd best get on and earn enough to keep you and them in style anyway, hadn't I?'

'You already do and we have a house I love in a place where we both want to live. I don't need any more.'

'Maybe an extra room or two for the babies when and if they happen to come along,' he suggested easily enough and she let out a quiet sigh of relief.

'Promise you'll never let my fortune come between us?' she said and twisted round to look at him with a plea to take her seriously.

'It's only money, love. I can manage on nothing much at all and Matty Caudle can turn a penny so many times I'm expecting the King to scream for mercy one day.'

'I really do wish I could have been with you when you first met her and her son, my darling,' she said truthfully and wriggled closer to show she meant it.

'I know you do and thank you, my love, but I never want you to find out at first-hand how hard life is for a girl on the streets.'

'Don't wrap me in cotton wool. You already know Ben's stepmama is Eiliane, Marchioness of Pemberley, and I'm sure you're aware she's set up an asylum for such children. I help out there when I can, so I'm quite aware of the things you're trying not to tell me. Those poor girls don't stand much chance of living long enough to become women at all, let alone happy ones, without the help of people like her.'

Wulf seemed to mull over the idea she knew a lot more than he thought she ought to about the darker side of London life. 'You Alstones and your web of powerful connections never fail to surprise me.'

'I'm a Haile now.'

'I'm not quite sure I am yet.'

'A Develin-Haile, then; it's a compromise I'm happy with.'

'If you are, then I shall have to learn to be, but I don't think I can ever be truly grateful the Earl of Carrowe was my father after all.'

'And why would you be when he treated you so harshly?'

'So our children don't have fingers pointed at them and other brats sniggering at them in corners. So you don't have to be married to a nameless man; so my mother isn't expected to be ashamed of me at every turn any more.'

'I don't think she ever was.'

'Then why did she let him get away with it, love? I know you would fight tooth and nail for our children if you had to, so why didn't she?'

'I can't answer that question, my darling, perhaps you should ask her.'

'I did and she palmed me off with some nonsense about him making such a mess of being a father to Gresley and Magnus she didn't want me to suffer it as well. Still, she's been hurt enough, and if believing that makes her feel better, so be it. At least she's not big or strong enough to kill a large and still-powerful man. So nobody can accuse her of making away with the Earl because it must have taken a man's strength to bludgeon and stab the old crow. It's only thanks to you that I'm not in Newgate awaiting trial for it right now myself.'

'I really am a paragon among wives, am I not?'

'Not if you don't stop doing that, no,' he told her shortly and removed her exploring hand from his intriguingly muscular belly.

'I've waited so long for you, Wulf. Even after I found you, you left me for what looked like for ever from this side of the Atlantic. So now I've finally got my hands on you I don't want to let you go.'

'It's your hands that are doing the damage right now, but I promise you I'm never going far without you again, love, if that will make you feel better and get them off me until you're more used to being my wife. I felt as if a vital part of me was being wrenched away when I sailed off to my new life swearing to forget you, but how could I stay here and long for you when you were going to marry my brother?'

'I lost faith in us before I even met you. I should have called off my betrothal to your brother the moment I set eyes on you, or at least I tried to set them on you, in the shadows—which was quite a challenge when all I wanted to do was feel what we could do to one another and never mind the rest of our senses.'

'I'm glad you didn't trust me that much then, love. I wasn't worth it.'

'You were always worth it,' Isabella said and told herself sternly not to turn into a watering pot because her failures had kept them so far apart for so long and he really thought he hadn't been worthy of her back then. 'And don't forget I learnt very young that Alstone women shouldn't trust devilishly handsome men and you're a devilishly handsome man, my darling. I suppose I had to find out for myself a deliciously desirable man like you doesn't have to have a devil living under his skin.'

'If your eldest brother-in-law hadn't dealt with him so effectively already, I'd castrate that piece of scum who pretended to marry your eldest sister all those years ago. His vicious misuse of an unfledged girl has made you distrust our whole sex ever since and I find that impossible to forgive.'

'Having to live openly with my cousin Celia is punishment enough for him.'

'Not for me it's not.'

'Miranda is worth a hundred of either of them and they did make her miserably unhappy, so I'm glad you hate them, too. But why are we talking about them when we could stare into each other's eyes and marvel at how we both finally managed to see sense at the same time, Wulf?'

'Distraction,' he said concisely.

'Oh, my love, I'm sorry. Let's go to sleep, then, so we can get to tomorrow and make love to one another again all the sooner,' she said and lay down on her side of the bed. She was going to have a lot to live up to, she decided as he reached for her hand and held it while they told each other silly stories to chase sleep so they could dream about the rest of their lives together.

* * * * *

LET'S TALK
Romance

For exclusive extracts, competitions
and special offers, find us online:

f facebook.com/millsandboon

◎ @millsandboonuk

🐦 @millsandboon

Or get in touch on 0844 844 1351*

For all the latest titles coming soon,
visit millsandboon.co.uk/nextmonth

*Calls cost 7p per minute plus your phone company's price per
minute access charge